Engaging the Earl

MINDY BURBIDGE STRUNK

Engaging THE EARL

~ *The* LEAGUE *of* ELIGIBLE BACHELORS ~

MINDY BURBIDGE STRUNK

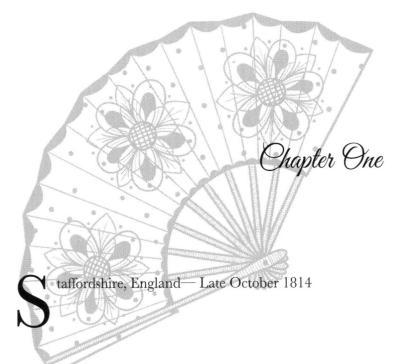

Chapter One

Staffordshire, England— Late October 1814

SARAH BROWN KNEW she would never be considered a great beauty. Her eyes were hazel. But not the sort of hazel that appeared bright brown or bright green depending on the gown she wore. They were simply hazel. Her hair was not truly blonde nor truly brown, and she had a completely unremarkable face, save, perhaps, for the scattering of freckles across her nose. But no one considered freckles remarkable— at least not in the favorable sense of the word. She drew the book in her hands tightly to her chest.

Such unremarkableness made her father's announcement more exciting but also more worrisome. Surely in a place like London, which boasted so many people, there had to be a man who might find her intriguing enough to marry.

That thought sent excitement tingling down her spine. But then the next thought always tempered it. She had little hope that a London Season would result in a marriage proposal.

She had heard of many ladies—ladies with large dowries and pleasant countenances—leaving London with no understanding. But still, there was a possibility, was there not?

Her father's recent elevation to knighthood made her family only slightly more socially acceptable, but the title came with no additional land or money. And as both things were required for her to make a good match, and she had neither, her chances seemed unlikely at best.

"Miss Brown, Lady Mariah is here to see you." Chadwick, the butler, stood in the doorway of their small library.

Sarah smiled. "Please, show her in."

The butler bowed and left the room, only to return a moment later with Sarah's dearest friend in tow.

"Mariah, how lovely to see you." Sarah tossed her book on the nearby couch and hurried over to her friend. "How fortuitous you should come when I have such news to share with you."

"As do I." Mariah beamed, her whole body shaking with excitement. But over what? Sarah had not shared her surprise yet. "But you should go first." Mariah tugged Sarah over to the couch.

Sarah clasped her hands in her lap. Even when one was near to bursting with excitement, it was no excuse for poor manners. Or that was what mama said. "You look as though you can barely contain yourself. Why do you not go first?" Mariah had never been one for propriety.

Mariah nodded. "You know me too well, Sarah. I have the best news you have ever heard."

Sarah scooted closer to her friend, her eyes widening as Mariah bit down on her lip. "Do I have to wait until I am an old maid to learn what has caused you such delight?"

Mariah reached over and pulled Sarah's hand into hers. "I spoke with Regi today and he has agreed that you may accompany us to London. He says you would do very well as my companion!" The squeal that sounded from Mariah's lips reminded Sarah of a piglet she once had. "You may come to London with me for the Season! Is that not the best surprise you have ever heard?"

Sarah nodded, quite certain it was not, indeed, the best thing she had ever heard.

Mariah patted her hand. "Now it is your turn. You said you had something to tell me also. What is it? I am certain it will not be so great as mine, but I wish to hear it nonetheless."

Sarah swallowed. Suddenly, her surprise did not seem so great as it had only moments ago. "It would seem our news is of a similar nature."

Mariah's brow creased. "Oh?"

"Yes, Papa told me at breakfast that he has secured a townhouse in London and is taking Mama and me for the Season." Her shoulders slumped. "Is that not wonderful? We shall still be together, but your brother need not provide for me while I am there."

Mariah's smile fell away. "But…" She sat back, putting some distance between them. "But what of our plans to be together? I had thought we could share the same maid…eat breakfast together…ready for balls and parties together…be as sisters."

Sarah scooted closer and took up Mariah's hand in her own. While some might see Mariah's response as selfish and superior, Sarah knew it was not so. Mariah often held imaginings in her head, and when things did not work out as she dreamed, she was disappointed until she could see the new picture clearly in her mind. "I do not see how this changes much. We will both be in London and can spend nearly all our time together. Besides, when you tire of your townhouse, you may come and visit me at mine."

Mariah smiled, but it was not as wide as it had been. It might take her a day or two before she saw the benefit of this plan. "Yes, I am certain you are right." Mariah nodded and her smile grew. "Yes, we shall see each other every day. It will be just as it is here, only we will have the splendors of London to enjoy. Oh, Sarah. It will be wonderful." She bit her lip and gave Sarah a side glance. "And we shall both fall madly in love and be married before the Season is done, to men of large fortunes."

Sarah laughed. "Oh, Mariah, you are a goose." She did not believe Mariah's assertions for a moment, but it did not stop Sarah from imagining it could happen. She could be content with a man of moderate fortune. Was that too much to ask?

"Where is your townhouse located?"

Sarah shrugged. "I do not know the address. Papa did not tell me." She smiled though, to hide her uneasiness. Their accommodations in London were another thing that worried her. Her family had enough money to support them and their small estate. Her father's income was not more than two thousand a year. As their only child, it provided a respectable dowry for the likes of a clergyman or solicitor. But there was surely not enough money for them to let a townhome in the fashionable London neighborhoods. Sarah did not know where they would stay, but she worried the address would hurt her prospects more than help.

Mariah waved her away. "I am certain you have nothing to fear. There must be hundreds of desirable townhomes in London to let." She sighed. "When do you leave?"

Sarah raised her brows. "Papa said we are to depart on Thursday next."

"We are to leave on Tuesday next." Mariah squealed again. "We shall arrive at nearly the same time. There shall be no end to the fun we will have. We should begin planning immediately."

Sarah sat back slightly. She had never seen Mariah in such a state. "How can we plan when we do not yet have invites to parties?" While Mariah knew much of the ways of country society, she had never been to London for the Season. In many ways, it was like one blind man leading another.

Mariah put a finger to her lips and tapped. "We shall only plan the afternoon events."

Sarah grinned. "Do you not want to leave the afternoons open? What if some gentlemen should wish to take us on a ride through Hyde Park and we must decline because we have already made plans?"

"Now who is the goose?" Mariah shook her head, a bland expression covering her face. "We shall simply have a rule that if either of us should have a need to cancel our plans— because of a gentleman, not a good book—" she eyed the book Sarah had tossed on the opposite couch— "then we shall reschedule whatever plans we had made."

Sarah nodded. "Very well." She rubbed her hands together. "What shall we do first?"

Mariah grinned wickedly. "What will gentlemen of large fortune be doing?"

Sarah laughed. "I am counting on you to guide me through this Season, but you make it very difficult to trust you when you look like that."

Mariah shrugged. "I have your best interests at heart, Sarah. Always."

Sarah squeezed Mariah's hand. "I know you do."

Chapter Two

London, November 1814

Reginald Thornbeck stood from his chair and moved around the desk. He stretched to one side and then to the other. It was nearly eleven. Surely his sister, Mariah, was up by now. He shook his head. She had taken to Town hours much faster than he had expected. Although perhaps that was due to their late arrival two nights before.

He had not seen the need to apply at another inn when they were so close to London, but he had not anticipated the overturned wagon that had brought their journey to a halt just outside of Town.

He rubbed at his eyes. Indeed, he had not completely recovered from the late night either. Although, he rarely slept well during the first few weeks in Town. The sounds were too different from those of Stoke-on-Trent. And the noises never seemed to stop. They continued well into the early morning hours.

His stomach grumbled. Whether Mariah was awake or not, he needed food. He closed the ledger on his desk and left his books for later. Unfortunately, they would still be there when he returned.

Stepping into the breakfast room, he grinned as he saw Mariah sitting at the table with a full plate. "Good morning, Mar. You seem to have your appetite back. I was beginning to worry after you. You hardly ate anything last evening."

Mariah smirked at him. "I was simply tired, Regi. That is all. But I awoke this morning well rested, and I am ready to see London."

Reginald laughed. "Oh, and what do you plan to see today?"

Mariah held up a small paper. "Sarah. She should have arrived last night, and we have a standing appointment for tea this afternoon."

He loaded up his plate with rolls, bacon, and eggs. The preserves sat on the table in small, lidded cups. "Has Miss Brown already written you with the address?"

Mariah shook her head as she chewed and waved the paper.

Reginald took the paper and looked at it. "This is it?"

"She sent me the address before we departed Stoke. And you may call her Sarah, Regi. You have known her for her entire life. I do not see why after all this time you insist on calling her *Miss Brown*."

"Because she is of age now. It would not be proper to call her by her Christian name." Reginald's brow furrowed. "This address is in Cheapside. I had best accompany you."

Mariah looked alarmed. "Is it dangerous?"

Reginald shook his head. "No. But it will be busy. Besides, it is not proper for you to go about London by yourself."

Mariah shrugged. "Are you to accompany me every time I visit Sarah?"

"Are you daft?" Reginald snorted. "I do not have that much time in my life, Mar. I do have Parliament and other business to attend to. But I should like to know where you will be when you are with her. After today's visit, you may take

Mills with you on your visits. She will likely welcome the chance to see a bit of London."

"But Mills is such a milkweed," Mariah whined.

"She is perfectly acceptable." Reginald refrained from rolling his eyes at his sister's arrogance.

"Business?" Mariah gave him a bland look. "Sitting at your club with your friends is hardly business, Regi." She put her elbows on the table and rested her chin in her palm. "Speaking of your friends—are they all to be in London this Season?"

Reginald raised a brow. What was Mar's sudden interest in his friends? "As far as I know, everyone will be in Town except Heatherton. His mother insisted he accompany her on a tour of the continent." His brow creased in question.

Mariah's smile faded. "A tour of the continent? Is that not what boys do when they tire of their parents meddling?"

Reginald shrugged. "His father died not six months ago. I believe his mother wished to escape the house and some of the more trying memories."

His sister scowled. "Then I suppose I will not see much of you?"

"Why would you believe that? I am your guardian. I will not leave you to yourself. This is your first Season."

Mariah's frowned deepened. "Then you are to always be about?"

"Which do you want, Mar?" Reginald shook his head. "Perhaps you could write me out a schedule informing me as to how much time you wish for me to be about, so I may let my secretary schedule you in."

She smirked, but it melted into a dazzling smile. A fist-like grip squeezed at his heart. It seemed unlikely she would come out of this Season without a husband. What would he do without her in his daily life? There would surely be fewer vexations, and the house would certainly be quiet without her in it. But still, he would miss her.

He sighed. He supposed it would simply be something he would grow accustomed to, just as he had when his father had died.

"What time are we to leave for Miss Brown's house?"

Mariah drained the last of her tea and set the cup on the table. "We agreed upon two o'clock when we made the plans."

Reginald nodded. "Then I should think it best if we left no later than half-past one. The roads are sure to be crowded at that time of day."

THE CARRIAGE ROLLED to a stop and both Reginald and Mariah stared out at the large windows of a storefront. "Why have we stopped? This is a shop, not someone's home."

Reginald opened the door and stepped out. He looked at the sign hanging above the door. Poking his head back inside the carriage, he extended his hand to his sister. "This is the address Miss Brown gave you. The family must be staying in the rooms above."

Mariah stepped out and stood looking up at the building. Her mouth hung slightly open. "There must be some mistake. Sarah's family would not let a place such as this." Her nose turned up.

Reginald grasped her elbow and directed her toward the side doorway. "You may wish to lower that nose of yours, Mar. I am certain it would hurt Miss Brown's feelings to see you acting so superior."

"But look at this place, Regi." Her voice dropped to a fierce whisper.

"I see nothing wrong with it. It is perfectly suitable. It is not as if there are many places to let in London. Especially for the budget the Browns likely have."

Mariah glared up at him. "Now who is acting superior?"

He shook his head. "I was casting no judgment."

"But Sarah's father has risen to the honor of knighthood. Why should he not be able to afford a better address?"

"While his title may have changed, Mar, his income has not." He ran a frustrated hand through his hair. His sister was not a dolt, but sometimes he wondered what she had in her brainbox. "It is a fact that Sir Winston has an income of two thousand a year. While respectable, that amount does not leave much to let a home in London."

Mariah bit her lip. "This will affect her chances of finding a match, will it not?"

Reginald lifted a shoulder, her comment giving him hope that perhaps she could think beyond ribbons and gowns. "Her chances were never very good, Mar. Her dowry is nothing to entice more than a country gentleman." He glanced at the empty shop. "Some may find this location a deterrent. But most will have discounted her before they ever even discover this." He did not like saying it. It made him feel terrible to cast Miss Brown in such low esteem. But he was only stating what was reality.

"Then we will simply have to spend more time at our house," Mariah lifted her chin.

They pushed through the doorway at the side of the shop and immediately started up the steps to the landing above. Taking a deep breath, Reginald rapped twice on the door.

Chadwick opened it wide.

"Good day, Chadwick. Is Sarah at home? We had arranged to have tea together this afternoon." Mariah smiled at the older man, but Reginald could tell she was ill at ease.

"Please, follow me to the parlor and I will see if Miss Brown is at home."

Reginald bowed slightly to the butler. "Thank you, Chadwick."

He led them into a pale yellow parlor. Reginald could not help but look around and was pleasantly surprised. He frowned at the realization that he had assumed the place to be untidy and ramshackle simply because of its location in Cheapside. Perhaps Mar had been right, and Reginald did think himself superior.

Mar moved over to a sofa of creamy white and sat down. Reginald continued to walk about the room. He was not here for tea but merely to accompany his sister. The paper on the walls, upon closer inspection, was of small, bright yellow flowers trailing in rows up toward the ceiling.

"Mariah," Miss Brown hurried into the room. Even with only the one word uttered, Reginald could hear the tenseness in her voice. "I was not expecting you." She glanced over and saw Reginald standing near the fireplace and her shoulders dropped. She dipped a curtsy. "Lord Stoke, I beg your pardon. I did not see you there."

Reginald dipped his head to her and smiled, hoping it would ease the tension around her eyes.

"You were not expecting me? How could you say such a thing? Did we not agree to have tea together?" Mariah's voice held a hint of disbelief.

Miss Brown swallowed. "I sent a note yesterday asking if we might postpone our plans. Did you not receive it?"

Mar shook her head. "No. But why should we postpone? You are obviously in London. And Regi and I are here now."

Miss Brown's shoulders drooped even more. "Yes. You are here now." Her voice held none of the cheer and confidence Reginald was used to hearing. She looked around the room. "You must think poorly of me. If I'd had any notion this was the type of home we could afford in London, I should surely have convinced Papa to stay in Stoke."

Mariah tilted her head to the side. "And miss out on all of our plans together?" She took an appraising look around the room. "This room is quite lovely. I see no reason you should be embarrassed by it."

"We are living over a *shop*, Mariah. Those of consequence do not live over shops—no matter how pretty the parlor is."

She sighed and dropped down on the couch near where Mariah stood. "Even if someone should wish to make my acquaintance, they will change their minds once they come for a morning visit."

Mariah shrugged. "I see no problem with it, but if it should make you feel better, you are welcome to take morning calls at our Townhouse." She turned her eyes to Reginald. "You do not mind, do you, Regi?"

Reginald clasped his hands behind his back. "As long as you do not involve me in the visits, I do not mind. However, I do not wish to offend Sir Winston in the least. I desire Miss Brown to seek her father's approval first."

Miss Brown looked over to Reginald and nodded, her countenance brightening for the first time. "Oh, thank you, my lord. I am certain Papa will not mind. I believe he was quite surprised when he saw the shop below." She shook her head. "Although, I feel certain they must have mentioned it in the ad. He must not have read carefully enough."

Mariah clapped her hands. "It will be wonderful! And just as I had planned. We may spend all our days together—just like we we're sisters."

A maid entered the room with a tea tray in her hands.

Mariah grinned at Sarah. "I had begun to think you would not allow us to stay long enough for tea."

"Surely you did not think me so rude." Sarah leaned forward and poured out three cups. "Will you join us, my lord?"

Reginald crossed the room. "If you insist, Miss Brown. But I only came here to accompany my sister. It was not my intention to intrude."

"You are not intruding." She handed him a cup and saucer. "My mother will be disappointed to have missed you. While she is not altogether happy with the location of the house, she is pleased that she mustn't walk far to the shops."

Miss Brown chuckled. "Although, I believe that is the point Papa regrets the most."

Mariah took a sip and put her cup down. "Now, Sarah, we must discuss what invitations you have received. As you have only just arrived, I assume your mother has not had time to accept many. That means we shall be able to accept those to which we have both been invited."

Sarah's smile faded. "I do not believe we have received any invitations yet."

Reginald placed his teacup on the table. "It is only because word has not circulated that you have arrived in London. Give it a few days, and I am certain you will see some invitations." It was a lie, and he knew it. It was not likely many in London even knew who Sir Winston Brown and his family were, let alone had intentions of inviting them to any parties or balls. But Reginald had influential friends and he would just need to convince them to direct a few invitations to the Browns. Perhaps once they were seen at a few fashionable parties, other invitations would follow. He stood up and straightened his coat. "Mar, I have a few errands I need to attend to. Is it acceptable with Miss Brown if you stay for an hour or two?"

He glanced at Miss Brown and his sister. They both nodded happily.

"Very well, I shall return at half-past four to collect you." He dipped his head to them and turned toward the doorway. He had not heard from Lord Ragsdale or Mr. Bancroft, but surely Lords Berwick, Montcort, and Ponsonby were about. And if Reginald knew his friends, they would all be at Brooks —which is precisely where Reginald planned to go.

Chapter Three

Reginald pushed through the doors to his club and immediately moved to his favorite room, the room he knew all of his friends would occupy if they were there.

It was his first time at Brooks since coming to London this Season, but it always felt like home. Perhaps not home, but like a very comfortable study. He stepped inside the large parlor and his eyes moved directly to the far corner. Two large couches and half a dozen chairs formed a cozy seating area. It was just far enough away from the rest of the groupings to be private, or as private as one could get in the crowded rooms of a gentleman's club.

A smile turned the corners of his lips when he saw his friends already occupying the seats. Lords Berwick and Montcort sat on one couch while Lords Ragsdale and Ponsonby occupied the other. Ah, Ragsdale *was* already in London.

Reginald moved over to the group and clapped Berwick on the shoulder. "Good day, gents. I was certain I would find you here."

Berwick turned partially and looked up at Reginald. "Reg,

it's about time you arrived. We began to think you were sulking."

Reginald smirked. "And just what would I have to sulk about? I am in London. It is not possible for one to sulk in London."

"I am able to sulk in London," Ragsdale cast a rueful look at the group.

"Ah, yes. I forgot about you, Rags. I stand corrected. Most cannot sulk in London. Is that better?" Reginald smirked.

"Oh, then you have not heard?" Montcort grinned up at Reginald.

"I have not heard what?" Reginald looked sidelong at his friend.

Ragsdale raised a brow. "Lady Clara is engaged."

Reginald's brows creased. "Actually, Rags, I had heard that news. Although I do not know why you think it would affect me. There was no agreement between us."

Berwick narrowed his eyes at Reginald. "I had thought there was some partiality on your part."

Reginald guffawed. "And give up all this? Never." He settled into a chair and stretched his long legs out in front of him, crossing them at the ankles. "Even Lady Clara was not enough to entice me out of bachelorhood."

Ragsdale released a deep breath. "I, for one, am glad to hear it. We were all afraid we would lose you to the Parson's mousetrap before the Season was out."

Reginald laughed and shook his head. "You need not fear, gents. I have no intention of marrying this Season or any Season in the near future."

Ragsdale grunted. "You're lucky your father isn't still around. The Duke reminds me on a weekly basis about what *my duty* is." He ran a hand over his chin. "He stopped for a bit when he was engaged to that chit, Miss Carter. But since she jilted him, he has been relentless."

Montcort shook his head. "I still cannot believe that woman chose a groom over a Duke. Who does such a thing?"

Ragsdale lifted a shoulder. "Supposedly he was a gentleman and she loved him." He drained the last bit of brandy from his glass. "But if love makes you do insensible things like that, I want nothing to do with it."

All the men raised their glasses and murmured, "Indeed."

Reginald looked around the group. He did not know what his life would be like if it were not for these men. Their friendships began back at Harrow when they were just boys. In the beginning, they were not all friends. Reginald, Montcort, and Berwick had become friends from almost the first day.

At the beginning of their second year, Ragsdale, who was a year older, took a disliking to Ponsonby, a scrawny, first-year boy with little experience in fisticuffs. Reginald, Montcort, and Berwick had come to Ponsy's defense, forcing Ragsdale to leave him be.

However, the tables were turned the next year when a bigger boy took a dislike to Ragsdale. When they all came to Rag's defense, the bond had formed. They had been friends ever since. Mr. Charles Bancroft joined them during their first year at Cambridge.

"Where is Charlie? Has anyone heard when he is to arrive?" Reginald looked around the group.

"Last I heard he is to arrive tomorrow next." Ragsdale set his glass on the table. Reginald had always found it interesting that Ragsdale, the heir to a dukedom, was the closest friend of the man who held no title at all. In all other aspects, Ragsdale held quite firmly to what society expected of his title.

"What invitations have you all accepted?" asked Berwick.

"I have not sent our acceptance to any yet," Reginald set his glass on the arm of his chair. "I was waiting to see what the rest of you did. The last thing I wish is to be the only one in attendance at any event hosted by the *ton*."

"My mother wishes to host a musicale," Ponsy grimaced. "I tried to dissuade her, but it is to no end. She is determined."

"That may work." Reginald perked up. "I promise to be in attendance and to bring Mariah if you will do me a favor."

Ponsy raised a brow. "And just what would that favor be?"

"It is not as bad as all that. I only wish for you to invite Sir Winston Brown and his family."

Ponsy's brow creased. "Who is Sir Winston Brown?"

Ragsdale and Montcort joined him. "I have not heard of him either. Who is he?" Montcort asked.

"He is from Stoke-on-Trent and has recently been knighted. He has brought his daughter to have a Season, but I'm afraid most of society has the same idea as you. His daughter, who is Mariah's dearest friend, was most disappointed to have not received any invitations yet."

Rags squinted at Reginald. "We are to take pity on this upstart, then?"

Reginald shook his head. "He was a gentleman before he was knighted. It is not as if he is an upstart, Rags." Reginald shifted in his seat. "And it is more for the daughter that I ask than for the parents. Although, they are a good sort of people and I believe they would get on well if they only had the chance to be invited."

Ponsy tilted his head to the side and leveled his gaze at Reginald. "And what do I get out of this? I think I deserve more than just your attendance at the musicale."

Reginald looked indignantly at his friend. "Did you miss the part where I said I would bring Mariah? She will be presented at court next week and I am certain she will be a diamond this Season."

"I still do not see how that affects me." Ponsy shrugged. "But if it means you all will attend, what do I care who else is invited. Give me the address and I shall see that Sir Winston and his family are on the list."

Reginald sat back in relief. But it was short lived. What

was he to do? If he gave Sir Winston's London address, Ponsonby might change his mind about the invitation and the others might be dissuaded as well. While Ponsy, as a baron, was not as high in the instep as Ragsdale, he still very much adhered to society's expectations. And society's expectations did not include those living in Cheapside.

"Why do you not send it to my house, and I will see that it is delivered to Sir Winston. I do not have their London address at present." He stretched the truth, but he did not regret it. Indeed, it was quite the opposite. He felt rather pleased with himself that he had secured an invitation for Miss Brown. And surely others would follow. Reginald allowed his chest to puff slightly. He rather liked the magnanimous feeling.

"Do you expect the rest of us to offer invitations as well?" Rags leaned forward and placed his elbows on his knees.

Reginald's good feelings slipped away.

He scowled at his friend. "I certainly do not expect it of you. However, I am certain once the rest of you meet Miss Brown and her family, you will see that it is not such an unpleasant notion."

Montcort smiled. "Perhaps this *Miss Brown* is the reason you are not sulking over Lady Clara."

Reginald shook his head. "I have no idea what you could mean. Miss Brown is a family friend, and I have known her since she was born. I only wish to see her have a successful Season. It is no different than I wish for Mariah."

Reginald lifted his glass to his mouth, but his mind churned. Did Montcort really think Reginald was doing this for his own benefit? Miss Brown, while a friend and sweet girl, was not the kind of lady he was looking for. Indeed, he was not looking for any sort of lady. Especially not one to marry.

"We never did establish what invitations we were to accept," Reginald grumbled.

"Lord Everton's ball is tomorrow next. I believe it will

have the best attendance. And he always has a lively card-room." Montcort stretched his legs out in front of him and pushed back into his seat. "I am inclined to accept that invitation. As for the musicales," he flicked his gaze to Ponsy, "I am inclined to reject them all. It is nothing more than an audition. And I do not wish to perform."

"Nor do I." Berwick grunted.

"But you all said you would come." Ponsy looked affronted.

"No, Reg said he would come and bring his sister. None of the rest of us promised anything." Berwick crossed his arms over his chest, looking smug.

Reginald cast his friends a narrow-eyed look. "Not to worry, Ponsy. We will *all* be in attendance."

"None of us are looking for a match." Montcort glanced at Reginald and quirked up the side of his mouth. "Except for you. You seem overly concerned about what happens to Miss Brown this Season."

Reginald grinned maliciously. "I would watch yourself, Cort, else you might find yourself accepting invitations to *all* the musicales. Indeed, you might even find your name on the list of performers."

Montcort scowled at him. "You do not want to start that challenge, Reg." His face softened, but it did not look any less menacing. "Because I guarantee you will not win."

Reginald steepled his fingers in front of him and stared just a little menacingly. "We'll see about that, Cort."

Chapter Four

Mariah sat in the chair near the fire, a pile of invitations in her lap.

"While I appreciate the invitation to Lady Ponsonby's musicale, I had rather hoped we would receive more." Sarah held up the one invitation in her hand.

She had not expected to receive as many invitations as Mariah and her brother, but she had expected more than one. Was there no other peer that her father was acquainted with? Or even any other gentlemen of means who held parties in London? Gracious, it was not even an invitation to a ball. How was she to make a match if she was not invited to a ball? Balls are where all matches started, were they not?

She puffed out her lips. Perhaps not all matches, but balls seemed to produce more marriages than anything else. Or that was what she supposed.

"I had hoped you would be invited to Lord Everton's ball on Saturday." Mariah put a finger to her lips and tapped. "Perhaps you could come as my companion. I know it is not what you hoped for, but my mother is not here to attend with me. And we both know as soon as we reach Lord Everton's home, Regi will bolt off to the cardroom with his friends."

Sarah pulled her bottom lip between her teeth and bit down, the slight pain distracting her for a moment. Attending as Mariah's companion would get her to the ball, but it was not the same as being invited on her own merit. She sighed. But if it resulted in a match, did she really care how she came about the invitation?

"Do you think it will work?" Sarah moved over and sat on the settee next to her friend.

Mariah patted Sarah on the leg. "Of course it will work. Why should it not?"

Sarah nodded her head. "It is not precisely as I had hoped, but I suppose it is better than sitting at home."

Mariah grinned. "Indeed, you are far too pretty to sit at home when there is a ball you could attend." She sat back and clasped her hands together. "Oh Sarah, this will be so diverting. It is just as I had imagined."

Sarah smiled, although she could not bring herself to be nearly as happy as Mariah. Growing up, Sarah had always known Mariah was of higher standing than herself, but Mariah had never made Sarah feel lower. At least not very often and not on purpose. While it was not Mariah's fault, Sarah had never noticed the disparity more than she did since arriving in London.

"You must bring your gown here, and we shall ready ourselves together. It will be much more convenient if we do not have to drive all the way to Cheapside to fetch you."

If she had not felt so put down, Sarah might have laughed at the irony. In this instance, Sarah knew that Mariah did not mean her words to be lowering, but she still could not help feeling as if she were simply a bit of charity work for her friend.

Mariah clapped her hands, even as Sarah sat back. "You see? It is as if we are sisters! Just as I planned back in Stoke-on-Trent."

Mariah frowned and tilted her head to the side. She

leaned forward and placed a hand on Sarah's forearm. "You need not worry, Sarah. Once you have attended a few events with me, the invitations will come on their own." She smiled softly. "Everyone will see your beauty. And once they speak to you and see your wit and intelligence, you will be much in demand."

Sarah sighed. Mariah was exaggerating, of course. No one would ever consider Sarah a great beauty. Especially not when she stood beside Mariah. But her words still lifted Sarah's spirits.

Mariah patted her arm. "Do you trust me?"

Did she trust her? Mariah was no more experienced than Sarah. But Mariah held the invitations, while Sarah did not.

She nodded, the tension dropping from her shoulders. Perhaps Mariah was correct. Perhaps it was just a matter of becoming acquainted with those in society for the invitations to start arriving for her family. "Of course I do, Mariah." Besides, if Mariah attended the ball, Lord Stoke would attend also. And at least he would ask her to dance, would he not? Attending some balls and parties as Mariah's companion might not be so terrible after all.

SARAH AND MARIAH followed Lord Stoke into Lord Everton's entryway. A line of people stood in front of the grand staircase, greeting everyone before motioning them into what Sarah assumed was the ballroom.

She sucked in a deep breath and ran her shaking hand down the front of her gown. She did not know why she was so nervous. She had attended plenty of assemblies back in Stoke, yet looking at this entryway, she knew she was very far away from a country assembly.

The gowns she saw just inside the door of the house were more exquisite than anything she had seen.

"Stop fidgeting," Mariah hissed in her ear. "If you fidget, they will know you are nervous. And if you are nervous, it makes them believe you do not belong." Mariah nodded her head and waved to several people across the room. "People of the *ton* always belong."

After several tension-filled moments, Lord Stoke held out his hand and motioned Mariah and Sarah forward. He looked very well in his black superfine coat and his blue-green waistcoat. But she shook those observations away as she stopped in front of their hosts.

Lord Stoke smiled as he motioned to his sister. "Lord and Lady Everton, may I introduce my sister, Lady Mariah, and her dear friend, Miss Sarah Brown."

Sarah tried to smile confidently, even though she did not feel it at all. However, Lord and Lady Everton seemed pleasant enough. They did not call her an imposter or throw her from the house, so it seemed the night was off to a good start.

Lord Stoke lifted one arm for Mariah and his other one for Sarah, smiling at her as she took it. A quiet gasp sounded, but she was not certain if it was from her or Mariah. She pulled to a stop in the middle of the doorway.

"It is magnificent, is it not?" Mariah said in a wispy voice. It made Sarah feel a little better to see that even Lady Mariah could be awed by something.

"There are some chairs on the other side of the ballroom. Let me settle you in, then I shall fetch you each a glass of champagne." Lord Stoke motioned them farther inside.

Sarah's stomach gave a slight tumble at the thought that he had included her in the offer. Perhaps she had not been so far off to think he might ask her to dance.

He led them over to a grouping of chairs at the far side of the room. Helping each of them to sit, he turned and made his way back through the crowd.

Sarah and Mariah were both quiet, each looking about the room and taking in every detail.

"Is there someone in particular you wish to dance with tonight?" Sarah asked.

Mariah sighed and slumped down in her seat. "No. The only man I wish to dance with is not even to attend the Season this year." Her nose curled slightly. "It seems he is *escorting his mother* on the continent." Her voice held the tone of a petulant child.

Sarah glanced at Mariah from the corner of her eye, her lips twitching as she tried to hold back a smile. "Are you still pining over Lord Heatherton? I had thought you had decided against him."

"I have tried to put him from my mind, but I cannot seem to do it. He is simply the only man I can picture myself marrying."

Sarah lifted her shoulder. "I suppose that is what love does, is it not? It makes us want what we cannot have."

Mariah turned and looked at her. "And why do you think I could not have him? Do you not think I am proper enough for him?"

"No, Mariah. It is not you that is the problem. It is him. Have not the whole lot of them, your brother included, declared they do not wish to marry?"

Mariah shrugged her shoulders delicately and shook her head, her gaze staring absently out at the dance floor. "I know they say such things, but I cannot help but think they do not truly mean it. If the right *lady,*" her voice took on a sing-song tone, "should come along, they would be helpless to resist." She lifted her chin. "I simply need to convince him that I am the right lady."

"How do you plan to accomplish that?"

"If he would only open his eyes and see me, I might stand a chance." Mariah looked completely defeated. "But that is difficult when he isn't even in England." A pout marred her features.

"Surely there is someone here who could amuse you in the absence of Lord Heatherton." Sarah continued to look about the room. There were a number of handsome gentlemen she could be happy enough with—not that they would notice her.

"Here you are, ladies." Lord Stoke handed each of them a glass of champagne and moved behind the chairs as if standing guard over them.

Mariah looked over her shoulder. "And just what do you think you are doing?"

Lord Stoke raised a brow at her. "I am your guardian and chaperone, Mar. Did you think I would abandon you?"

She looked at him blandly. "I most certainly hoped you would. I expected you to disappear to the cardroom as soon as we entered the house. Indeed, I counted on it."

Lord Stoke grinned mischievously. "Now, what kind of a brother would I be if I did not stay and supervise the gentlemen who might think themselves worthy to dance with you?" He folded his arms across his chest, placing a fierce look on his face.

Sarah smiled. This was a side of Lord Stoke she had never seen. And from the look of utter confusion on Mariah's face, neither had she.

"This is precisely why Sarah came with me. There is no need for you to stand over me like a sentry. You will scare away any gentleman who wishes to ask me to dance." Mariah clenched her fingers tightly together in her lap.

"That was the idea." Lord Stoke raised a brow but looked between the two. His gaze rested on Sarah and her stomach flipped again. "If I leave, do you promise to report to me every gentleman who asks Mar to dance?" He was going to leave? While it may have been in Mariah's plans for him to leave, it was not in Sarah's. Who would ask her to dance if he was not there?

Mariah swatted Sarah's leg and she nodded. "If that is what you wish, my lord."

Lord Stoke's face did not soften in the least. "It is, indeed, what I wish."

Sarah nodded again. "Very well." She glanced at Mariah from the corner of her eye. "You are both fortunate I have a very good memory." She looked straight ahead and smiled even as she felt her evening slipping away from her.

"I shall be in the cardroom if you need me," Lord Stoke said as he moved around the chairs.

"Do not fear, my lord. We shall be perfectly fine without you." Mariah called after him. Once Lord Stoke was out of hearing, she turned to Sarah. "Now, is there anyone you wish to dance with?"

Sarah shrugged. "I do not know anyone here. How should I know if I wish to dance with them?"

They both turned to look toward a crowd making a bit of a ruckus with loud laughter and voices echoing through the large room.

Amid the crowd was a man—easily seen as he stood at least a head taller than anyone else in the group. But that was not the only distinguishing feature. His dark brown hair curled around his ears and an easy smile seemed to capture the attention of everyone around him. He moved and the crowds flowed along with him.

Sarah could not pull her eyes away from him. Who was that man and how could she be introduced to him?

A soft chuckle sounded next to her. "It looks as though you have found someone you wish to dance with after all."

Chapter Five

Reginald walked casually through the ballroom, making sure not to look any lady in the eye and risk having to ask her to dance. If he need not be with Mariah, he did not wish to be in the ballroom at all. The card-room would prove much more diverting and relatively free of women and their marital eyes.

Reginald grinned as he spotted his friends. Montcort and Ponsonby were seated at a table with cards in their hands. Ragsdale occupied a wholly different table. Reginald could not decipher what games they each played, but each man focused on their cards. He patted his pocket, even though he knew his fish were there.

Several tables still had empty chairs, but Reginald was not about to sit in on just any game. If he were playing against just one person, his preference would be Piquet. But in a group setting such as this, he preferred Vingt-un. It was the game he was most proficient at. Mariah would say it was just luck. But Reginald knew better. He knew skill was involved.

Berwick sidled up beside him, his arms folded across his chest. "Are you just going to stand here? Or are you going to take up a table?"

Reginald glanced over at his friend. "You know I like to have a feel for the room before I commit to one."

"Just do not feel for too long or else you will find yourself out of a game."

Reginald shrugged. "What are you to play tonight, Ben?"

Berwick sighed. "I have not yet decided. My last two bouts with Loto were less successful than I had hoped. I believe I might try my hand at something else."

Reginald glanced out the door. The cardroom was farther from the ballroom than he had hoped. He could not see the dance floor at all. It would make watching over Mariah impossible. Perhaps he should go check on her before he settled in. He had seen Lord Muckrake—his lip curled at the appropriateness of the man's name—in the ballroom, and he would not put it past the man to try and secure Mariah's affections—or at least her twenty thousand pounds.

Reginald grunted out a laugh. He would be cold and in the ground before Muckrake would ever spend time with Mariah.

"Have you heard a word I've said?" Berwick's irritated voice sounded next to him.

"My apologies, Ben. I was just thinking about Mariah. She is in the ballroom with her friend, Miss Brown, as her only defense against the less savory gentlemen in attendance tonight." He ran a hand along the back of his neck. "I should be there, watching out for her."

Berwick turned slightly and looked in the same direction. "Who, in particular, do you wish to save her from? I did not even enter the ballroom. That only leads to trouble."

"I saw Lord Muckrake as I was leaving the room. As usual, he had a flock of followers around him."

Berwick shook his head. "I do not understand what the ladies see in him."

Reginald shrugged. "I am certain all their fathers have

28

warned them against him. And what better way to push a daughter in his direction."

Berwick squinted. "I wonder how I might get fathers to warn their daughters away from me?" He grinned.

Reginald rolled his eyes. "Because you have difficulty with the ladies? Besides, you are not the same kind of man as Muckrake. You would not trifle with a lady's affections knowing full well you have no intention of offering for her."

"You are correct. Although, I have thought about it. It is utterly boring showing a woman proper respect all the time." Berwick shrugged. "I confess I have desired the company of a charming young lady from time to time. Besides, have you seen the flocks around Muckrake?"

"Yes, but have you seen the ladies?" Reginald's nose flared slightly. "They are not the kind of ladies I should like hanging on my every word."

Berwick stared at the doorway a moment before flicking his brows up in resignation. "Then are you to swear off the cardroom for tonight?"

Reginald glanced at the tables and then at the door. "Perhaps if I just check in on the ballroom, I can see for myself that Mar is safe."

"I shall come with you. There isn't a seat at the table I wish to join at present." He clapped Reginald on the shoulder and they both turned toward the door. "But we may not stay long. I do not wish to be trapped into a dance. For then I shall never be free of the ballroom."

"I thought you wished to avoid the ballroom altogether," Reginald raised a brow at his friend. "Why the sudden interest?"

"I just thought to see those ladies you did not wish to hang on your every word one last time, before I make my final decision." His lips quirked up.

"You're ridiculous." Reginald shook his head. "I shall just take a quick peek. Mariah did not seem pleased when sʰ thought I was staying in the ballroom. I do not wish for her to see me, lest she thinks I'm checking in on her."

Berwick walked beside Reginald. "Except that you *are* checking in on her."

Reginald huffed. "But I do not need her to know that. If she finds out, she will be rather out of sorts. And Mariah is unbearable when she is out of sorts."

Berwick grunted. "Yes, I've witnessed it before."

They reached the ballroom doors and Reginald stuck his head inside. Mariah and Miss Brown sat where he had left them. Mariah watched the dance floor, while Miss Brown watched the group buzzing around Lord Muckrake. He moved ever closer to Mariah.

Reginald swatted Berwick on the shoulder and motioned him to follow. They entered the ballroom and moved to the opposite side from Miss Brown and Mariah. The crowd had swelled enough that it would be easy to remain hidden.

"There she is," Berwick motioned to Mariah. "She seems to be fine. And Muckrake is over there." He motioned with his head to the far corner. "Can we return to the cardroom now?"

Reginald watched Mariah and Miss Brown. From the corner of his eye, he caught movement and shifted his gaze toward it. Mr. Montgomery made his way toward the ladies. Reginald leaned back on his heels and crossed his arms.

Montgomery was not a rogue like Muckrake, but he was not what Reginald had in mind for his sister either. But it was only a dance, was it not? He need not be overly concerned. Unless the gentleman took the dance as an opportunity to expand their acquaintance. A dance was how it all started, was it not? His hand fisted tightly at his side. Why had he ever agreed to bring Mariah to London? He had done little else but worry over her since they arrived.

He glanced around the room, noting how many unworthy gentlemen were in attendance. Must he protect Mar from all of them?

"Oh, hang it. I do not think I shall be returning to the cardroom. I need to remain here."

Berwick followed Reginald's gaze. "Montgomery is not such a terrible man. Why must you save Lady Mariah from him?"

Reginald cleared his throat. "It is not that he is terrible. I just do not wish him to set his sights on my sister."

"Perhaps he is intending to ask Lady Mariah's friend. What did you say her name was?"

"Miss Sarah Brown."

"Oh, yes, now I recall. Perhaps Mr. Montgomery wishes to dance with Miss Brown."

Reginald squinted at the man. "He is not right for Miss Brown either."

"Oh?" Berwick held the word out longer than necessary. "And who is right for Miss Brown?"

Reginald sighed at his friend's inference. "She is Mariah's companion for the evening. Does that not make it my responsibility to watch out for her also? I would wish for Sir Winston to do the same for Mariah if the tables were turned." There was a little too much bite to his words for his comfort. Berwick would likely take it to mean something that was not true.

He fastened his gaze on the two. It seemed Miss Brown was safe for the next set as Mr. Montgomery bowed in front of Mariah and offered his hand. She smiled and nodded, placing her hand in his.

Reginald scowled and clenched his fists.

Mr. Montgomery led her to the dance floor.

Reginald grunted. "You see, if I had been there, she likely would not have to be subjected to Mr. Montgomery."

Berwick shrugged. "I do not believe your presence would've made a difference. Montgomery has never been overly observant. I doubt your stern look would have deterred him in the least." He glanced over at Reginald. "Besides, if she is dancing with Mr. Montgomery, she is not available to dance with Muckrake. I should think that would make you happy."

Reginald watched Miss Brown. Her eyes seemed to travel in whatever direction Lord Muckrake moved. Was Sarah taken with the man? He had always thought her rather clever. How could she be smitten with the likes of Muckrake? Surely she knew of his reputation, and if not, she could see what kind of man he was just by those who followed him about.

Reginald squinted at his pretty young neighbor and grunted. Perhaps it was not Mariah he needed to save but rather Miss Brown.

But how exactly was he to save her? Muckrake had yet to look in her direction. He turned toward Berwick but continually glanced over to Miss Brown. "I am happy to have Mariah saved for the moment. But Miss Brown may not be out of danger." He motioned to her, watching as she continued to follow Muckrake's procession around the ballroom.

"He does not seem inclined to dance, at present. Perhaps your worries are unfounded." Berwick looked at his pocket watch and cast a longing look toward the door. "I fear we have been here too long. There are several gazes following us even as we speak," he whispered.

"If I could turn her attention elsewhere, I would feel better about returning to the cardroom."

Berwick raised a brow. "Are you to play matchmaker now?"

Reginald smirked. "No, but Miss Brown is a nice, sensible girl. She does not know the kind of man Lord Muckrake truly is. I do not wish to see her hurt. If I might change the direction of her gaze to someone more suitable, then I shall not worry so much about Mariah either. They are inseparable, you know." It was not completely about Mariah, but Reginald could not fully say why he was concerned for his sister's friend.

"What does Miss Brown's affections toward Lord Muckrake have to do with Lady Mariah?" Berwick fiddled with his pocket watch, flipping it open and closed over and over.

"I simply prefer to keep Muckrake as far away from Mariah as possible. If Miss Brown, however unlikely it may be, turns the head of Muckrake, it would place Mariah in close proximity. I simply cannot risk it."

Berwick shook his head. "Are you certain it is not you who has an interest in Miss Brown?"

Reginald looked at Berwick, his brow furrowed. "Don't be bacon brained. I have known Miss Brown her entire life. I simply do not wish to see her hurt. If Miss Brown is hurt, it will hurt Mariah."

Berwick shrugged but motioned to the far side of the room. "Mr. Croft is a good sort of man."

Reginald sought out the man and gave him an appraising look. "He is, but he is rather dull, don't you think?"

Berwick shrugged. "What about Mr. Pond?"

"He is a spitter. I do not think Miss Brown would appreciate a man who spits every time he speaks."

Berwick glanced over at Reginald. "What of Mr. Lancing?"

Reginald shook his head. "The man is not yet thirty and is very near bald. No. He will not do."

"It is just a dance, Reg." There was a question in Berwick's voice, but Reginald ignored it.

If Mariah were not dearest friends with Miss Brown, Reginald should not care who she set her sights upon. But Mariah changed everything. He would make certain his sister married well and was not taken advantage of.

"Perhaps Croft would be tolerable for a dance." Reginald moved along the outskirts of the dance floor, Berwick trailing along behind him with his eyes downcast until they reached Mr. Croft's side.

"Croft, I have not seen you in some time. Why are you not dancing?" Reginald saw no need for small talk.

Mr. Croft shrugged. "I have not been here long. I am still assessing the room."

Reginald clapped him on the back. "Let me introduce you to Miss Brown. This is her first Season in London, and she is one of my sister's dearest friends. I think you will find her very diverting."

"But—"

Not allowing the man a chance to answer, Reginald grabbed Croft by the arm and guided him to where Miss Brown sat.

"Miss Brown, I would like to introduce you to my friend, Mr. Croft. We were at school together at Cambridge."

Mr. Croft shrugged slightly before he bowed. "It is an honor to meet you, Miss Brown. If you are not otherwise engaged, might I have the next set?"

Miss Brown flicked her gaze toward Lord Muckrake quickly but turned it back to Mr. Croft. She nodded and smiled. "My next set has not been spoken for. I should be honored to dance with you, Mr. Croft."

Croft clasped his hands behind his back, bouncing on his toes several times. "Capital. I shall fetch you at the start of the next set."

Miss Brown smiled, although Reginald did not think it looked very sincere, which surprised him. Miss Brown was usually very sensible. Why would she not be pleased to dance with the likes of Mr. Croft? He was much more suitable for her than Lord Muckrake—in both status and character.

Mr. Croft turned away and moved back into the crowd. Reginald glanced out at the dance floor where Mariah was beginning the next dance with Montgomery. Who would ask her next?

As much as he knew it would vex her, Reginald knew he could not return to the cardroom. He would lose a mountain of money at the tables as his mind would not be on the game.

"Are you having a nice time, Miss Brown?" Berwick asked.

Miss Brown looked over as if just seeing Berwick standing beside Reginald. She smiled. It was much more genuine than what she had offered Mr. Croft.

She cocked a brow. "Yes, my lord. I have not danced as much as I would like, but I am enjoying watching everyone." She looked from Berwick to Reginald. "I thought you had retired to the cardroom?"

Reginald shrugged. "I realized I was leaving Mariah unprotected. There are several gentlemen in attendance that I do not wish for her to associate with."

"Then you are to stay?"

Reginald could not tell if Miss Brown was happy about that or not. She always was harder to read than Mariah.

"I think it will be best." Reginald clasped his hands behind his back, his skin prickling. Why did he care if she approved?

"Then *I* shall return to the cardroom. I am certain a spot has opened by now." Berwick gave Reginald a bland look. It was obvious he did not agree with Reginald's decision, but Reginald did not care. He was not Reginald's father. Nor did he have a sister. He did not know what it was like to have such a responsibility.

But Reginald knew. And he took the responsibility very seriously.

Chapter Six

Sarah sat in her seat, watching Mariah dance while she waited for Mr. Croft to return. Lord Stoke stood behind her, looking out over the dance floor. Had he convinced Mr. Croft to ask her so he did not have to dance with her himself?

Sarah released a wistful sigh. She missed the easy relationship they'd had as children. There had not been the same rules of propriety to follow then. She was simply Sarah and he was Reginald. They had never been intimate friends, as she was six years his junior. But by virtue of her relationship with Mariah, they had spent considerable time together.

She glanced back at him. Looking at his stiff form now, no one would ever guess they had once called each other by Christian names. Now he did not even wish to dance with her. She twisted her hands in her lap. She had been just fine sitting there by herself. But now her stomach lurched, and she felt uncharacteristically nervous.

The set ended and Mr. Montgomery led Mariah back to their seats. But just as she sat down, Mr. Croft approached and offered Sarah his hand. She took it and allowed him to lead her to the dance floor.

It was not that she did not like Mr. Croft. She did not know him well enough to have an opinion. She was simply disappointed he was not the man with the crowd of women around him.

Sarah looked over Mr. Croft's shoulder, seeing the tall gentleman leading a woman to the dance floor. He did dance then. She had begun to wonder if he only went about the room talking and laughing with the ladies that followed him. If he danced as gracefully as he walked, he would be an amiable partner—one she would not hesitate to accept.

But she doubted she would ever have the chance to dance with him. She did not even know his name. Propriety would not allow him to ask her without a proper introduction. And judging from those ladies that followed him about, she was not the sort of lady he would seek out, anyway. She was far too plain...far too unremarkable. All the ladies were far more handsome than the likes of Sarah.

She pulled her gaze to Mr. Croft. What was she doing pining over an unknown man when there was a perfectly acceptable man in front of her? A man who had singled her out—perhaps after a bit of persuasion. But he had asked her, nonetheless. Did he not deserve her full attention? How had she allowed herself to be so rude? Her mother would be rather appalled and disappointed.

Sarah vowed to make amends from that moment on.

She smiled pleasantly at Mr. Croft. The music started and she bowed to him. He was not an unpleasant man to look upon, and he seemed to be interested in her. His eyes did not dart around the room as hers had done earlier.

She lifted her hand to press it against his. "Mr. Croft, where do you hail from?" The question had barely passed her lips when they moved to other partners. Reels were never an easy dance to hold a conversation during. Partners changed too quickly.

She let out a breath. How did people form attachments at

balls when there was so little time for conversation? It was much easier at their country assemblies. There was time to speak over the refreshment table. Even the dances seemed to allow more opportunities. This ballroom was so large and held so many people that even if the opportunity arose, Sarah was not sure how much she would hear of Mr. Croft's reply.

He came even with her again. "My estate is in Durham," was all he got out before he moved away again.

Gads, at this rate she would know very little about him, even if he asked her for a second set. Perhaps she had been wrong, and balls were not the place for her to meet the gentleman she would marry. *If* she was to meet someone in London. She had only been here a few days, but she had seen little that gave her hope that it would happen.

She frowned. When had she become so dull? The gentleman in front of her frowned also. "Is something the matter, Miss Brown?"

Sarah shook her head. "Nothing is the matter. I thought I saw my friend wave to me. But it must have just been a trick of the light." She smiled, trying to prove she told the truth. But they turned in a circle and he moved on before she could tell if he believed it.

The set seemed to last forever, yet she still did not feel as if she had learned much about Mr. Croft, apart from the location of his estate. Perhaps if she mentioned that she was thirsty, he might lead her over to the refreshment table. It would be easier to engage him in a conversation when they could stay face-to-face for longer than a moment.

The set ended and Mr. Croft bowed to her. He lifted his arm and led her back to her seat. Mariah was not in her chair, but Lord Stoke still stood with his arms crossed behind the chairs. He gave a slight dip of his head to Mr. Croft, but otherwise seemed to ignore her.

Sarah looked from Lord Stoke to Mr. Croft and back.

"Thank you for the dance, Mr. Croft." She cleared her throat. "It does seem to have made me rather thirsty though."

She waited for him to volunteer to escort her to the refreshment table, but he did not. Sarah frowned. Had he noticed her poor behavior at the beginning of their set and now did not wish to pursue their acquaintance? Or had he not enjoyed their dance together? Perhaps he was not aware that the refreshment table was where conversations happened. Or maybe he did know, and he just did not wish to converse with her.

He helped her into her chair, then bowed. "Thank you for the dance, Miss Brown." He turned on his heel and disappeared into the crowd without so much as a pause for her response.

Sarah heaved out a sigh. This was not a fortuitous beginning. She did the unthinkable and slouched down in her chair. No other gentlemen appeared anxious to be paired with her.

Her first ball—and she was an utter failure.

Lord Stoke cleared his throat behind her. "I hope you found Mr. Croft acceptable."

Sarah nodded. "He was a fine dancer. I only wish we'd had more of an opportunity to converse."

Lord Stoke did not respond, as he continued his sentry duty behind the chairs. Sarah would even enjoy a conversation with him. But he seemed disinclined to speak.

Mariah returned to the chair. Her face was flush, and she waved her fan furiously. "Lord Candlewood is fetching me a glass of champagne." She smiled at Sarah. "I never knew dancing could make me so thirsty. It was never like this at the assemblies back in Stoke."

Sarah smiled. It was hard not to respond to Mariah's enthusiasm.

"Sarah, who was that you were dancing with? He looked to be a fine dancer."

"His name is Mr. Croft." Sarah glanced behind her quickly. "Your brother introduced us."

Mariah turned in her seat and half scowled, half grinned at her brother. "Do not think your kind act will prevent me from scolding you."

Lord Stoke glanced down at his sister briefly then resumed his scowl at the room. "And what will you be scolding me about this time, Mar?"

"That you are standing here watching over me like I am your prisoner, and you are afraid I might escape. You promised you would occupy your time tonight in the card-room." Mariah pouted.

"There was no seat at the Vingt-un table. I thought I might as well occupy my time here."

"You thought wrong, Regi. I can assure you of that." Mariah lifted a brow and pursed her lips together tightly.

A man approached and Sarah sucked in a breath. It was *him*. It was the tall man she had been watching most of the evening. Was he coming to ask her for a set?

He bowed before them, looking up from beneath his lashes. "Lady Mariah."

The breath whooshed from Sarah's lungs and tears stung at her eyes.

He was there for Mariah, not her.

Sarah bit the side of her cheek, willing the tears back. Why was she surprised? She had known for years that Mariah was more desirable in both appearance and dowry. Why would this gentleman single out Sarah over Mariah?

She shifted away from her friend. Knowing the differences between them did not make the acknowledgment of them hurt any less.

"I hoped, Lady Mariah, you would do me the honor of dancing the next set with me?"

Sarah turned at the same time as Mariah to look at Lord

Stoke. His jaw was set in a hard line, the muscles in his cheeks working.

His eyes narrowed and Mariah's eyes widened slightly, but she turned around and looked at the gentleman. "I am afraid we have not been properly introduced, sir."

The gentleman raised a brow at Lord Stoke. "Come now, Stoke, do introduce me to your sister so we might dance the next set."

Lord Stoke was quiet, his gaze staring just over the gentleman's shoulder. After what seemed an eternity, Lord Stoke opened his mouth. "Lady Mariah, may I introduce you—" he paused, his jaw clenching again— "to Lord Muckrake." He nearly spat out the man's name.

Sarah glanced at Mariah.

A smile played at her lips, but it was not a jovial smile as much as it was trying to dispel the tension surrounding them.

Lord Muckrake extended his hand to Mariah. "Now that introductions have been made, may I claim your next set?"

Lord Stoke cleared his throat. "I am afraid her next is spoken for."

Lord Muckrake looked around. "I do not see anyone coming to claim the set."

"Miss Brown, would you please hurry to the cardroom and inform Lord Berwick it is time for the set he claimed?"

Sarah glanced from Mariah to her brother and then to Lord Muckrake. She had met Lord Berwick, but she did not recall him ever claiming one of Mariah's sets. But why would Lord Stoke lie?

Lord Stoke gently nudged her shoulder. "Go on now, Miss Brown. If you do not hurry, he shall miss the whole set."

Lord Muckrake narrowed his eyes. "Then perhaps I may claim the next."

Sarah paused half standing, half sitting, watching the men. Lord Stoke swallowed hard. "Lord Ragsdale has claimed that set."

Mariah's brows rose.

Lord Muckrake's smile leveled out into a hard line. "What of the next set? Surely your friends have not claimed them all?"

"I'm afraid they have claimed her next five sets." Lord Stoke smiled smoothly.

"Ah, excellent." Lord Muckrake matched Lord Stoke's grin. "Then her supper dance is free?"

Lord Stoke's smile dropped as he did the figures in his head. "Oh, you are correct. I do not believe she is otherwise engaged," he said through clenched teeth.

Lord Muckrake laughed, his chest puffing out. "Excellent. Then I shall return and claim your supper dance." He bowed to them and turned into the crowd that seemed to form around him.

When Lord Muckrake was out of hearing, Mariah sat forward on her chair and twisted around, her hands on her hips. "Why did you say Lord Berwick and your other friends had claimed those sets. No one has claimed my next set because I am thirsty and needed to rest." She nodded her head toward the refreshment table.

They all looked to see Lord Candlewood moving slowly toward them, two shaky glasses of champagne in his hands.

Lord Stoke shook his head. "Well, it will not do for you to skip your dance with Berwick. If you do, you may not be able to dance for the rest of the evening. Although, if that is the case, we may as well return home."

Mariah scowled at him. "We are not leaving."

He nodded toward the door. "Then will you please go fetch him, Miss Brown?"

"But he did not ask me!" Mariah nearly shouted. Frustration and confusion clouded her face.

Sarah straightened but turned slightly to see if Lord Stoke had changed his mind.

He motioned her towards the doorway. "You may as well bring them all in."

Bring them all in? But she did not know them all. Lord Berwick was the only one she was familiar with. How was she to retrieve the others when she had not been properly introduced to them?

She made her way toward the cardroom thinking about what she had just witnessed. It was obvious that Lord Stoke and Lord Muckrake were not friends, but what was it that made them dislike each other so completely? Did Muckrake not like Lord Stoke, or was he simply reacting to Lord Stoke's cold reception?

She glanced back at the ballroom and immediately spotted Lord Muckrake. It was not difficult to see his tall frame and the crowd of women following him. But it also did not give her any answers. She did not even know what title he held. For all she knew, he could be an earl or a viscount, which would place him firmly out of her reach. She did not bother to remind herself that a baron was not within her reach either. But she had not completely given up on that dream.

She allowed herself one last lingering look. Perhaps, if she were very lucky, he would be a baron.

She turned back toward the cardroom, walking quickly to make up for the time she had dallied away watching a man she hardly knew.

Lord Stoke did not like him, of that she was certain. But did that change her interest in him? Something told her it should. But she was determined to discover the reason before she made any decisions.

Chapter Seven

Sarah reached the cardroom door and timidly poked her head inside. It did not seem a proper place for a lady. Smoke clouded the room and the definite smell of spirits wafted out the door. She wrinkled her nose.

That, it seemed, was only the beginning of her problems. Tables full of gentlemen filled the whole of the large parlor. Most of them had their heads bent low, and those who did not, faced away from her—not that seeing their faces would help her much.

A gentleman standing just inside the door gave her a curious look. "May I help you, Miss?"

Sarah nodded. "I was sent to fetch Lord Berwick."

"I saw him at the Ecarté table. Let me fetch him for you." The gentleman turned and made his way around several tables before leaning over and talking to a man with his back to Sarah. Lord Berwick turned and looked over his shoulder, his brow furrowed.

Tossing his cards on the table with a frown, he scooped up his fish and stood up. He leaned over the table and said something, sending the other men into uproarious laughter.

Sarah's face heated as all the eyes at the table turned to

her. What had he said to them? She swallowed, deciding it was best if she did not know.

He came and stood beside her. "Miss Brown, was it?"

She nodded and smiled, trying to make this situation less awkward than it was. "Yes, that is correct." She clasped her hands in front of her. Why was she so nervous? It was not as if she had sent herself to fetch this man. "Lord Stoke asked me to come and fetch you."

Lord Berwick's brow creased even more. "Is something the matter?"

Sarah pulled her bottom lip between her teeth. Did she tell him the whole story? Or did she leave that to Lord Stoke? She pushed out her lips slightly. If Lord Stoke had wished to keep his behavior a secret, then he should have come to fetch the men himself.

"Lord Stoke needs your assistance. Lord Muckrake asked Mariah for a set and Lord Stoke may have inferred that her next five sets were already claimed."

"Five sets?" Lord Berwick cursed with a huff. But it quickly deteriorated into a laugh. "I am now involved in keeping Lady Mariah safe from that rake?"

Lord Berwick thought Lord Muckrake undesirable also? He had called him a rake. Could Lord Muckrake not be the respectable man she had hoped him to be? She grimaced. "It would seem so."

His face clouded. "Wait, did you say five sets?" He shook his head. "Not a chance. If I dance even two sets with Lady Mariah, it will be seen as a near proposal. Not that I have anything against Stoke's sister, but I will not marry the chit just to save her from dancing with Muckrake." He folded his arms across his chest and looked around the room. Was he searching for a means of escape?

Sarah shook her head furiously. "Oh, no. He does not expect you to claim them all." She glanced around him at the other tables. "Lord Stoke has claimed a set for each of your friends."

Berwick threw his head back and laughed. She thought she even detected a bit of moisture in the corner of the man's eyes. "Did he now?" That was his only response? She had thought he would be angry with her. But he did not seem angry at all. Indeed, he seemed to think the whole thing a rather good joke. If he were not a marquess, Sarah might be persuaded to set her sights on him.

Lord Berwick raised his brows, his lips still twitching with laughter. "I wonder how Rags will take the news." He looked over his shoulder, but Sarah could not tell at which table he directed his gaze. "He is on a winning streak, and I can't say he will be happy to leave."

Sarah bit her lip. What was she to do? It was not as if she could drag any of these men into the ballroom. "Perhaps he could take one of the later sets?"

Lord Berwick turned back and grinned down at her. "Don't worry. I will collect them all and bring them to the ballroom."

Sarah released a breath. "Thank you. But could you make haste? It is of a rather urgent nature. You are at this very moment supposed to be dancing with Mariah."

Lord Berwick shook his head and made a growling noise deep in his throat, though his lips were still turned upwards. He motioned to a man standing at the far side of the room watching a game. The man strode over. He dipped his head to Sarah and then looked at Lord Berwick. "You beckoned?"

"Charlie, our presence has been requested in the ballroom."

The man gave Sarah an appraising look. "And why should we be needed in the ballroom?"

"Do not blame her." Berwick motioned to Sarah, but his eyes still scanned the tables. "Bancroft, this is Miss Brown. She is a dear friend of Lady Mariah Thornbeck."

Bancroft gave a slight bow, but suspicion still hung in his gaze.

Bancroft? Was he Lord Bancroft or Mr. Bancroft? Lord Berwick had not offered a proper introduction. If she called him '*my lord,*' and he was not, it would tell the gentlemen that she did not belong there. Taking the easy way out, she curtsied. "It is a pleasure to meet you, sir." While it was not technically incorrect, calling him '*sir*' was not technically correct either. But then neither had been Lord Berwick's introduction, so perhaps no one would notice.

"The pleasure is all mine, Miss Brown." His tone said the complete opposite.

He turned back to Lord Berwick. "I'm afraid I am not inclined to make an appearance in the ballroom." He nodded toward the interior of the room. "A seat has opened up at Whist."

He turned to go, but Lord Berwick reached out and grabbed hold of his arm. "Not so fast, Charlie." He nodded toward the ballroom. "Firstly, you hate Whist. And secondly, it seems our friend, Stoke, has committed each of us to a set with Lady Mariah. I was to be first, but as it will take me some time to remove Cort and Rags from the tables, I thought it best if you went along first."

Bancroft curled his nose. "But if we step foot in the ballroom, we will surely be stuck there for the rest of the evening. Or at least until the supper dance."

Lord Berwick nodded and then grinned, rather wickedly. "Perhaps. But do not think about that. Instead, occupy your mind with what we are to do to Reg after the dancing."

Bancroft grinned. "Oh, that is a rather pleasant thought." He turned to Sarah, and as if seeing her in a different light, he lifted his arm. "Come along, Miss Brown. We mustn't keep Lady Mariah waiting."

Sarah walked beside Bancroft and glanced at him from the corner of her eye.

He was the opposite of Lord Muckrake. Where Lord Muckrake was tall and slender, this Bancroft fellow was stocky. Muckrake's hair was dark and curled up around his ears in a rather handsome way. Bancroft's hair was similar to hers, not quite brown but not quite blond. He was rather unremarkable in every way except, perhaps, for his eyes. His eyes were quite possibly the most beautiful blue eyes she had ever seen. They reminded her of the sea just before the sun dropped below the horizon.

"Why did Reg claim his sister's sets for us?" Bancroft's brow creased.

Sarah pulled her gaze away when he turned toward her. "He was trying to protect her from Lord Muckrake."

"Ah." He nodded his head. No more explanation was needed. What was wrong with Lord Muckrake that all these men disliked him?

"Such a fitting name for him." Bancroft's lips curled up in disgust. "I can understand why Reg would take such a high hand in this situation. If a man like Muckrake ever asked Madi to dance—" He let the sentence fall away.

Who was Madi? And what would he do to Lord Muckrake? Although, perhaps the more pertinent question was what did he believe Lord Muckrake would do to Madi?

Sarah was genuinely intrigued. "I do not believe it went as Lord Stoke planned though." Sarah motioned Bancroft toward Lord Stoke and Mariah.

"And how is that?" He lifted a hand in acknowledgment to the dip of Stoke's head.

"I believe he thought it might deter Lord Muckrake by making him wait until after the supper dance. However, he did not count the number of sets correctly and left her supper set free." She lifted her shoulder. "He was short one friend."

Bancroft shook his head. "If only Heatherton were here."

"Indeed, Lord Stoke is not the only one to wish him here."

Bancroft glanced over at her, and Sarah frowned. Why

had she said that? Mariah would be mortified if her brother or his friends learned of her affection for Lord Heatherton.

Bancroft shook his head but laughed. "Poor Reg. Tonight is not his night. First he must remain in the ballroom, then his plans go awry."

"I do not believe Mariah thinks her night much better." Mariah's lips still sat in a firm line.

"But Lady Mariah enjoys balls. Reg does not. And to have the whole thing come to naught? He stayed in the ballroom to keep Muckrake away, yet still the man secured a set. Yes, I say poor Reg, indeed."

"And his poor luck has not yet come to an end." A man fell in step with Bancroft.

Bancroft glanced over and smiled. "How do you mean, Rags?"

Rags? Was this Lord Ragsdale? Sarah had heard Lord Stoke mention that name to Lord Muckrake. She squinted at him. The name was either a shortened version of his title or it was meant as a joke. Lord Ragsdale was the finest-dressed gentleman Sarah had ever seen. She could not detect even a hair out of place. And he had more of a regal air about him than any of the others she had met.

Rags shrugged, looking none too happy to be there. He nudged his way between Sarah and Bancroft, hunching down as if to make himself less visible. "Not only is Lady Mariah to dance with Lord Muckrake, but Reg now owes me sixty pounds to replace what I left at the table."

Bancroft laughed again. "Perhaps he should leave after supper. He can't afford to stay longer."

Sarah swallowed hard. Sixty pounds? How was such an amount to be won or lost in a single night? And what kind of man could laugh over such an amount? Should her father be so careless, her family would feel the strain. She glanced at Rags and Bancroft from the corner of her eye. Any man who could laugh about losing sixty pounds was obviously a man flush in the pockets. She glanced over at Bancroft. Just how flush was Lord Muckrake?

They made their way to Mariah and Lord Stoke.

Lord Berwick and another man joined them as they came to a stop in front of Mariah. Lord Berwick tilted his head to the side. He glanced back and forth between brother and sister. His gaze finally settled on Mariah. He held out his hand. "It seems I am late for our set, my lady." He winked at her as he helped her from her seat.

Mariah giggled. "I had nearly begun to lose hope you would come."

"I thought I was to take the first dance." Bancroft raised a brow.

"It was not as difficult as I thought to lure Rags away from the tables." Berwick led Mariah out to the dance floor.

Lord Stoke's brows rose. "It is never easy to lure Rags from the tables. Why was tonight any different?"

Lord Ragsdale smirked. "Ben promised you would pay me what I left at the table plus an additional twenty pounds for my trouble."

Lord Stoke jerked his gaze to Lord Berwick, but then turned back to the group and nodded.

Sarah swallowed. Sixty pounds! And Lord Stoke had simply nodded his head as if it were nothing of consequence. She had always known Mariah's family had deep coffers, but it had never been so evident as it was then.

Sarah settled into her seat and forced herself to watch Mariah and Lord Berwick dance what was left of the set. Thinking about the repercussions of sixty pounds had given her a headache.

"As I was all prepared to dance, Miss Brown, would you do me the honor." Bancroft held out his hand.

Sarah glanced back at Lord Stoke. She had not technically been introduced to Bancroft. Or at least it had been a very poor introduction.

"Go ahead, Miss Brown. I have no objections."

Sarah's shoulders dropped. Lawkes, he was no help at all.

She placed her hand in Bancroft's, allowing him to lead her to the dance floor.

They positioned themselves at the end of the line and Sarah smiled uncertainly at him.

"Where do you hail from, Miss Brown?" Bancroft asked as they came together.

"Staffordshire. Mariah and I are neighbors."

"Ah, then you are familiar with Oakdale Grove?"

Sarah nodded. "Yes. I have spent most of my life there."

"It is a fine estate."

They parted and moved to other partners. Sarah chided herself. Why did she not ask after him? It seemed no one was to tell her his proper name, so she might as well try to discover it for herself.

When they came back together again, her brow slightly raised. "And where do you hail from, sir?" There it was again...*sir*.

If he was a lord, would he not have said something?

But he did not seem bothered in the least. He grinned down at her. From all she had seen tonight, he seemed to be a rather amiable gentleman—full of smiles and laughter.

"My estate is in Cornwall."

Sarah smiled genuinely. "I have never been to Cornwall. But I have heard the coastline there is lovely, but also very harsh."

Bancroft nodded. "Some might call it harsh, but I can't think of it as such."

They separated again, ending their conversation for a moment. Sarah frowned. What question would give her the answers she needed—apart from the direct one? She was about to go mad not knowing how to properly address him.

She cleared her throat, readying herself as they met in the middle. "Have you spent much time in Parliament?"

51

His brow furrowed. "No. I find the matters of Parliament rather tedious."

Sarah bit her cheek. That was no help at all. Was he a lord that just did not attend or did he not attend Parliament because he was not allowed to?

"Do you have any siblings?" Perhaps this question would offer her some insight.

He nodded his head, and a soft smile curved his lips. "Yes, I have a sister. Madeleine is eight years my junior."

Sarah nearly scowled. While she did discover who Madi likely was, she had not discovered what she wished to know about Bancroft.

"Then you have no brothers?"

He shook his head. "No, it is just the two of us."

They moved away again, and Sarah took the opportunity to think of more questions to ask. Although she was running out of ideas rather quickly. And time. They were nearly done with the reel, and they had missed the first dance completely.

"What of your mother and father?" She grinned to herself. Why had she not thought of that before? Surely in a discussion about his parents, if there was a title, it would come out, would it not?

His face clouded slightly. "My father died when I was still attending Cambridge." The sadness seemed to lift in the next moment. "But my mother is still living. She is a rather remarkable woman. But she detests London and remained in Cornwall."

Sarah should be happy with all that she had learned about the man. She knew more about him in this one dance than she had learned about Mr. Croft in a whole set. However, the one thing she wished to know still eluded her.

The set finally ended. Mariah and Lord Berwick arrived at the chairs just as Bancroft helped Sarah into her seat.

Mariah curtsied to Bancroft and grinned up at him. "Mr. Bancroft, I do believe it is your turn for a set."

Sarah nearly squealed. There it was! The answer she'd been trying to learn for the last half of an hour. She relaxed back into her chair. Calling him *sir* had not been the slight she had imagined it to be.

Mariah took her turn with each of Lord Stoke's friends and Sarah watched. None of the other men asked her to dance. Indeed, each one snuck out of the ballroom once their set was over. They had all seemed rather good-natured about the situation, save for Lord Ragsdale. She wondered if it was the situation or if he was always out of sorts.

When Lord Montcort helped Mariah into her chair, Lord Muckrake appeared at his elbow. "Ah, Montcort. I see you finally pulled yourself away from the cardroom to fulfill your claim." He raised an eyebrow, and Sarah realized he was not as handsome as she had originally thought. There was a look in his eyes she could not quite place. It was not kindness. She knew that much.

The humor dropped from Lord Montcort's face and his jaw set in a hard line. "Keep your hands where we can see them, Muckrake."

"Not to worry. I am not taking her from the ballroom... tonight." Lord Muckrake smirked then held out his hand to Mariah. "It seems my time has come at last."

Mariah smiled stiffly but allowed him to lead her toward the dance floor. She glanced back over her shoulder, giving her brother a wide-eyed look.

"Thunder and turf," Lord Stoke muttered. "This was just what I wished to avoid." He craned his head to the side. "And now he has led her so far into the crowd, I cannot see her." He grunted and moved around the chairs.

He glanced down at Sarah. "Miss Brown, would you do me the honor of dancing the set with me?" He extended his hand toward her.

"You seem to have things in hand, Reg. I will take my leave." Lord Montcort turned and hurried through the crowd.

Sarah looked around her as if she thought he might be speaking to another Miss Brown. When she looked back, he nodded expectantly.

"Yes, of course." She put her hand in his and allowed him to lead her to the dance floor. She had only dreamed of dancing with him but had not thought him to actually ask her. Now that he had, she was not certain where to look. She blushed. This was not the dancing lessons they had paired up for all those years ago. This was an actual ball. The champagne she had sipped at earlier sloshed about in her stomach.

Lord Stoke led her deep into the crush. They took their places in line, and both looked to the side where Mariah and Lord Muckrake stood.

Chapter Eight

Reginald looked down the line and spotted Mariah. She stood across from Muckrake but looked everywhere but at the man. *That's a good girl.*

Reginald smiled. At least his sister was not a complete dolt. She obviously saw Lord Muckrake for what he was.

His shoulders relaxed and he smiled across at Miss Brown. Perhaps it had been unnecessary to join the set. But now he was here, he could not take it back.

At least not without embarrassing and disappointing Miss Brown. He grunted. Perhaps he should have just stayed in the cardroom. It is not as if his presence in the ballroom had done anything to deter Lord Muckrake from Mariah. All it had accomplished was to force Reginald to dance when it was the last thing he wished to do. And he now owed more than one hundred and twenty pounds to his friends to cover their losses. All in all, it had been a rather disastrous evening.

He scowled but then caught Miss Brown's gaze. It was not her fault that he was in this predicament. He should not be ill-tempered with her.

He smiled, remembering when she had been just Sarah. It

had been many years since he had felt comfortable calling her by her Christian name. But he still found himself thinking of her in that way more times than not.

He remembered it as if it were yesterday. He had returned home from Cambridge for the summer and found Sarah was no longer the little girl he remembered before he left. In the beginning, he had not been altogether comfortable with the changes. But after a time, he did not notice it as much.

He glanced down the row at Mariah. It had been the same time he realized Mariah was no longer a little girl either. And from that time onward, he had dreaded this moment, the moment when someone like Muckrake would take notice of her.

"I am surprised you decided to dance," Sarah said as they came together.

"While I do not do it often, I find I enjoy dancing now and then." He grinned. "Especially when the partner is agreeable."

Sarah smiled and it felt like the old days when Reginald was learning to dance from the dancing master. Sarah had been his partner on many occasions, as Mariah often cried off early. The memories allowed Reginald to relax. There were no expectations with this dance. It was just Sarah.

"Are you going to dance more sets this evening?"

Reginald gave her a wide-eyed look. "Not if I can help it."

A laugh bubbled out and she covered her mouth with her hand. "You are to return to the cardroom for the rest of the evening, then?"

Reginald lifted his shoulder. "I have not decided. I am not yet certain that Mariah is safe, now that Muckrake has had his dance with her. And there are other men in attendance which are not much better." He frowned. "Perhaps it is best if we leave after dinner."

They separated and moved to different partners. Coming

back together, Reginald glanced over at his sister. "Mariah will not be pleased if we leave early. I am certain she wishes me back to the cardroom."

Miss Brown returned his smile. "I am certain you are correct. Mariah does not like to be watched over."

"If she knew what I know about some of these men, she would appreciate my watchful eye."

Miss Brown raised a brow. "I do not believe we are speaking of the same Mariah. Her knowing what you know would only make her more determined to be on her own. To prove she does not need you."

Reginald shrugged. "You are surely correct. Mariah is nothing if not stubborn." His brow creased. "You do not think she would deliberately seek out Muckrake just to prove a point, do you?"

Miss Brown shook her head. "No. I know for certain Mariah's affections lie elsewhere."

They came together in the middle, nearly face-to-face, and turned in a tight circle. His pulse ticked up slightly. He raised his brow and tilted his head slightly to the side. "Oh? And what do you know of Mariah's affections?"

They backed away from each other and Miss Brown ducked her head, a guilty expression on her face. "That is not for me to discuss. But I do not believe you have any reason to worry in regard to Lord Muckrake." She glanced down the row. "She does not look to be fawning over him as many of the other ladies do."

Reginald followed her gaze. Miss Brown was correct. Mariah smiled politely at the man, but Reginald could not see any sign of affection or even fondness. He sucked in a deep breath. "That is, indeed, a relief."

"It is a pity he is so objectionable." Miss Brown looked down the row and sighed.

"Do not make me worry about you now, Miss Brown." He

smiled at her. "Although you have always been far more sensible than Mariah."

Miss Brown's features clouded, but then she smiled so quickly that Reginald almost wondered if he had seen correctly.

"Yes, I am nothing if not sensible." Did he detect a hint of annoyance in her voice?

Reginald shrugged it away. Why should it annoy Miss Brown to be known to have sense? It was not something many ladies her age possessed.

"What exactly is so objectionable about him?"

Reginald's nostrils flared. "He has ruined at least six ladies, although I am certain there are more of them that I do not know about. He takes what he wants and then leaves them to face the repercussions alone. He is deplorable and no lady of sense would cast her eyes in his direction."

Miss Brown frowned, then glanced toward Mariah and Muckrake, as if she were trying to reconcile what Reginald had just told her with what she had previously believed.

Reginald hoped she was not like so many of the other young ladies who chased after Muckrake, even after knowing what he was.

The set ended and Reginald led Miss Brown back to their seats. Muckrake deposited Mariah at the same time. He looked over at Reginald and winked. "Your sister is a fine dancer and a very handsome lady."

Reginald balled his hands at his side. He placed a protective hand on her shoulder and narrowed his eyes. "Yes, it seems we both had very handsome partners."

Muckrake looked at down at Miss Brown. He studied her for a moment, then looked back at Reginald. A lazy smile spread across his face. "I had not thought her the sort of lady you would find agreeable."

Just what did Muckrake mean by that? Sarah was a perfectly amiable partner. Reginald's hands tightened on

Mariah's shoulder until she winced, and he dropped his hands to his side.

Muckrake bowed to Mariah. "Lady Mariah, may I claim your first set after supper?"

Mariah looked back at him and let out a nervous chuckle. "Oh." She stammered.

What was this man about? Two dances with Mar back-to-back? Was he purposely trying to tell others that he was taking Mariah for himself? Or was he simply trying to ruin her in the eyes of any proper gentleman? That was the last thing Reginald wanted and the last thing Mariah needed.

"I am afraid we are not returning to the ballroom after supper. I have an early appointment and it would not be proper for me to leave the ladies behind without a chaperone."

Mariah jerked her head around and stared at him. Emotions warred within her gaze. She did not want to dance with Muckrake, of that Reginald was certain. But she did not wish to leave the ball early either.

He gave her a slight shrug. What else was he to do? If she declined to dance with Muckrake, she would not be allowed to dance the rest of the evening. And if that were the case, what was the point in staying? Perhaps he could convince his friends to return to his townhouse and have drinks there.

She turned back to face Muckrake and gave him a tight smile. "I am sorry, my lord, but we seem to be leaving early tonight. Perhaps at the next ball, we will have the opportunity to dance."

Reginald smiled smugly. He may not have succeeded in preventing Muckrake from dancing with her one time, but he would make certain Muckrake did not dance with her again. Ever.

The lazy smile spread across Muckrake's face again. "Of that, my lady, you may be certain." The rake turned on his heel and disappeared into the crowd, a flock of ladies following him.

Reginald released a sigh. He tilted his head side to side and twisted, stretching out his tight and knotted muscles. Lud, this was going to be a long Season.

Chapter Nine

Reginald stood up from behind his desk, stretching out his back and rolling his neck several times. He knew keeping current on the ledgers was of great import, but it did not make the task any less tedious.

He looked at the cord hanging in the corner of his study. He should call for tea, but the thought of having tea by himself did not set well. What was Mar up to this afternoon?

Stepping into the corridor from his study, he looked in both directions. Where should he begin to look for her? If they were at Oakdale, he would look for her in the orangery. But he was not sure where to look for her here. This was her first time in London, and he was not certain what rooms had become her favorite. Perhaps he should find a servant and ask if they had seen her.

He moved along the corridor, his hands clasped behind his back. Mariah had not been happy leaving the ball early last evening, but she would thank him when she learned the full story of Lord Muckrake. Or at least he thought she would. He frowned. But then it was Mariah, and she was never one to be grateful for his protection. Or overprotection, as she saw it.

He breathed out heavily through his nose. She had no idea

what Muckrake was capable of and Reginald did not intend to let her find out.

He rounded the corner and stopped outside the Bird Parlor. The lilting tones of a female voice drifted from the room.

Reginald grinned. It seemed he would not need to ask a servant after all.

His smile widened when he heard another voice. Sarah had come for a visit. She would make an amiable addition at tea. It was always pleasant when Sarah came. She seemed to put Mariah in better spirits. And when Mariah was in high spirits, the entire house was calmer.

He stood outside the door and listened for a moment. It was not completely acceptable, and Mariah would ring a peal over him if she discovered him. But he could not help himself. He knew once he entered the room, they would change their conversation to something of less substance.

"I thought your affections had turned towards Lord Muckrake," Mariah said.

Sarah leaned in slightly, her voice quiet. Reginald leaned forward also, straining to hear what she said. But he could not determine her words. The shaking of her head made him think she was dismissing the idea, which was a relief.

"Do not let Regi's opinion sway you. If Lord Muckrake is who you desire, I shall help you win his affections."

He swallowed hard. Did Sarah still desire his affections? While she was not under his guardianship, he still did not wish to see her with that man. He had hoped she had seen him for what he was. Or at least had taken his words of caution seriously.

Mariah's eyes lit. "Indeed, you are in earnest?" She clapped her hands together. "Oh, this is very exciting. He is much better than Lord Muckrake. He has ten thousand a year! And I do believe you would make a very good match with him."

Then Sarah did not wish to pursue Muckrake. But who was Mariah talking about? Had Sarah discovered she had affections for another gentleman? Reginald leaned closer to the door and twisted his head so his ear turned fully to the room. What was his name? Was he reputable? Did Reginald know him?

Mariah babbled on but made no mention of the gentleman's name. A maid walked past and darted a glance at him as she walked by. Reginald's face heated. Lud, he had been caught by a servant listening at the door. It was so lowering. He was an earl, for pity's sake.

He straightened his waistcoat and pushed into the room. He was learning no new information and was only looking suspect to the servants. He may as well make his presence known.

"Good afternoon, Mariah." He moved to the sofa and placed a kiss on his sister's cheek then offered a smile to Sarah. "And to you, Miss Brown." As he had suspected, their quiet chatter ceased as soon as he entered. He sat in the chair opposite the ladies. "What were you so intently discussing just now?"

Mariah lifted her chin. "We were speaking of the ball last evening and how disappointed we were to leave it so early. I believe we were the only ladies in London abed before midnight." She scowled at him.

"Yes, you informed me of your displeasure last evening, Mariah. I should think you would have exhausted that subject by now." Reginald picked up his newspaper off the side table and held it up in front of him. "Was that all you were discussing?" He did not believe they would actually give the name of the man Sarah wished to pursue, but it was a possibility, was it not? Perhaps if he were very quiet...

Mariah sighed. "We were discussing the gentlemen present. There were many fine dancers in attendance. But there were none I found particularly interesting."

Reginald tipped the corner of his paper down and looked at his sister. "None were particularly interesting? You danced with nearly every one of my friends. I should have thought you found them somewhat intriguing. After all, they did quit the cardroom in order to save you from Lord Muckrake's attentions."

Mariah raised a brow. "And a lot of good it did me. I still ended up dancing with the gentleman."

Reginald let out a guffaw. "Gentleman, indeed."

"Whatever you wish to call him, your efforts were in vain. And I believe it is quite possible it will happen again at the next ball. I am certain your protests only gave him a challenge to overcome."

"Then I shall just have to send our regrets for all invitations to balls. I will not allow you to dance with that man again." Reginald grinned at the sharp intake of breath he assumed could only be from Mariah. Gads, if only he could find her a husband. He would certainly miss her, but he did not know if he could handle another Season of this. Not when this one was going to be his demise.

"But Regi, you can't. If that is your plan, you may as well send me back to Stoke."

"Now there is an idea." He admitted there was far too much enthusiasm in his tone, but the idea was appealing. It would solve all his problems. Or at the very least, delay them.

He heard the rustle of fabric and the top of his newspaper pushed down. "I shall not allow it."

Reginald flicked his glance at Sarah. What did she think about the whole situation? Did she sympathize with Mariah or find her as tedious as Reginald did?

Sarah sat on the sofa, her gaze darting back and forth between the two. But her face gave nothing away.

"Then how do you suggest I keep it from happening again?" Reginald said with a sigh and raised his paper high, pretending to read it once again.

"I suppose you will have to make more friends," Sarah chuckled, but it quickly became muffled as she must have placed her hand over her mouth.

Reginald lowered his paper. "I beg your pardon?" He raised a brow at Sarah, and she pinked rather handsomely. His lips turned up of their own accord.

Her face sobered, but merriment still danced in her eyes.

Reginald tilted his head to the side. Had he ever noticed her eyes before? They were rather pretty—much browner than he had remembered—when there was mischief in them. And while he usually did not find hazel eyes all that remarkable, something about Sarah's were. He gave a slight shrug. Pretty eyes would be helpful in securing her a match. It was much more difficult to marry off an ugly *and* poor woman.

She dropped her hands into her lap, fidgeting with her fingers. "I only meant that there will be more sets than what your friends can claim. Otherwise, as Lord Berwick told me last evening, everyone will assume there is an understanding between them and Mariah."

Reginald's brow creased. "You believe people will think five gentlemen have an understanding with my sister?"

Sarah curled her lips inward. "I am only repeating what Lord Berwick told me last evening."

Reginald shook his head and raised the paper in front of him, even though he was not reading it. "Then I suppose I shall have to formulate a better plan before I accept another invitation to a ball."

"I hope you figure it out soon, Regi. I do not wish to miss all the balls this Season." A slight breeze fluttered the corner of his paper as Mariah returned to her seat.

"I am most pleased that you found a gentleman that intrigued you."

Reginald's focus on the words blurred but he kept the paper in place. This was better than listening in the corridor.

It was as if they forgot he was even there and there was no risk of the servants discovering him.

"I do not know why you are so pleased, Mariah." Sarah's voice held a note of frustration. "It is not as if he is interested in me. He spent most of his evening in the cardroom."

Cardroom. Reginald released a breath. At least he could be assured that she was not speaking of Lord Muckrake. Not that he believed Sarah was cotton-brained enough to set her sights on that gentleman once she had learned of his reputation. But there were others of similar ilk.

"We must come up with a plan to gain the gentleman's notice."

"And how do we do that?" Sarah sounded uncertain.

Reginald peaked discreetly around the paper.

Mariah tapped her finger over her lips. "Simple. I will teach you how to flirt with a man."

Reginald coughed to cover his laughter. Mariah teaching Sarah how to flirt? Where had Mariah gained her proficiency? What did she know of such things?

The corner of his paper curled over again. Mariah peered at him. "Is there a problem, Regi?"

Reginald shook his head and patted his chest. "No, no. I just had a tickle in my throat. I am well."

Mariah studied him for a moment, but then shrugged and released his paper.

"What do you know of flirting?" Sarah's voice had quieted from before, but he could still hear her. Had she discovered he was listening?

"Trust me, Sarah, I am quite proficient in the art."

It took all his concentration to stop the laugh before it came out again. Surely, they would realize he was listening if it escaped. His sister was beyond the pale, offering to teach Sarah something she knew nothing about. And what was this nonsense that flirting was an art? Art required pencils or oils. Certainly not whatever trick Mariah thought to teach. If Reginald was not trying so hard to be invisible, he might have just argued that point with her.

"I do trust you, Mariah. But what do you suggest I try first?"

How could Sarah be so daft? Was she seriously considering this nonsense? He heard someone shift on the couch, but he did not know if it was Mariah or Sarah. "The first step in flirting with a gentleman is you must laugh at all his jokes. They like to be thought of as witty." Mariah's voice had lowered, but her words were still clear.

He could not listen for another second. It could not be worth all this just to discover the name of a gentleman. He lowered his newspaper and scoffed. "That's ridiculous." What did Mariah know of what a gentleman wanted? And if she did have this knowledge, why had she never done anything Reginald wished her to?

"And what is so ridiculous, Regi?" There was a distinct huff in Mariah's voice.

Reginald folded his paper and placed it on his lap. "No man wishes to have a giggling girl beside him. Much less take her for a wife."

"And just what do you know of finding a wife?" Mariah's scowl furrowed her brow and pursed her lips. "Are you not one of the men who has vowed to stay a bachelor? How are you to say what is desirable when looking for a bride?"

Reginald shook his head. "It has little to do with finding a bride, per se. It has more to do with tolerating a person enough to learn if you are compatible. And I know plenty about that." He gave Mariah a pointed look. "Why do you think I have vowed to stay a bachelor?"

Sarah's brow creased. "Perhaps your brother is right. It might be best if we tried another approach."

Mariah turned her scowl on Sarah. "I thought you said you trusted me. Are you really going to take the advice of a man with so little experience at courting?"

Sarah's gaze shifted between them, and she pulled her bottom lip between her teeth. "I think you both make very good points."

That was very... diplomatic of her. She was surely wasting her skills for diplomacy in the ballrooms of London.

Reginald shrugged and rolled his eyes at Mariah. "Do what you wish, you usually do. But do not come moaning to me when your ploy does not work."

Mariah shrugged. "When have I ever come moaning to you?" Reginald opened his mouth to start listing examples, but Mariah hurried on. "I will help Sarah to find a match. After-all, is that not why she came to London?"

Reginald spread out his paper and lifted it in front of him. If they did not want his opinion, he would keep it to himself. However, he would only admit to himself that he was the slightest bit interested in observing the results of Mar's experiment. And perhaps even more interested to discover the gentleman they would use it upon.

Chapter Ten

S arah tried to slow her steps as she followed the butler down the corridor, a paper crumpled tightly in her fist. But her excitement kept pushing her faster, until she ran into the older man's back and stepped on the back of his heel, causing them both to stumble slightly.

He cast her an annoyed expression and motioned her into a room. "Lady Mariah, Miss Brown is here to see you."

Mariah stood up from her place on the couch, her stitchery dropping to the floor.

Normally Sarah would have raised her brows at the carelessness, but today she had news that made the stitchery unimportant.

She hurried over to the couch and reached out her hands to Mariah. She wished to let out a squeal of delight but held it back because she knew it would not be proper. Not that such things had ever stopped Mariah from squealing when she was excited. But Mariah was the daughter of an earl, and such things could be overlooked. It was not likely to be overlooked coming from Sarah.

"Sarah, what is it? You look as though you are positively bursting with excitement."

Sarah nodded and thrust a paper forward. "Look, look at this."

Mariah took the paper and looked down at it. "It is an invitation to a card party?"

Sarah nodded her head. "Yes, it is for Mr. Harvey's card party." Her eyes widened. "Mariah, it has started. The invitations have started to arrive."

Mariah laughed and patted Sarah's arm. "Is it not just as I said? Did I not tell you once you started to attend other events the invitations would follow?"

"Are you to attend?" Sarah pulled her lip between her teeth. "I do not know what I should do if I have to go alone with my parents."

"Have you already sent your acceptance?" Mariah sat down on the couch and studied the paper.

Sarah shook her head. Her mother had wished to accept immediately, but Sarah had convinced her to wait until she spoke to Mariah. *You need not have Mariah with you at every event*, her mother had chided.

But Sarah did not agree.

Her mother was a gentleman's daughter. But that did not make her knowledgeable about the upper tier of society. Her father, like her husband, was not a gentleman of great wealth.

Mariah smiled widely and reached for a pile of letters off the nearby tray. "I have not replied to any that I received today. Let's go through them together and we can see which ones would be to our best advantage."

"But—"

Mariah frowned. "But what? Would it not be better for us to attend a party hosted by Lady Greenspan or Lord Wellsby? I should not like to decline an invitation to an advantageous party in favor of one at Mr. Harvey's."

Sarah looked down at the paper in her hand, her shoulders dropping. But this party was different. Her family had been particularly singled out. It was not one that she would be attending as Mariah's guest. Did that not mean something?

Lord Stoke entered the room and took his seat in his usual chair. "And what are we discussing today, Mariah? Are you deciding which laugh is best for each kind of joke?" He picked up his paper but looked over at the ladies before opening it. "Or perhaps it is simply a matter of tone?"

Mariah smirked at her brother. "No, Regi. As a matter of fact, we were discussing which parties we are to attend this week."

Lord Stoke put his paper aside, an interested look on his face. "And where am I to escort you?"

"Sarah wishes to go to a card party on Wednesday next hosted by Mr. Harvey." She tilted her head to the side and pushed out her lips, showing him she did not care for that idea. "But I contend that we should check our invitations and see what parties will be of most benefit."

Lord Stoke frowned. "But Mr. Harvey is a friend. Why would you not accept his invitation?"

Mariah gave him an exasperated look. "Are you suggesting we send our regrets to the likes of Lady Greenspan in favor of Mr. Harvey? Why would we do such a thing?"

"For one, he is our friend, while Lady Greenspan is merely an acquaintance." He raised a brow. "But it does not matter one way or another. I cannot escort you to either event on Wednesday next. I have a meeting with Lord Everton from Lords and Mr. Carver from Commons. We are discussing a new commerce bill that we wish to present together in Parliament."

Mariah pouted.

Sarah studied her for a moment. From her experience, when Mariah pouted, she usually received what she wanted. Would Lord Stoke change his plans so Mariah could attend Lady Greenspan's party?

He shook his head. "I'm sorry, Mar, but there is nothing

for it. I have already committed to the gentlemen, and I cannot cry off. Especially not for a card party."

"Then I am to miss them both? How is that acceptable?" Tears filled the bottom of Mariah's lids. She was very proficient at conjuring tears if her pout did not work. Some might find it distasteful, but more times than not, Sarah benefitted from her actions. And besides, it was just Mariah's way. You could not accept only parts of her. It was all or nothing. And Sarah had decided long ago that Mariah's friendship was worth the few vexations here and there.

Sarah sat up taller. "Oh, Mariah. Perhaps this is not so terrible. We were invited to Mr. Harvey's also. My parents could escort us to that party."

Lord Stoke smiled patiently at Mariah. "You see, you shall not have to miss a party. Sir Winston and Lady Brown will surely have no objection to taking you along."

Sarah nodded. "Indeed, they will quite enjoy it. This shall be their first party in town."

Mariah looked down at the pile in her lap. Cards and papers were turned in varying directions. She pulled a section from the middle. Setting the rest aside, she stood and threw the papers in the fire. "If we are to go to Mr. Harvey's, I suppose I have no need of those."

Sarah jumped up. "Oh, Mariah, have you sent your regrets yet?"

Mariah frowned down at the flames engulfing the papers. She glanced up at Sarah and then at her brother. "Oh, I seem to have forgotten that." She shrugged a shoulder. "There is nothing for it now."

Sarah swallowed, staring at the flames. "But Mariah, it is completely improper not to send your regrets. Do you remember who they were from?"

Mariah put a finger to her lips and thought, then shook her head. "The only one that comes to mind is Lady Greenspan. I do not recall the other three."

"What about Lord Wellsby?"

Mariah smiled and nodded. "Oh yes, he was one of them."

"That is only one of three. Surely you can remember the others." Sarah's stomach twisted at the thought that an invitation might go unanswered.

Mariah shrugged. "I cannot imagine every person invited sends their regrets or acceptance." She frowned at Sarah. "Do not act as though I have done something criminal, Sarah. They are just invitations."

Sarah glanced over at Lord Stoke. His hand covered his face and his fingers rubbed at his eyes. Was he doing it out of frustration or were his eyes simply bothering him?

He looked up at Mariah, but his usual smile was missing. "Then we agree? You shall accompany the Browns to Mr. Harvey's party on Wednesday next?"

Mariah clasped her hands in front of her and nodded. "Yes, I suppose that is the best plan."

Lord Stoke pushed himself out of his chair and moved toward the doorway. "Will you send your acceptance or must I do it?" There was a touch of agitation in his tone.

Mariah pushed her hip out, placing her hand on it. "Of course I will send my acceptance, Regi. Do you think I would attend a party without sending an acceptance? Mama did teach me etiquette."

"Sometimes, Mar, I'm not sure what to think about you." Lord Stoke turned from the room, his head shaking slightly.

Mariah glared at his back, but then moved over to the couch and sat next to Sarah. She picked up Sarah's hands and grinned widely. "We shall have so much fun. Have you received any other invitations?"

Sarah frowned, her head shaking. "No, just the one from Mr. Harvey." She looked down at her hands. "And the one from Lord Ponsonby. But I'm sure it is as you say, more will come. I simply need to be patient."

But when? When would more come? She had been in London for more than a fortnight, and they had only received two invitations. And one of them she was certain was because of Lord Stoke.

But she smiled because Mariah seemed so happy.

Mariah pulled her stack of cards and letters onto her lap. "Why do we not go through the rest of these, and we can decide together which we shall attend."

Sarah sighed. "That is a large pile." While she appreciated Mariah including her in the invitations, it was not the same as being invited on her own merit. Still, she would likely see Mr. Bancroft while attending a party with Mariah, whereas she was guaranteed not to see him if she attended nothing at all.

Sarah and Mariah peered out the window of the carriage together, looking up at the front of Mr. Harvey's townhome.

Sir Winston and Lady Brown sat on the opposite bench, waiting for a footman to open the door. Lady Brown flipped open her fan, waving it furiously in front of her. It could not be because she was hot, as the nighttime temperatures had cooled greatly in the last fortnight. The action had become more of a habit than a need to cool herself.

"Are you not excited, girls?" Her eyes widened as she allowed Sarah's father to help her from the carriage.

Sarah ran her hands down the front of her gown and swallowed. She did not know why she was so nervous. It was just Mr. Harvey, not a lord or duke. This should feel no different than a party at his home in the country.

She clutched her box of fish and moved to stand up.

Mariah put her hand out and gently pushed her back into her seat. She pulled the fish out of Sarah's hands and set them on the bench between them.

Sarah's brow creased. "What are you doing? How shall I play if I don't have my fish?"

Mariah raised a brow looking rather pleased with herself. "If you do not have fish, you shall have to borrow some from a gentleman." She grinned widely as if this were her most brilliant idea yet.

Sarah bit the side of her cheek, questioning whether she should follow Mariah so blindly. "Are you certain? It seems to me it shows a certain amount of stupidity to come to a card party and forget your fish."

Mariah shook her head. "If you know so much about this, why did you ask for my help?" Her voice was clipped, and Sarah knew she had hurt her feelings.

Sarah glanced down at the box on the bench and nodded. "If that is what you think is best."

Mariah nodded. "Now come along. Your parents are almost to the door." She stepped out first and waited for Sarah on the walkway.

Sarah closed her eyes and clutched her hands tightly in her lap. This was it. This was the night she would make certain Mr. Bancroft noticed her.

"Do not forget what we discussed, Sarah," Mariah hissed in Sarah's ear as they entered Mr. Harvey's townhome.

Sarah glanced around the modest sized entryway. Black and white marble floors created a checkered pattern on the floor and a large chandelier hung above. It was not as grand as Mariah's townhome, but it was in a respectable neighborhood and did not have a shop beneath it.

"Which part?" Sarah glanced over at her friend. "We have discussed a great many things this week."

Mariah's eyes widened slightly. "If Mr. Bancroft is here, you are to flirt with him, remember? It is the only way he will pay you any mind."

Sarah nodded reluctantly. While she knew Mariah did not

mean to infer that Sarah's own attributes were not enough to draw his attention, the inference was still there.

There were many things Mariah was very knowledgeable about. As the daughter of nobility, she had been trained by her mother as such. However, Sarah was not convinced that flirting had been part of her lessons. She simply could not picture in her mind the Countess teaching Mariah to giggle at things that may not actually be funny. And Lord Stoke seemed to find the notion utterly ridiculous. Indeed, he had used that exact word.

But, as Sarah had no other ideas, she did not believe she should disregard Mariah's ideas completely.

Besides, she did remember seeing Miss Ashdown giggling rather frequently at everything Mr. Rosen said to her at the last assembly. At the time, Sarah had not realized what the girl was doing. But the couple were to be wed within a fortnight, so perhaps Mariah was not so wrong.

"What if he is not here?" It was not the first time she had wondered. Mr. Harvey was a well-liked man in Stoke-on-Trent, as far as she had witnessed. But she did not know if his influence extended to those of Lord Stoke's friends. Perhaps Mr. Bancroft would not even be here. And then what would she do? Should she practice on someone else?

She shook her head. That seemed to be a poor idea. And likely would only lead to misunderstandings.

She sighed. Perhaps tonight was not the night she would know if Mariah's instructions were correct.

Mariah's hand swung to the side, her fan hitting Sarah in the upper arm.

"Ouch," Sarah said as she rubbed her arm. "Why did you hit me?"

Mariah nodded her head and Sarah looked in that direction. A slow smile spread across her face when she saw Mr. Bancroft standing across the room speaking with Lord Montcort.

"It is just as I thought," Mariah said behind her fan. "This was the most advantageous event for us tonight."

Sarah opened her mouth to correct her, but then shut it knowing it would not make a difference. If Mariah had had her way, they would be at Lady Greenspan's party tonight, not at Mr. Harvey's. She lifted her chin slightly and smiled. It seemed Mariah was not always right. Sometimes Sarah knew the right of it.

Mariah grabbed her hand and pulled her in his direction. Once they reached the men, Mariah pulled to a stop and grinned up at them. "Good evening, Lord Montcort," she turned her gaze to the other men. "Mr. Bancroft. I was uncertain we would see you here tonight. I know Lady Greenspan also had a party this evening."

The two men looked down at them and Sarah's stomach lurched. Mr. Bancroft looked very handsome this evening in his deep blue tailcoat and pink and blue striped waistcoat.

Neither man looked directly at her, nor did they look directly at Mariah. She could not say she detected any amount of interest on either man's part. But they didn't ignore them, so she decided there might still be hope.

Mr. Bancroft shrugged. "I find Lady Greenspan rather a bore."

Mariah cleared her throat loudly and gave Sarah a wide-eyed stare.

Indeed? That was what she wanted Sarah to laugh at?

Sarah thought of Miss Ashdown, happily engaged, and let out a giggle while trying not to roll her eyes. "Really, Mr. Bancroft, you are terrible speaking in such a manner."

Mr. Bancroft's smile fell away and he looked at her as if she had just said the earth was flat.

He cleared his throat and looked just over Sarah's shoulder. "Anyhow, Mr. Harvey is a good sort of man and far more diverting."

Both men looked around Mariah and Sarah. "Where is Reg?" Lord Montcort asked.

Mariah lifted her shoulder. "He had a meeting with several gentlemen from Parliament." She rolled her eyes. "And tonight was the only night they could meet." She leaned in closer to the men. "But I think perhaps he just did not wish to accompany me."

"If Reg did not bring you, who did?" Lord Montcort asked.

"Mariah came with my parents and me," Sarah finally found her voice.

"Reg took the night off, did he? Well, isn't he the lucky one," Mr. Bancroft said.

Mariah shoved another elbow into Sarah's ribs. Lawkes, at this rate, Sarah's side would be black and blue, come morning.

But still, she let out a loud laugh.

Mr. Bancroft's brow creased. "Are you well, Miss Brown?"

Sarah smiled widely and nodded. "Of course. Why should you think I was unwell?"

"I thought you must have been coughing," his brow creased deeper.

Sarah raised a hand, patting lightly her neck. She cleared her throat. Mariah's plan was not working in the least. Or was it Sarah's laugh that was the problem? Either way, Mr. Bancroft must think Sarah the most ridiculous person in the room. "Oh, no. I just had a slight tickle." Heat traveled up her neck all the way to the tips of her earlobes. Next time she would need to control her laughter, perhaps simply giggle as she had the first time.

She closed her eyes briefly, praying that there would not be a next time.

Mariah looked out at the tables and then turned back to the gentlemen. "Have you decided which game you are to play tonight?"

Lord Montcort nodded his head. "I believe I will try my hand at Hazard."

Mr. Bancroft raised a shoulder. "I had the devil's luck at Ecarté last time I played. Quadrille will be my game tonight."

Sarah let out a sigh but then hurried on before Mariah had the chance to elbow her again. "I was thinking of joining the Quadrille table also." She smiled at him, hoping it looked dazzling, rather than as dreadful as she felt. "If you are amiable, sir, perhaps we could play beside each other."

Mr. Bancroft nodded slowly, but he did not look thrilled by the idea. Sarah glanced away, her smile falling. This was not going at all how she'd planned. Perhaps it would have been best for her to practice on a different man. At least when it did not work on them, it would not be disheartening.

She turned to Mariah. "What about you Mariah? What game are you to play?"

Mariah lifted her shoulder and grunted. "Perhaps I shall just watch for a bit."

Sarah moved over to the Quadrille table standing behind an empty seat. Mr. Bancroft pulled out the chair and motioned her to it. "Miss Brown."

Sarah smiled up at him. Was he just being a gentleman or was he happy she was sitting next to him? She sat in the offered seat and ran her hands down the front of her gown.

As the cards were dealt, Mr. Bancroft leaned over. "You may wish to keep your fish on the table. You would not want someone to accuse you of cheating when you withdraw the box later."

Sarah looked down at her hands. She tried to pretend that she only now noticed she had no fish with her, but from the look on Mr. Bancroft's face, she had not fooled him.

"I seem to have left my fish in the carriage." She laughed nervously. "Perhaps I should excuse myself and allow someone else to play." She moved to push her chair out, knowing Mariah would be extremely disappointed in the performance.

Was she not supposed to ask to borrow some fish from Mr. Bancroft? But she couldn't do it. He surely already thought her a complete nodcock.

Before she could stand, Mr. Bancroft put out his hand and stopped her. "You need not go, Miss Brown. I shall lend you some of my fish."

Sarah smiled and ducked her head. He would surely think this was part of the performance, even if her embarrassment and gratitude were genuine. "Thank you, sir. You are too kind."

Mariah leaned forward, hissing in her ear "Did I not tell you it was a good plan?" Her voice hummed with excitement.

It had worked. However, Sarah was uncertain she was completely happy with the results. Yes, Mr. Bancroft had shared his fish, but not without Sarah appearing slow-witted and ridiculous. And glancing at Mr. Bancroft from the side of her eyes, she could not help but think he would not be interested in a lady who forgot something so simple as to bring fish to a card party.

Chapter Eleven

Reginald handed off the reins of his horse to the groom and strode towards the house. It felt good to take a ride, even if it was more sedate than what he would get in the country.

While Rotten Row allowed Jack Spavins to have his head, it was rather short-lived as the path was not very long.

But Reginald did not mind. He had exercised Jack enough and was now ready to return indoors. A shiver traveled up his spine and he shook it off. It seemed Winter had taken hold of the city.

Rubbing his hands together, he allowed a smile to turn the corners of his lips. Now he could speak to Mariah. And dared he hope Sarah would be present also? She had come to the house nearly every day since she arrived in London. The house would not feel the same without her there. Besides, Mariah would simply mope if she had no one to entertain her.

His grin increased. Besides, he was anxious to discover how the evening of flirting had gone. Indeed, he had nearly canceled his meeting just so he might witness what was surely an entertaining display.

His brow creased slightly. Although, he had yet to discover just who the gentleman was that Sarah was trying to attract.

He pulled out his pocket watch, checking the time. Mariah should have finished breakfast already, and if today was the same as most days, Sarah would have arrived for morning calls.

He quickened his pace, taking all three stairs to the terrace in one bound. He pushed through the doors and headed toward the parlor. But pulled up short when he caught a whiff of himself. Lud, it would not do to see Sarah—and Mariah—smelling like a horse.

He hurried up the staircase, taking them two at a time. Unfastening the buttons on his coat, he hurried into his room, shutting the door behind him.

His valet, Jones, stepped from the dressing room. "Ah, my Lord, you're back. How was your ride?"

"It was just what I needed. Thank you, Jones. It is nothing to a bruising ride in the country, but it was quite refreshing nonetheless." He tugged at the sleeves of his coat and shrugged out of it. "I need to change before I see Mariah. She would be most displeased should I join her for tea smelling like Jack."

Jones chuckled. "No, sir. I do not believe she would appreciate it." He stripped off Reginald's waistcoat and shirt, throwing them on the chair next to him. "Do you have a waistcoat in mind, my lord?"

Reginald shook his head. "No, you pick what you think is best."

Jones disappeared into the dressing room but soon returned with an arm full of clothes. He handed Reginald a pair of trousers. While Reginald changed, Jones took the riding clothes and draped them over the wardrobe door.

Reginald slipped the shirt over his head, the coolness of the fabric feeling good against his still-warm skin. He looked in the mirror at his valet standing behind him. "Do you know if Miss Brown has arrived for morning calls?"

Jones met his eyes in the mirror and his brow rose a fraction. "I have not heard, my lord."

Reginald raised his own brow high. He and Jones were close, but it would not do for the man to believe himself too intimate with Reginald's life. "Miss Brown and Mariah went to Mr. Harvey's card party last night. I was in my meeting with Lord Everton and Mr. Carver when Mariah arrived home. I was unable to speak to her last night and was out on my ride while she ate breakfast."

His valet nodded. "As I said, sir, I have not heard if Miss Brown has arrived yet." The man's tone and expressions were in check, as they should be, even if there was a twinkle in his eyes that Reginald did not like.

He put his arms back and his valet slipped his tailcoat up and over his shoulders. He moved them from side to side until the coat settled perfectly on his frame. Something did not feel right. Although, he was uncertain if it was his coat or his valet's look.

Jones stepped forward with the brush, taking long strokes down Reginald's back and arms. After several swipes, Reginald shook him off. "That will do." He stepped away and looked one last time at his reflection in the mirror. His hair was a bit disheveled, but he ran his hand through it, and it settled back into place.

Jones disappeared back into the dressing room as Reginald left his chambers. Now to find Sar—Mariah. He was going to find Mariah.

He walked into the parlor but pulled up short. Mariah was there, sitting on the couch. But Sarah was absent.

He cleared his throat. "Good morning, Mariah. How are you today?"

She looked at him over her shoulder. "I am well, Regi. You

were gone rather early this morning." She turned back to whatever she held in her lap. "I missed you at breakfast."

He moved around the couch and settled in his favorite chair. It was the chair his father had always occupied. "I took Jack out for a ride. He has not had a good bout of exercise since we arrived in London."

"I should have known you would be with Jack. I could not imagine any of your friends would be up and about so early after how late Mr. Harvey's card party went." Mariah slinked over, standing beside his chair. "Regi, what are your plans today?"

He eyed his sister, knowing she had already made plans for him. "I was to have tea with Ben and Cort. Why?"

His sister sighed dramatically.

Reginald rolled his eyes. "What did you wish my plans to be, Mar?"

She turned a dazzling smile on him. Gads, no gentleman stood a chance when she looked at them like that. His chest tightened. What would he do then? He'd be all alone in this big house.

"Sarah and I wished to visit the museum. I suppose we could go by ourselves…" She looked up at the ceiling innocently.

He let out an irritated grunt, even though he was grateful she had asked him. It was much easier to keep track of her when she asked him along. He had worried he would be forced to sneak around, out of sight.

"I suppose I could alter my plans if it is important."

She beamed down at him. "Oh, thank you, Regi. I knew you would not disappoint me."

He looked at the clock. "When shall we leave?"

Mariah hurried toward the door. "I told Sarah we would fetch her just after ten." She glanced down at her gown. "I shall hurry and change, then we may be on our way."

Reginald chuckled. "I do not believe I have seen you hurry in all of your life."

She cast him a bland expression over her shoulder and then rushed from the room.

SARAH AND MARIAH sat across from Reginald in the carriage, whispering back and forth so quietly he could barely hear a word of it—which he found much more vexing than he wished to admit. Were they discussing the card party? He laid his head back on the cushion, pretending to sleep. Perhaps if they thought he was not listening, they would speak louder, and he could hear what they were discussing. It had worked in the parlor.

He shook his head lightly. What had his life come to that he must resort to fake sleep so he might secretly listen in on his sister's conversations? Lud, the gents would make hay if they ever found out.

He was simply trying to protect Mariah. If he was not worried about her, he would not care what she spoke of with Sarah. Yes. That was all there was to it.

If he could just discover who the gentleman was that Sarah had set her sights on, he would not care anymore. As Mariah's friend, Reginald felt a certain obligation in keeping a watchful eye on Sarah also. Besides, her associations would affect Mariah. And if it affected Mariah, Reginald wanted to know the particulars.

"Sarah," Mariah's voice rose in volume making it unnecessary for Reginald to strain to hear. "I wish to hear your opinion about how last evening went. What do you feel went wrong? And what went according to plan? You need a bit more practice."

He cracked an eye open ever so slightly, trying to see Sarah's face as she answered.

Her brow creased. "I think it went well enough. You were correct about leaving my fish in the carriage. He did stop me from removing myself from that game and offered to share his with me."

Mariah had convinced Sarah to leave her fish in the carriage? They had been attending a card party. Of all the cotton-brained things to do. Surely the gentleman thought Sarah quite daft.

"Yes, well that did work out better than I anticipated when you first sat down. I nearly pushed you back into your seat when you offered to leave the table." Mariah sighed. "But it seemed to work out for the best, so I will not visit that again."

"Thank you, Mariah." Sarah's head nodded slowly, although she seemed uncertain of what she was grateful for. "However, I do not believe laughing at what he said was very successful." Sarah tugged her lower lip between her teeth. Reginald's cracked eye focused on her lips. They looked very soft and smooth.

"That is because you did it completely wrong." Mariah's voice snapped him out of his trance, and he shifted.

He pinched his eyes shut, not needing to look at the ladies to know they were staring at him. Their gazes bored into him.

After several moments of silence, Mariah continued. "When I said to laugh at his jokes, I did not mean for you to laugh so loudly. I believe he thought you might be near bedlam." She cleared her throat and tittered. "You see? That is how it should be done."

What a ridiculous bunch of cow dung. Reginald had not heard Sarah's laughter last evening, which he found he regretted, so he could not compare it to Mariah's. But her tittering laugh was as annoying as anything he had ever heard. Besides, it did not sound sincere in the least.

He dared to crack an eye open once again. Sarah's head hung down and she twisted the fingertips of her gloves. "I'm sorry, Mariah. When you nudged me, I did not have time to think."

Mariah smiled at her friend and patted her on the arm. "I know. I was not trying to be harsh. I just wish for you to be successful this Season."

Then why was she filling Sarah's head with a bunch of rubbish?

Sarah nodded her head, but her face held a look of resignation.

Reginald resisted the urge to glare at Mariah or give her a good talking-to. Sometimes he wondered what Sarah received from her association with his sister. From what he could see, all Mariah gave her was bad advice and undue criticism.

"It is no matter," Mariah sighed. "I have been thinking about it, and I do not believe that is the best way to go about flirting. I have several other ideas that I believe will prove much more successful."

Reginald rolled his eyes behind his closed lids. This should prove amusing. He had heard nothing from Mariah that seemed the least bit helpful thus far.

The carriage stopped and Reginald heard the ladies shift on their seats. He opened his eyes to see them staring out the window.

"Look at it, Sarah."

"It is wonderful, is it not?" Sarah said, her tone nearly reverent.

Reginald twisted his head from side to side, stretching out his muscles from holding so still. "Well, do you plan to just sit there gaping? Or shall we go inside?"

Both ladies turned smiling faces to him, nodding quickly.

The carriage door opened and Reginald stepped out, breathing in the cool air and stretching out his aching muscles. He had not realized how stiffly he had held himself while trying to appear asleep. It had been a rather taxing exercise.

The sky was gray, and he wondered if they might not see snow before the day was out.

He held his hand out, helping Mariah and then Sarah out of the carriage. He lifted his arm, but Mariah stepped past him, wrapping her arms around Sarah's and leaving Reginald by himself.

He frowned. They did not need his assistance. He could not remember a time when Mariah had dismissed his arm. It was a stark reminder that her days under his protection were coming to an end. What would he do then? With no wife or children to look after, what would he do with all of his time? His friends proved entertaining, but they would not always be with him in the country. The summer months could prove dreadfully long and tedious without Mariah about. He let out a mournful sigh.

"Regi, what is the matter?" Mariah glanced back at him.

"Nothing. I was just looking at the sky and hoping we make it home before the weather turns."

"Perhaps we should not linger too long at the exhibits," Sarah said.

"Nonsense, even if a storm should come, we will be fine." Mariah raised a warning brow at Reginald. "Please do not make us rush through, Regi. It is our first time here."

He waved her words away. "You may stay as long as you wish, Mar."

She smiled back at him. "Thank you, Regi. You truly are the best brother."

He clasped his hands behind his back and smirked. "Perhaps you will remember that the next time we leave a ball early." He had not said it overly loud, and when Mariah did not react, he assumed she must not have heard him. But Sarah looked back at him and grinned.

His stomach tingled as if a dozen caterpillars took a turn about inside him.

They entered the museum and Reginald moved toward

the anteroom, writing his name and residence in the book. Nine other names were above. He looked at his pocket watch. It looked as though they would make it in with the next group. They should only need to wait another few minutes before they would be admitted.

He returned to Mariah and Sarah. "What do you wish to see first?"

The ladies looked around the hall. "I have heard that the Greek and Roman antiquities are very impressive." Sarah peered into a room on the first floor.

"Have you heard? There are even mummies in one of these rooms." Mariah gave a little shudder. "They sound a bit eerie, but I find I am very anxious to see them."

Reginald nodded his head. "We should be in the next company admitted. Then we may go wherever you wish. I am at your service." He bowed exaggeratedly and Mariah giggled.

Reginald looked up at Sarah from his bow. Had she giggled too? Why did he hope she had? Lud, perhaps Mariah was not so far off on her flirting. Although Reginald would never admit such a thing to her.

If she had, she was no longer giggling. But he was satisfied to see a soft smile on her lips. She may not have found him as witty as Mariah, but she had found him humorous. Or was that simply a kind smile? Or even worse, was it a smile out of pity? Gads, that would be the worst of the scenarios.

He rubbed his fingers over his brows. What did it matter? He tugged down his waistcoat and looked for something to capture his attention. Something that was not Miss Sarah Brown.

A little man, with thinning hair and round glasses perched on his nose, entered the anteroom and looked over the book. Turning, he called out the names of the people on the list. As the crowd moved forward, Mariah leaned toward Sarah. "I have another idea I think you should try." Her voice raised over the murmurs of the crowd and Reginald—for once—was grateful for the crush.

Sarah glanced over at Mariah. "Oh?"

Reginald could hear the hesitation in her voice. It did the girl credit that she was leery of Mariah's schemes. Although, that credibility was diminished when she followed Mariah's other ridiculous ideas.

"Yes, I found one of my mother's old fans several months ago. I had forgotten about it until our conversation the other day."

"Your mother's fan?" Sarah sounded confused and Reginald did not blame her. What did his mother's old fan have to do with anything?

"Yes," Mariah's eyes sparked. "I pulled it out of my trunk after last evening was such a dismal failure."

Sarah frowned. "I would not say it was dismal. Or even a failure."

Reginald grimaced. His sister was not always aware of how her comments were interpreted.

She waved away Sarah's objections. "The fan has instructions printed on it."

"Instructions for what?"

Mariah smiled. "For flirting, of course."

Sarah blinked several times at Mariah. "I do not understand. You wish for me to use a fan to flirt?"

"Yes! Is it not a clever idea?" Mariah beamed with enthusiasm.

Reginald groaned. The giggling did not seem quite so ridiculous now. However, fan flirting should prove amusing to watch. Perhaps he should allow their schemes to continue.

The ladies turned to look at him and he feigned interest in a nearby exhibit. "Regi, what are you groaning at?"

He pointed at an idol from the Sandwich Islands exhibit. "It was not a groan as much as an *Ah, interesting*, kind of grunt."

Mariah switched her lips to the side, but then shrugged. "What is it anyway?"

"It is an idol." He squinted at the sign. "Supposed to aid in fertility."

Sarah's face pinked and Mariah swatted his arm. "Such things should not be mentioned in the presence of ladies, Regi. Do you know nothing of propriety?"

He was to receive a lesson on propriety from Mariah? "But that is what the sign says..." They moved on, leaving him pointing at the plaque. He grinned to himself. At least now he knew what to do should Mariah grow too taxing.

He hurried to catch up with them. How had he never realized the British Museum could be so diverting?

Chapter Twelve

Sarah sat in the library reading, while her mother and Mariah worked on stitcheries, waiting for her father and Lord Stoke to join them after dinner. It was one of the few nights when Mariah and her brother did not have an engagement to attend—one night when Sarah was not to be dragged along as a sort of pity companion.

Sarah reread the page again, her mind not entirely on the words. It had been kind of Mariah and Lord Stoke to invite them to dinner. Indeed, it reminded Sarah of the country. There were many evenings when their families dined together.

She frowned at the page, even though she knew not what was on it. It was not that the content was overly challenging, but rather her attention to it was challenged. She knew she should not be angry with Mariah for their lack of invitations. Lord Stoke had used his influence to have Sarah and her family invited to a musicale at week's end. And an invitation to a dinner party at Mr. Bancroft's had arrived just that morning.

Still, there had been few other invitations outside of Lord Stoke's sphere of influence. Why were others not coming? Had people learned of their address and dismissed them? Or were they simply so unknown in society that no one even thought to invite them?

Laughter sounded from the corridor and Sarah looked up. She set the book in her lap. It wasn't as if she had been paying it any attention anyway.

Lord Stoke and her father entered the room and Sarah's breath hitched at the sight. She could not say exactly what it was that made her throat constrict and her heart beat a little faster. The sight was not an uncommon one. But tonight it felt different. Tonight, it felt right.

Sarah shook her head. What was she doing? This was Lord Stoke. She had been his dancing partner as a boy and spent a great part of her life at his home—with his sister. But most importantly he was an earl. And while he cut a very handsome form, she could not let her affections be turned. She had a plan and it involved Mr. Bancroft. Not Lord Stoke.

Her father sat on the couch next to her mother, patting her softly on the knee. She turned and smiled up at him.

Sarah's heart constricted. She longed for a marriage like her parents had. Theirs had been an arranged marriage. But they had been fortunate that theirs had developed into love.

Sarah sighed. She was only one and twenty, but she was beginning to lose hope. It was as if the lack of invitations was just a manifestation of her future. A love match seemed impossible when an arranged marriage seemed completely out of reach.

A sudden restlessness overtook her, and she pushed off the couch and moved to the other side of the room. Perhaps she needed to find a different book. One that would stretch her mind enough to crowd out her unsettling thoughts.

She looked at several shelves of books, but nothing captured her attention until she discovered a book of charades. She pulled the book free and clasped it to her chest as she moved to the far side, looking at the portraits covering the wall from the chair rail to the ceiling. Only two faces did she recognize—those of Mariah's parents. What would they think of Mariah now? It had been over five years since they died. Would they approve of her friendship with Sarah? It was one thing to allow girls to play together as children. But now that Mariah was out, would they feel the same? They would surely not be pleased with the Cheapside address Sarah resided in.

"Miss Brown, were you able to find a book to your liking?" Lord Stoke sauntered over to her.

She nodded, tipping the book toward him so he might see the cover.

"Charades? Do you enjoy them?" His brows rose. "I have never been very good at them myself."

"I do enjoy them. They can be challenging at times, but I find I enjoy that also." Sarah smiled up at him. It was easy to feel comfortable around Reginald. And at times like this, he felt like Reginald—Reginald from the country. Reginald from the neighboring estate. Just Reginald. She had missed that Reginald since coming to London. Here he tended to feel more like Lord Stoke.

He narrowed his eyes at her. "It is easy to claim you enjoy them, but it is quite another to actually prove it."

She gasped. Her eyes wide with offense. But she could not keep the smile from her lips. "Are you inferring I might be lying to you, my lord?"

He shrugged. "I have no proof to the contrary."

Sarah opened the book to an indiscriminate page. "Then perhaps I should give you proof."

He slowly nodded his head. "I think it would be best."

Sarah pointed to a charade and read it aloud.

"My first a blessing sent to earth,
Of plants and flowers to aid the birth.
My second surely was designed

To hurl destruction on mankind.
My whole a pledge from pardoned Heaven,
Of wrath appeased and crimes forgiven."

SHE LOOKED up at him when she finished. "Do you know the answer?"

He shrugged. "I have no notion what it means."

"It is a rainbow." She gave him a triumphant grin, daring him to tell her she was incorrect.

Reginald's brow furrowed. "How is a rainbow the answer to that? I simply do not see it."

She pointed to the charade. "The clue for the first part of the word is here where it says *my first.*" She looked up at him, but his brows were still deeply creased. "What is a blessing that aids plants and flowers from the time they are only seeds?"

Reginald folded his arms. "The sun."

Sarah chuckled. "Yes, that could be it. But not when you look at the next part. The second part of the word is *a design hurled on mankind.*" You must think about destructive things that affected all mankind."

"I would say that is a flood. But that is not part of the word." He looked down at the pages as if trying to see if the answer had been printed there.

"True, we must look at the rest to obtain the full clue. But I think the clue is speaking of the bow. It has killed many people since its invention." She pointed to the text. "But here is our final clue. '*My whole pledge from pardoned Heaven, of wrath appeased and crimes forgiven.*" She stared up at him, his face creased in concentration. Gracious he was handsome. She had always known it, but tonight it was more pronounced, as if her heart and head were working together in an ill-advised scheme.

"Ah, so the pledge from Heaven is when God sent the rainbow as a promise never to flood the earth again?"

She nodded. "Yes. You see? It is not so difficult if you break it down into pieces."

He lifted his chin. "Let's try another one." He winked at her, and her knees went weak. "Just so I know that you did not pick one you already solved."

She raised a brow and handed him the book. "That will be the true proof for you?"

He nodded his head and opened the book, turning several pages until he grinned. "Here. Tell me what the answer is to this one."

> *"My first is in harvest rarely known,*
> *Nor would it welcome be.*
> *My next in country or in town,*
> *Each miss delights to see.*
> *And when dreary winter's dress is shown,*
> *In joyous play my whole is thrown."*

Sarah grinned up at him. "The answer is a snowball."

Reginald looked down at the page, his mouth gaping slightly. "How did you figure it out so quickly?"

Sarah lifted a shoulder. "The answers just come to me."

He shook his head. "You are a very intelligent woman, Miss Brown."

"Thank you, my lord. But I do not believe solving charades makes one intelligent."

"I beg to differ, Sarah." He said her name so quietly she almost did not hear it.

Almost.

Her weak knees now nearly shook, and a warmth spread from her chest to her arms and neck. Gracious, she smiled over at him, this may not have been a wise idea.

Chapter Thirteen

Reginald cleared his throat. "What do you find so captivating among my family's portraits?" He stared at the wall of paintings.

"I was just looking at the portraits of your parents. It has been a long time since I saw them."

He moved closer to her, staring up at his parents' likenesses. "Yes, it has been a long time."

She glanced at him from the corner of her eye. "Does looking at them bother you?" She had not intended to make him melancholy.

He shook his head. "No. I sometimes wonder what they would think about everything…if they would approve of how I am doing as Mariah's guardian."

A faint smile turned Sarah's lips at how alike their thoughts had been. "What could they have to be disappointed about? Mariah is perfectly lovely."

He released a heavy sigh. "She is."

"But?" Did Reginald disapprove of Mariah's friendship with Sarah? She had never considered it before, but now she had to wonder. His sigh made her think he had something unpleasant to discuss.

He glanced over and gave her a tenuous smile, which only made her worries increase. "But I'm afraid she tends a bit toward the ridiculous at times."

"Ridiculous? Whatever could you mean?" Worry for herself vanished only to be replaced with indignation on behalf of her friend.

His brow creased as if he were regretting his comment.

"Come now, we have been friends for a long time, my lord. You need not keep things from me—especially concerning Mariah."

Reginald shrugged. "I have overheard bits and pieces of your conversations of late. And her plans for you to gain a gentleman's attention is beyond the pale."

Sarah's face burned with humiliation. She had not thought he was paying them any mind when Mariah had brought up the subject of flirting. He always seemed so disinterested. "And what is so ridiculous?" Sarah snapped a bit too forcefully. While Mariah's ideas were not improper, many in society might find them inappropriate. Perhaps it was guilt that made her take offense.

He gave her a pitying look. "Flirting with a fan? Are you seriously considering such antics?"

"What would you know about such things?" She raised her chin, offended on Mariah's behalf.

"I am a man, and I know what I thought when a lady tittered at everything I said." He shrugged. "Frankly, a fan has never been emplo—" He paused and looked upwards. "I am mistaken. I believe Miss Waterston used a fan, although, until this moment, I had not realized what she was doing with it." He dropped his gaze back to her. "But as you can see, it all came to naught. If anything, it turned my eyes away from them, not toward them."

Sarah looked back to the portraits and grunted. "You are hardly the typical man, my lord. You have sworn off marriage." She frowned. But had not Mr. Bancroft also? Perhaps Reginald had more insight than she gave him credit.

"I have not sworn it off forever. I know I have a duty to fulfill. But it doesn't have to be now." He raised his brows as if knowing her thoughts. "Trust me, I know of what I speak."

"It is humorous. Both Mariah and you have asked me to trust you, but you have opposing aims. Who am I to trust more?"

Reginald raised his brows. "I would trust whomever has a closer connection to the person you wish to attract. And from any direction you look at it, I am that person."

Did he know about Mr. Bancroft? What did he think about it? "Then you believe I may have already ruined my chances? Or perhaps you believe that flirting isn't even necessary?"

He clasped his hands behind his back. "I did not say that. I believe Mariah is correct in that some men may need more of a nudge than others. The key is knowing what kind of nudge."

Sarah looked straight ahead, blinking several times. A nudge? Now she must determine a gentleman's nudges? What exactly was a nudge, and how was she to learn such a thing? Was there some sort of outward indication to help her know what Mr. Bancroft's nudge was? Or perhaps a book she might study? "As a gentleman, you know what these nudges are?" Her voice came out sounding uncertain and vulnerable—both of which she disliked.

He shrugged, tilting his head to the side. "I may not know what will work on every man, but I can surely guide you better than Mariah and her fans."

Was he offering to help her? It seemed odd that he should help her try to secure the affections of one of his friends. Perhaps Reginald did not know her aim was Mr. Bancroft after all. "Are you saying you will…teach me?"

Reginald looked at her from the corner of his eyes. "Do you wish for my help?"

Sarah looked at the portrait in front of her without seeing it and sucked in a deep breath. Is that what she wanted? Was this what every lady went through in order to secure a match? It was rather exhausting. She was surprised anyone ever made it to the actual nuptials.

She looked over her shoulder at her parents, sitting close to each other on the couch. Would it be worth the humiliation if she could have something close to what they had?

She nodded. "Yes. I would like your help."

"Very well." Reginald pushed out his lips and nodded. "Again, I must commend you on your intelligence."

Sarah was uncertain whether it was intelligent or dim-witted to agree to have him help her. But she could not see that he could be any worse of a teacher than Mariah. "How do we proceed?"

"We should begin immediately. The Season will be over before you know it."

Sarah nodded her head. "Where do we begin?"

"What are you two talking about over there?" Mariah called from across the room.

Sarah's face heated. What was she to say? Her parents were there, and they did not even know about Mariah's plans for flirting. What would they think if they discovered Reginald was a part of it too?

"Miss Brown was simply showing me how to discover the answers to the charades in her book," Reginald called back without even turning his head. "And then we were speaking about memories of mother and father."

"Why does she not come over here and share? I should like to hear the memories also." Mariah's tone had taken on her usual pout. "Although, you can skip the part about the charades. I find I do not like them in the least."

"Oh, yes. I should love to share some memories also. Lady Stoke was, after all, a dear friend of mine." Sarah's mother turned in her seat and smiled at them.

"I suppose we must join them now," Sarah whispered. She moved to turn back toward the group, but Reginald reached out his hand and stopped her. Heat crept up her skin where his hand rested on her wrist.

He grinned. "That is your first lesson, Miss Brown. A slight touch or brush of the hand will do far more to attract the attention of a gentleman than a misplaced giggle."

Sarah licked her lips and pulled her arm away, uncomfortable with the tingles dancing up her arm. What had just happened? Never had a simple touch left her arm warm and cold at the same time. Would this happen every time she touched Mr. Bancroft?

She moved over and sat on the couch beside her mother. Casually, she rubbed at the spot where Reginald had touched her. The tingles had lessened, but not so much that she could not feel them.

The cushion next to her sunk down as the rustle of fabric caught her attention. Her eyes widened at Reginald sitting next to her, their legs as close as they could be without touching. What was he doing? Her parents and Mariah were all there, able to see everything.

She glanced over at him, but his face betrayed nothing. Was she the only one who felt as if her body was about to ignite with fire? Was his heart not about to pound out of his chest?

Looking anywhere but at their nearly touching legs, Sarah cleared her throat. It was so dry and tight. Where was a cup of tea when she needed it?

There looked to be a small amount of space between her and her mother. If Sarah scooted just a little, she would put a small amount of much-needed distance on her other side.

Wiggling to the side was not enough. She dropped her hands on the cushion to push herself to the side, but before she could move, Reginald's hand settled atop hers. At first, he simply rested it there. But then, his thumb slowly moved up and down the side of her hand. With each brush, an explosion of heat and tickles radiated across her hand and gooseflesh dotted her upper arms. Her heart galloped as if it were running a race inside her. She was both in agony and bliss.

What was she supposed to do? If she lifted her hand, he would know she was affected, but if she did not move her hand, she would surely go mad.

She glanced over at him. The half-smile gracing his face told her little of what he was thinking or feeling. Indeed, he seemed perfectly capable of carrying on a conversation with her father, while she could barely think at all. However, the glimmer in his eye told her far more. He was enjoying this. He certainly knew what he was doing to her. He knew he was making her uncomfortable, and he thought it amusing!

"What memories were you telling Reginald about?" Mariah smiled at Sarah. Had she noticed their hands?

Sarah pulled her hand from the couch, not caring what Reginald thought about it. Unlike him, she could not carry on a conversation with him teasing her so.

"I was recalling the time she took us to the milliner's shop and Mrs. Garvey was there buying the newest silk from India. Do you remember, Mariah?" Sarah clasped her hands in her lap, trying to force her awareness of the man next to her away. This feeling was far worse than her earlier restlessness. If only she had stayed seated, she would not be in this muddle. Or perhaps she would. After the evening's demonstration, she would not underestimate Reginald again.

"Was that not a good joke, Sarah?"

Sarah lifted her eyes to meet Mariah's expectant ones. Lawks, what had she said? She smiled and nodded. "Indeed, it was very humorous."

Mariah lifted a brow ever so much. Most people would have missed it. But Sarah knew Mariah well enough to know her look of suspicion. Her friend suspected that Sarah had not been listening. And she was correct. But it was not Sarah's fault. It was Reginald's. His presence beside her was leaving her with barely a thought in her head that did not involve him.

Reginald cleared his throat and Mariah turned her probing gaze away.

Sarah released a breath, her shoulders sagging. She leaned back onto the couch, only half-listening to Reginald's memory of his mother. It did not matter if she wasn't listening this time. The memory involved Mariah, not Sarah. No questions would be directed her way.

Sarah rubbed at the spot between her brows where a dull ache thudded. What had she gotten herself into with Reginald? She had not realized when she agreed to his offer that it would entail him *showing* her what to do. Could he not simply use words? She was a relatively intelligent girl with a wide vocabulary. Surely there were words to explain how to touch a man without Reginald having to demonstrate.

Her face heated again. Gracious, she had surely been red-faced since the men entered the room. What would her mother say? She was an observant woman and would surely have noticed.

"Sarah? Are you listening to me?" Mariah's pouty voice penetrated Sarah's thoughts and she let out a soft moan.

"No, I'm not." She lowered her fingers from her forehead. "I'm sorry, Mariah. I know I have been dreadfully rude, but I have a dull ache in my head. It is making it very hard for me to concentrate."

Her mother tsked. "Oh, dearest. You do look pale. Perhaps it would be best if we returned home."

"Yes, yes." Her father said as he pushed to his feet. "You do look very ill, indeed."

Sarah smiled gratefully at her mother. While she was disappointed to have her evening with Mariah end so early, she would not be disappointed to remove herself from Reginald. Or at least his touch. She frowned. That was not true.

She yearned for the feel of his touch on her skin. She just did not wish to have others there to witness it. Goodness. What did that say about her? Rubbing at her brow again, she tried to take the thought back.

"Oh, Sarah. I had no idea you were feeling so unwell." Mariah looked at Sarah with worried eyes.

Sarah offered her a small smile. "It came on rather suddenly. You need not concern yourself. I am certain I simply need to rest. I do not believe I am used to Town hours yet."

Reginald stood up next to her and placed his hand on the small of her back. The tingles tickled up her spine, making her question if she would be able to walk to the doorway, let alone to the carriage. But it also made her crave his touch even more.

"I am sorry you are feeling ill, Miss Brown. I do hope you will be recovered enough to join us at the theater tomorrow night." He glanced at Sarah's parents. "The invitation includes you as well, if you are not otherwise engaged."

Her mother shook her head and grinned happily. "No, my lord, our evening has not been claimed."

Reginald dipped his head, his hand still lingering on Sarah's back. Was his thumb rubbing circles there? She had no idea when she would ever have an opportunity to use these techniques Reginald was demonstrating. Surely, he must realize that as well. But if he did, why was he continuing to do it? Was it just to tease her?

She stood rooted in place, afraid if she moved her feet that her legs would dissolve beneath her.

He finally pulled his hand away and took several steps to the side, speaking to her father.

Sarah released her breath, even as she longed to move

closer to him again and feel his warmth. Slowly, her legs recovered, and she moved closer to the safety of her mother.

Looking at him from the corner of her eyes, she had to admit he knew what he was about. If his tutoring on flirting worked half as well on Mr. Bancroft as it worked on her, she would be engaged before the Season even reached its peak.

Chapter Fourteen

Reginald walked purposely toward his study. The Browns were on their way home and Mariah had taken a book to her chambers. The house was quiet at last.

He grinned to himself as he recalled the look on Sarah's face when he had touched her wrist. Although, that look was nothing to the wide eyes she had given him when he had set his hand atop hers.

He chuckled as he pushed open the door and made his way straight to the small table in the corner. He removed the stopper from the decanter and poured the liquid into a glass.

Moving over to the fire, he stoked the coals in the grate just enough to start the flame. A maid would be along shortly to add another log. Settling himself into a chair, he kicked off his shoes to the side and rested his feet on the low table. Crossing his ankles, he took a deep swallow of his drink.

What had happened tonight? While he could not deny he felt great pleasure in unsettling Sarah so much, he also could not deny that he had been equally affected.

Which made no sense. He had touched Sarah many times

over the years, and his skin had never warmed and his heart had never raced as it had in the drawing room that evening. Perhaps it was simply that he was more skilled at flirting than he realized.

The evening had started out mundane enough, but it had taken a turn when he and Sir Winston returned to the library after dinner.

He rubbed at his eyes. He had likely made a mistake. He should never have offered to teach Sarah to flirt. What had he been thinking? He may think it all a joke, but what was Sarah's impression? She was a kind girl, and he did not wish to hurt her.

Perhaps he should cry off and offer her no more advice. But then Sarah would be left to Mariah and her fans. And that was simply unacceptable.

He took another gulp from his glass. Perhaps it was not what he was teaching that was the problem. It seemed a shame to not help Sarah when he could.

Perhaps the problem was his demonstration. He could have told her how to accomplish the task without showing her, could he not? The showing was when everything had changed.

He shook his head. The thought of simply explaining what Sarah needed to do left him feeling unsatisfied. Indeed, he was nearly certain he had seen gooseflesh on her arms when he had brushed his thumb along her hand. Why did that thought bring him so much pleasure? It was surely not him, but rather the motion that had caused her reaction.

He twisted the glass around on the arm of the chair as he considered his options. Should he withdraw as her instructor or continue?

The thought of quitting left a dull ache in his stomach and chest. She needed him and the things he could teach her, of that he was certain.

He brought the glass to his lips. He would not quit. But he may need to change his approach. It would certainly be best if he simply told her what to do. It was something he needed to think about.

A maid came into the room and placed another log on the grate.

Reginald stood and walked over to his desk. He was not yet sleepy. He would look over the ledgers he had just received from the bailiff at his estate in Hampshire. That would certainly make him drowsy in no time.

———

REGINALD STOOD on the walkway outside the shop beneath the Browns' Cheapside Townhouse. Sir Winston had already assisted his wife inside the carriage. Reginald motioned him inside. "I will help Miss Brown and Mariah up."

"Capital," Sir Winston grinned as he bounded up the steps.

Reginald turned to Sarah and put out his hand. "How are you this evening, Miss Brown? Is your headache gone?"

She glanced at his hand and then up at his eyes. A hint of wariness hovered there.

He grinned. She was surely thinking of their lesson last night, just as he was. Indeed, he had thought of little else all day.

"I am well, my lord. Thank you for inquiring." She placed her hand in his and he handed her up into the carriage.

Warmth spread through his gloves and across his hand and fingers. He glanced down. It was the same thing that had happened last evening when he touched her. Curious. He handed up Mariah, allowing himself to think on it only a moment longer.

He climbed inside and caught Sarah's gaze. She had

settled in the seat next to her parents. He tilted his head to the side as he settled in next to Mariah. Something had happened between them, although he was not completely certain what it was.

"Are you not excited, Sarah?" Mariah started talking as soon as the carriage set into motion.

"It will be great fun." Sarah flicked a glance at Reginald.

He folded his arms across his chest and watched the fading daylight out the window as Sarah, Mariah, and Lady Brown chatted about the upcoming play. Should he continue with lessons tonight? He had to confess the idea intrigued him. But what could he teach her in the dimly lit theater? He had already made a small mental list of things she should try. Showing an interest in topics the gentleman was interested in. Speak intelligently on subjects the gentleman might not already know about. Those types of things. But they were not lessons for the theater.

A slow grin spread across his face. Ah, yes. He had the perfect lesson for the evening. His foot tapped up and down excitedly. Now if only the carriage would move along, he could start on his plan immediately.

"Regi, who else will be attending tonight?" Mariah nudged him.

He glanced over. "Many of the *ton* will be in attendance, I would guess." He knew what she was asking, but sometimes he enjoyed vexing her by pretending he didn't.

She let out a sigh and he smiled. "I am certain of that. But I meant in our box. Who else have you invited?"

Reginald feigned dawning understanding. "Oh, yes. Our party will fill our box. Lords Ponsonby and Montcort will be in the box on our left, and Mr. Bancroft has purchased the box to our right. Lords Ragsdale and Berwick will be in his box."

Mariah frowned. "Are there not enough seats for the gentleman to sit in our box?" She flicked a glance at Sarah.

What was that about? Had Mariah developed a tendré for one of his friends? He glanced at Sarah. Or was it Sarah? His brows rose. Which of his friends could she be interested in? His stomach turned sour as he thought about each of them with her.

Reginald shook his head. "Even if they were not bringing ladies with them, we would not all fit."

Mariah's lips flattened into a frown, and she glanced at Sarah again. "They are bringing ladies with them? All of them?"

Reginald nodded. "Yes. When last I spoke to them, that was their intention." He eyed his sister.

She harrumphed.

Sarah cleared her throat. "Do not be glum, Mariah. I am certain we will have a lovely time in our box."

"Yes, of course, we will." Sir Winston chimed in, adding his enthusiasm.

Mariah crossed her arms and grunted an indiscernible response.

Reginald lifted a brow. Perhaps Mariah was the one he should be instructing on flirting. He was certain none of his friends would find her pout endearing. If her affections were for one of his friends, she would likely end up disappointed with the result.

The carriage fell silent, and he dropped his head back and closed his eyes. Even if it were only for a moment, it would surely help. While he loved his sister, her pouting and whining often left him with a headache and sore neck.

When the carriage finally stopped in front of the theater, Reginald stepped out onto the walkway, gently rubbing at his temple as he waited for Mariah to appear.

He handed his sister down, and when Sarah appeared before her parents, he helped her out of the carriage as well. He released her hand as soon as she was safely on the walkway. She did not look in the mood for a lingering touch just then.

He dropped his hand to his side, gently shaking it in hopes of cooling it down at least a small bit.

She looked up at the front of the Drury Lane Theatre. "It is lovely, is it not? Mr. Holland could not have designed a more fitting building."

Reginald pulled his eyes from the building and looked over at Sarah. Did she know about architecture in general or just this architect? He scratched at his earlobe. He had known Sarah all her life, and yet, since coming to London, he had learned several things he had not previously known. How had he never known she loved charades or that she knew about architecture? What else did he not know about her? And why did he want to discover it so badly?

Mariah pointed to a statue. "Who is that?"

Sarah smiled. "That is Shakespeare, Mariah. Do you not recognize him?"

Mariah lifted a shoulder and turned her attention to the door. "I suppose if I had recognized him, I should not have asked who he was." She moved toward the doors, but Reginald noted the pink of her cheeks. She was embarrassed that she had not known. Although Reginald did not know why. It was not as though everyone in England knew who Shakespeare was or what he looked like.

He placed his hands on Mariah's and Sarah's backs and led them into the semi-circular saloon. Sarah flinched slightly but did not look back at him. She continued to look around the large room, taking in all there was to see.

Reginald chuckled to himself. He was rather enjoying these flirting lessons. It was a side of Sarah he had never seen before and he had to admit he rather liked it.

They moved to the staircase. "How far must we climb, Regi?"

"To the top, Mar. Our box is on the upper tier."

Lady Brown looked up the staircase and flicked out her fan, waving it furiously. "Oh, dear. That is a climb."

Sir Winston took his wife's hand and tucked it into the crook of his arm. "Do not fear, my dear. I shall be here to help you."

She smiled lovingly at her husband. "Thank you, Sir Winston."

Reginald grinned. The Browns were an endearing couple. He was certain they loved each other deeply, and sometimes he felt himself studying them when he thought no one was looking.

Their relationship was so very different from that of his own parents. His mother's and father's marriage had been arranged, which was not wholly uncommon. To his knowledge, the Browns' marriage had also been arranged. However, unlike the Browns, Reginald's parents had never taken to each other. They were civil, but there had never been any warmth or love between them. Indeed, Reginald did not believe his parents had even been friends.

The Browns, however, were not afraid to show affection for each other in public, as Reginald had just witnessed. They did tend toward the more formal when they were outside their home. Lady Brown called her husband "Mr. Brown," or she had until he had been knighted last year. Reginald could see the pride in her eyes when she referred to her husband as "Sir Winston" now. But when they were at home or among their small group of friends, they called each other by their Christian names. Unlike his parents who had only referred to each other by their titles.

Watching them together had made him wonder why Sarah needed Mariah's help in securing the affections of a man. Had Sarah not observed her parents? Although, perhaps observing a couple who had been married for decades only showed her what she wanted but not necessarily how to obtain it.

They reached the top of the staircase and Lady Brown stopped, leaning against the railing. "Lawks, that was trying."

"But you did it masterfully, my dear." Sir Winston patted her hand and waited patiently for her to catch her breath.

Reginald held out his hand and led Mariah and Sarah toward their box. "Here we are." He led them inside.

Lady Brown moved to the row of seats in front and peered out into the theater. "Oh, look, Sir Winston. Is that not Lady Mayfair?"

"Upon my word, I do believe you are correct, my dear."

Lady Brown continued to point out prominent members of society to her husband.

Mariah took the only other seat in the front row.

"Mariah, do you not think I should sit next to my parents?" Sarah asked.

Mariah looked back and her eyes widened in what would certainly be a pre-pout. Lud, if she did not receive what she wanted, she would turn on the full effect. It was rather maddening. But his parents had done nothing to curb it when she was young, and she was far too old for him to change her now.

Sarah glanced over at him as if to ask him to do something.

He shrugged. He would not be the one to change up the seating. Indeed, he was quite happy with this arrangement. It would work very well for the evening's *lesson*.

She looked back at Mariah, obviously vexed at Reginald's lack of assistance.

"Come now, Sarah. It is my first time at the theater." Mariah added a slight whine to her voice.

Sarah raised a brow. "It is not my first time also?"

Mariah giggled. "Oh yes, of course. But you are only interested in the architecture and the actors, whereas I am interested in who is in attendance. You may see what you came to see from the second row. But I must be on the front row to be fully seen by others."

Mariah blinked several times as if allowing her words to settle in as if she knew Sarah would see it her way once she had a chance to think clearly about it.

Sarah let out a sigh. "Oh, very well. I will sit in the back with Lord Stoke." She glanced over at him with altogether too much wariness. "You will keep your hands to yourself, will you not?" She whispered.

Reginald feigned hurt and leaned toward her. Thankfully, Mariah, Sir Winston, and Lady Brown were far too busy pointing people out to pay Reginald's conversation with Sarah any mind. "My dear, Miss Brown. You act as though I have behaved inappropriately toward you. Did you not request my help? I have done nothing but instruct you."

Sarah narrowed her eyes at him.

He grinned and held up his hands, clasping them together in a very exaggerated manner. "They shall remain in my lap for the entirety of the evening."

Sarah swallowed but nodded. "Very well. I am sorry if I implied you have been anything less than a gentleman."

He held out his hand to her and she stared down at it. "I only intend to help you into your seat."

Sarah accepted his help, settling into the seat directly behind her mother.

"Good evening, Reg." Montcort poked his head into the box.

"Good evening, Cort." Reginald dipped his head to his friend.

Montcort glanced around the box and nodded as if he approved. "We will all meet in the Egyptian Hall at intermission?"

Reginald nodded. "Indeed."

Montcort nodded and ducked back out.

Sarah opened her mouth to say something, but the actors

came onto the stage and the theater quieted—or as quiet as it can be with more than three thousand people in attendance— and she turned away from him. He would never know what she was going to say.

Sarah settled back into her seat, her eyes watching the movement on the stage.

Reginald smiled. It was time for his lesson to begin. He leaned over close to Sarah. "Miss Brown," his whispered voice lifted the shorter hairs around the back of her neck that had escaped her knot, "I just realized this would be a perfect setting for your next lesson."

Sarah gave a slight full-body shiver and swallowed.

He grinned widely. It was just as he had hoped.

Turning to look at him, she shook her head. "I am not certain this is the place for a lesson, my lord," she whispered back.

Reginald shook his head. "On the contrary. It has already begun."

She frowned.

He scooted in closer. "You see, you must find opportunities, such as this, to whisper in the gentleman's ear. Not only does it afford you the chance to sit close together, but it will also have a decided effect on him. There will be little question in his mind on where your affections lie."

She lifted a hand to her head, pushing those short hairs back up into place. "But it feels far too bold," she whispered behind her fan.

He shook his head. "Nonsense. I would not recommend using this in the early stages of your flirting. But perhaps once he has called on you a time or two, it would be appropriate." He grinned. The lighting was not bright, but he could still see gooseflesh dotting her neck and upper arms. He was rather impressed with the control she was otherwise showing.

She looked straight ahead but nodded.

Reginald straightened in his chair. There was not much

left to say on the matter and he thought she may need a respite anyway. If he kept her in gooseflesh the whole of the evening, she would surely not enjoy the play.

And it was likely she may never let him near her again— which was something he could not abide.

Chapter Fifteen

Gads! Sarah had thought the touching was distracting. It was nothing to Reginald whispering in her ear. It was as if every nerve in her body was on full alert, tingling and sparking with every word.

She cursed Mariah and her insistence she sit on the front row.

Sarah glanced at Reginald. Did he realize what he was doing to her?

Her eyes narrowed slightly. Of course, he did. Had he not told her what it would do to the man she did it to? If only she could give him a lesson of her own. It would serve him right.

But what could she do? What could she say to teach him the lesson he needed to learn? It must be something be good.

Sarah bit the side of her cheek, paying no attention to the actors on stage. Perhaps it did not really matter what she said. It was not the meaning of the words that had affected her as much as the breaths involved. In truth, it could be complete gibberish but have the same effect.

She grinned, feeling as if she had the upper hand for the moment. Scooting closer to him, she leaned in and made certain she was speaking into his neck just above his collar.

"My lord," she added a bit more breath than she normally would, "Are you not impressed with the costumes this evening?"

Reginald shuddered and Sarah sat taller in her seat, a satisfied grin on her lips. He was not the only one to play the game.

He looked over at her, his brow creased.

She smiled at him. Should she tell him she was *practicing*? Or that she just wished to do to him what he had done to her? No, she would let him wonder over it for a while longer.

He leaned over. "Yes, they are quite lovely."

Sarah tilted her head, willing her body not to react.

He stayed, breathing on her neck several heartbeats longer than was necessary before he straightened. He glanced down at the small strip of skin showing between the top of her gloves and the bottom of her sleeve and a satisfied grin covered his face.

Sarah ran her hand over the skin. Ah, gooseflesh! Curse her body for not doing as she instructed it.

She sat chafing. What she needed was to come up with something containing several *h*'s. That letter gave a heartier breath and, therefore, induced an extra effect.

Drumming her fingers on her thigh, Sarah searched her memory for as many *h* words as she could remember.

She leaned over. "How do haberdashers spend their holidays?" It was complete nonsense, but she did not care. She earned her desired result. Reginald gave another full-body shudder.

He turned to her. "I beg your pardon?"

Mariah turned and looked over her shoulder at them. "Hush," she scowled.

Sarah rolled her lips between her teeth but grinned.

He was giving her the opportunity to say it again? She could not have asked for a better result. She leaned in even closer than before, lowering her voice but using even more breath than before. "I asked how do haber—"

He held up his hand. "No. Do not say it again," he hissed. Shifting in his seat, he stared at her for a moment. His eyes lit and a look of understanding—admiration, even—dawned. He leaned in, his lips so close to her ear she could feel the heat from them. "Have you not heard? I hardly ever hire a haber-dasher." His words were slow and heavily enunciated.

Sarah gripped the arms of her chair, her knuckles surely bleached white. *I will not react...* The sensations pulsing through her skin, causing her heart to make erratic beats, finally lessened and she loosened her grip. She glowered at Reginald.

His shoulders gently bounced. He was laughing! He was terrible. A terrible, unkind man. A man who had not learned his lesson.

He believed he had beaten her. But he had not. She had to come up with something better. Something that would prove she could win this game he had started.

She scooted her chair closer, and their thighs rubbed each other. The touch nearly pushed her back, but she persisted and leaned in. "A happy herd of hippopotami happened upon a plentiful pile of peppers," Sarah drew out each word as long as she could, taking at least three times longer to say it than was necessary. She placed her hand on his arm before moving it over her mouth to quiet the giggle bubbling up in her throat.

Reginald sat very still with his eyes closed and his hands clenched together in his lap. His Adam's Apple bobbed several times.

Sarah lifted her chin in victory. She had done it. She had left him speechless. She would like to see him top that.

He leaned over with a wicked grin on his face.

On second thought, she would not like to see him top it.

She hurried to scoot her chair away, but she was not fast enough.

He placed his arm behind her chair, his hand lightly gripping the small band of skin between the top of her gloves and her sleeve. His thumb began its rhythmic sweep.

"You promised you would not touch me tonight."

"Shush."

Her eyes fluttered shut.

His breath hit her skin. Warm. Tickling. Lifting each little hair on her neck.

Her muscles twitched in anticipation. How long would his torture continue?

Applause sounded and Reginald sat bolt upright.

Sarah sagged against her chair and closed her eyes. *Saved by intermission*! Lawks, she had never been so happy to stand up. And judging by how fast Reginald shot out of his seat, he must have felt the same.

She rubbed one hand along her neck and the other over her arm. Her brain could not focus on a single thought while her nerves were so overstimulated. Gads! The play was only half over. How was she to survive the rest of the play? Perhaps she needed to wave a white flag and call a truce.

REGINALD LED Sarah and Mariah down the stairs to the Egyptian Hall. All of his friends were already there waiting with young ladies hovering at their elbows. Sarah glanced from beneath her lashes at the woman beside Mr. Bancroft.

She was pretty. Far prettier than Sarah. And from the looks of her gown, she was far wealthier also.

Sarah held back, standing slightly behind Mariah. This was her society, not Sarah's. She did not belong among these people of wealth and status. Even if her father was a knight, most of these people would not think any higher of him than they had before his elevation. It was a stark reminder of her position. Why had she thought it a good idea to come to London? She was even beginning to question her intentions toward Mr. Bancroft. He did not seem out of place.

Reginald stepped away from them. "I will go and fetch us all some refreshments."

Mariah nodded. "Thank you, Regi."

He frowned at her. It was not proper to use such informal names in such a public setting. But Mariah completely ignored her brother's look of disapproval.

Reginald shook his head and moved off, disappearing into the crowd.

Mariah moved back next to Sarah and nodded toward the lady with Mr. Bancroft. "Her name is Lady Josephine." Her tone held a mark of disapproval. "Can you imagine—after all Napoleon has done— to have the same name as his wife?" She crinkled her nose. "I should have changed my name if I were her. Or at least used a nickname."

Mariah may have had a point, but Sarah felt it was something she should not be discussing openly in the middle of the theater saloon for everyone to hear. It simply was not proper. But it was not Sarah's place to correct her friend. "She seems lovely."

Mariah shrugged. "How would you know that? You have not said a single word to her."

"Her face looks nice. She has done nothing but smile since I first set eyes on her."

"Smiles may be faked, Sarah. I am certain Mr. Bancroft only asked her to come because of the size of her dowry."

And there it was. Another reminder of how out of place she was among these people. Even Mr. Bancroft, with his ten thousand a year, wished for someone with a sizable dowry. What hope did someone like Sarah have?

"You do not know that, Mariah," Sarah said in whispered tones. "Perhaps they have many of the same likes and interests." She took several steps away from the group. She did not know whether she hoped Mariah was right or wrong. Neither option seemed to give her any hope of winning Mr. Bancroft.

"You would make him a better wife, I am certain."

Sarah gasped. "Mariah, please keep your voice down. I do not wish for all of London to know of my preference."

Reginald arrived with three glasses of lemonade in his hands and a plate of small cakes and biscuits perched on top rather precariously considering the crush of people. Had he heard Mariah's declaration? The thought that he may have made Sarah's stomach clench.

"Mariah, please take the plate before it falls or the food slips off."

Mariah secured the plate just as Sarah's parents stepped up beside her. Her father looked at the plate in Mariah's hands. "The refreshments look tasty. Shall I fetch us some, my dear?" he asked Sarah's mother.

She nodded excitedly. Sarah looked around, wondering if others noticed. There were surely some in the room who would consider her mother's excitement at a simple plate of refreshments a show of low breeding. But would Mr. Bancroft?

Lords Berwick, Montcort, and Ragsdale returned with refreshments for their partners, and they all formed a rather lopsided circle. Most of the ladies said nothing, looking around at the others gathered and quietly sipping on their drinks. The young lady with Lord Ragsdale, however, commented on everything that was said. Normally Sarah would not see that as a problem, except for the fact that most of her comments showed a complete lack of intelligence. It would have been better for the lady to stay quiet and unseen. The gentlemen's looks at each other indicated they were of a similar mind.

Sarah stayed slightly behind Mariah, watching the inter-actions.

"What did you think of Mrs. Davison's performance?" Mr. Bancroft directed his questions to the whole group.

"I've heard she is comparable to Mrs. Siddons." Lord Ragsdale grunted a laugh. "I simply do not see it. Mrs. Davison was proficient enough, but she will never equal Mrs. Sarah Siddons."

Lords Montcort and Ponsonby rolled their eyes.

"I thought she was marvelous." Lady Josephine spoke up.

Mariah glanced over her shoulder at Sarah, an annoyed look on her face.

"What did you think of her performance, Stoke? You frequent the theater often and have a point of comparison."

Sarah glanced over at Reginald and tilted her head. She was very interested in what he would say. She could not imagine Reginald had seen much of the lady's acting abilities. At least not at this performance.

He cleared his throat and glanced over at her. When he caught her eye, the tips of his ears reddened. "I, uh, thought her performance very proficient." He ran his hand along the back of his neck.

"Proficient? That is not very high praise." The woman standing beside Lord Ragsdale spoke up. Apparently, she had not yet discovered that staying quiet was to her advantage. "A person may be considered proficient, but if it is lacking in the proper warmth and emotion, it will not have the same effect."

Sarah raised a brow. The lady did have some sense in her brain. Who would have guessed?

"Indeed, Lady Mary is correct." Lord Montcort gave Reginald a pointed look. "What part did you enjoy the most?"

"I do not like to dissect the play into pieces and analyze it. I prefer to look at it as a whole. And in that regard, I found the performance very satisfying."

Lord Montcort raised a brow.

Mariah looked at her brother. "Regi, what is the matter?

You look unwell." She lifted a hand to his cheek and then his forehead.

He gently batted it away. "I am well, Mariah. It is just deuced warm in here."

A bell sounded, indicating the intermission was ending. Everyone turned toward the staircase, but Lord Montcort reached out a hand and held Reginald back. Sarah also hung back.

Lord Montcort leaned his head toward Reginald. "I noticed Lady Clara was in the box across from yours. I thought you said you cared not that she was engaged."

Reginald's hand clenched at his side. He glanced over at Sarah and then looked straight ahead. "I was not aware Lady Clara was even here."

Montcort raised a brow. "Then what had you so distracted? I have never known you to have so few opinions on a play."

"No one distracted me. It was simply too hot and stuffy inside there tonight. I do not know how anyone could concentrate on the stage."

"I'm not convinced." Lord Montcort waggled his brows. "Tell me, what is the distraction's name?"

"It has no name." Reginald nearly yelled at his friend. "Can we please be done with this conversation?"

Lord Montcort shrugged. "If that is what you wish." He turned and joined the crowd moving toward the staircase.

Reginald cast another glance at Sarah. His stern face relaxed and one corner of his mouth quirked up. He moved in closer to her and leaned in. "I meant to congratulate you."

"Congratulate me? On what?" She placed her empty plate on the tray of a passing servant.

"Your herd of hippopotami and their pile of peppers." He grinned widely. "A game well played, Sarah. Very well played."

She ducked her head to hide the large smile covering her

face and her undoubtedly pink cheeks at the use of her Christian name. She did not wish for him to think that she condoned his earlier behavior. Indeed, she should not have continued to engage in it. It was completely improper. But she could not make herself regret the decision.

The question was, would he continue their game into the second half? She had her doubts. After overhearing the conversation with Lord Montcort, she would not be surprised if he were not watching Reginald to see if his distraction did have a name other than Lady Clara.

Sarah frowned. Who was Lady Clara? If Sarah held any place in society she would surely know. And if she asked, it would only point out to others that she did not belong. She shook the thought from her mind. It was none of her concern.

Mr. Bancroft moved past her as they made their way through the crowd to the staircase.

Sarah reached out and gripped his arm before she could think about it.

He pulled to a stop and looked at her. "Yes, Miss Brown? Did you need something?"

Sarah blinked rapidly. She should have planned out her conversation in advance. What was she to say?

"Uh…" She swallowed. Think…think. "I meant to tell you the night of the ball but then I seemed to have forgotten."

He raised his brows and leaned slightly forward as if urging her to explain further. When she did not answer immediately, he prodded. "What did you forget?"

She bit the inside of her cheek, hoping the pain might bring her to her senses. Her loud, awkward laugh from the night of the card party burst out. "I wanted to thank you for the kind invitation to your dinner party. We are looking forward to attending."

His brow creased, but then he nodded. "But you need not concern yourself, you expressed your thanks when you sent your acceptance."

She nodded. "Yes, well, I wanted to thank you personally as well. My mother always says words have more meaning face to face." Her mother never said anything of the sort. Why did this man bring out the idiot—and apparently the liar —in her? She hated being a liar and now she had involved her mother in her lies. Why was this all so hard?

He smiled. "Your mother is very wise." He looked down at her hand still on his arm. "I hope you enjoy the rest of the play."

She looked down too, only then remembering it was there. Yanking it back to her side, she smiled awkwardly at him. He turned his back on her and she frowned. Wiggling her fingers, she wondered. Where was the heat? Where were the tingles running up and down her arm? She had felt nothing when she touched Mr. Bancroft. Not even a spark.

Which was odd, was it not? When Reginald had touched her, she had felt its effect for minutes after he released her. Indeed, she could still feel where his thumb had rubbed her arm before intermission.

Was it possible that only the receiver of the touch felt its effects? It seemed possible. Reginald never seemed affected when he touched her. But if that was the case, how could she arrange for Mr. Bancroft to touch her?

They arrived at the staircase and Reginald put his hand on the small of her back as he led her before him. The heat blossomed up her back and into her stomach and chest.

Sarah shook her head. How was she to know if Mr. Bancroft had felt anything by her touch? When he had looked down at her hand, was that because he felt the heat? Gads. She would need to ask Reginald about this, no matter how much she dreaded—and longed for—how he might answer her questions.

Chapter Sixteen

Sarah stood at the window watching the street below. Carriages and horses streamed past the window constantly. Indeed, there had hardly been a time when she saw the road completely empty. But that was to be expected, she supposed, when one lived above a shop *in Cheapside*.

She glanced at the card in her hands, rereading it for at least the hundredth time.

Miss Brown,

Please accompany me on a walk at two o'clock this afternoon.

Yours,

Stoke

She glanced over her shoulder at the clock on the mantle. He would be here in little more than five minutes. Her stomach rippled. She did not know why he had asked her and the uncertainty was causing her much anxiety. She placed her hand over her stomach.

What could Reginald mean by taking a turn with her? Were they to walk in Hyde Park where everyone could see them? Her stomach flopped again.

She stared at the street below. Perhaps he wished to apologize for his *lesson* the evening before. She felt a moment of regret for her participation. It had been entirely improper. And she was embarrassed to admit how much she had enjoyed the whole thing. Perhaps not in the moment. But reflecting upon it later always brought a smile to her lips.

She grinned. Lord Montcort had watched Reginald rather closely during the second half of the play. Which meant Reginald had never been able to retaliate against her herd of hippopotami comment.

That must be what he wished to speak to her about. Her stomach twisted again, and she turned away from the window just as a familiar carriage came into view.

Reginald. Just thinking about seeing him made her pulse quicken and her cheeks heat. If she just knew what he wanted to discuss with her, she could relax.

He was early.

Sarah grabbed her short gloves off the side table and hurried to the door. She wished to meet him in the entry and leave before either her father or her mother could ask too many questions.

She stepped on the entryway floor just as Chadwick opened the door and admitted Reginald.

She sucked in a gasp. Gracious, he looked handsome standing there in the entryway. A rustling started in her stomach, and she placed her hand over it. Why had he asked her to go for a walk? What could he mean by it? What if he had discovered her desire for a match with Mr. Bancroft? Was he there to dissuade her?

Mariah had said it was a good match, but Sarah could not fully agree. While Mr. Bancroft did not hold a title, he was good friends with many men who did. His social circle was not much different than that of Reginald or even Lord Muckrake —not that she had set her sights on that gentleman again. Perhaps Sarah needed to set her sights lower than even Mr.

Bancroft. A lesser gentleman like her father. But there were not many of them about London. It was far too expensive.

Reginald caught her eye and he grinned. "Ah, Miss Brown. I see you have anticipated me."

She shrugged. "My bedroom window overlooks the street. I saw your carriage approach." Her face heated as she realized he would know she was watching for him. Would he think her too eager for their walk?

She shook it off. It could not be helped now. She would simply need to show more restraint in the future.

He dipped his head and motioned to the front door. "Then we shall waste no more time and set out at once." Chadwick approached her with her pelisse and bonnet. "Thank you, Chadwick."

He nodded and held the pelisse while she slipped her arms inside. Sarah pulled her bonnet on and tied the strings as she stood beside Reginald. "I am ready."

He placed his hand on the small of her back and she flinched only slightly. Anticipating it had helped her not to react too much. Hopefully, he had not noticed it at all.

"Lord Stoke." Her mother called from the landing above. Sarah let out a frustrated sigh. They had been so close to leaving unimpeded. *Please do not say you will come along.*

Reginald looked up and tipped his hat. "Good day, Lady Brown."

Sarah's mother hurried down the stairs. "Good day to you, my lord." She looked around. "Is Lady Mariah waiting in the carriage? Sarah indicated that your sister would be joining you."

Reginald glanced over. "I did not bring my sister. She says it is too cold to enjoy a turn about the park."

Sarah's mother looked at her. "I shall call Becky and have her accompany you."

Sarah nodded and released the breath she had been holding. Yes, Becky was a far better option than her mother as a chaperone.

Her gaze dropped to the floor and guilt wormed its way through her belly. She loved her mother, truly she did. But Sarah was certain the conversation Reginald wished to have with her was not one either of them wished for her mother to hear. Becky, on the other hand, would hang back far enough that she would not overhear anything that might indicate just how improper they had been last evening.

"Robert, please have Becky fetched immediately. I am certain Lord Stoke has a busy day and has no time to wait around." The footman scurried away, leaving the three of them standing awkwardly in the entryway. Her mother finally spoke. "Are you to walk about Hyde Park?"

Reginald shook his head. "I have tired of Hyde Park. I thought we might take a turn about the Green Park. I have not been there in years." He glanced at Sarah. "Unless you object, of course."

She shook her head.

Her mother nodded knowingly, even though Sarah doubted her mother had ever set foot in the Green Park. Indeed, Sarah doubted her mother had even visited Hyde Park. But she could not be certain.

"Yes, I find the Green Park much more amiable than Hyde Park. The fountain is particularly pretty at this time of year. The water is not completely frozen, but a layer of frost covers the stones. When I was there last week with Sir Winston, the ducks were still in residence." She sighed. "Although, it has turned much colder this week, so I cannot promise they will still be there."

Sarah's mouth dropped open. "You have visited the Green Park and Hyde Park?"

Her mother gave her a bland look. "Of course, dearest. Do you believe your father and I simply sit at home and do nothing while you are off at Lady Mariah's?"

Sarah shut her mouth. She had not really thought about how her parents spent their time while she was away. She assumed her mother did a fair amount of shopping, even though her father could scarcely afford it. But now that Sarah thought about it, she had not noticed any new items in the house.

Becky came down the stairs, bundled in her warmest coat.

"Ah, Becky is here." Lady Brown smiled. "Off you go." She turned and left them standing in the entryway.

Reginald smiled. "You heard your mother. Off we go."

Sarah cast one last glance over her shoulder. But her mother had disappeared down a corridor.

Reginald replaced his hand on her back and gently guided her forward. All thoughts of her mother fled, and Sarah was acutely aware of the man beside her. Would he keep his hand on her back the whole time?

Gracious, she hoped not. She would be a very poor conversationalist if he did.

He was quiet in the carriage as they made their way through the London streets to the park. He did not look unhappy or angry, maybe just pensive?

She was uncertain if it was because Becky was in the carriage with them or if he simply had nothing to say. But if that were the case, why had he asked her to accompany him?

He could wish to discuss something pertaining to Mariah. If it was about his sister, it would not be proper for him to discuss it in front of a servant. But neither would anything about his *lessons*. So perhaps Sarah should just relax and enjoy the carriage ride. They would be at the park soon enough and then he would, at last, tell her what he was about.

She relaxed and the ride to the Green Park moved rather quickly. When the carriage stopped, Reginald bounded out and waited to hand Sarah down. Once she was standing beside him, he clasped his hands behind his back, and they walked toward the entrance of the park. He was quiet as they walked the pathway along Constitution Hill.

He glanced behind them and sighed. "I wished to speak to you about last evening."

Sarah's shoulders relaxed. "I wondered if that might be the reason behind your note." Sarah smiled. "You need not apologize, my lord. While it was completely improper, I did learn something new."

His steps slowed and he stared at her. "I did not ask you here to apologize. I regret nothing about the evening." A smug smile curved his lips. "Except perhaps Montcort and his never-ending questions."

Sarah narrowed her eyes. "You regret nothing?"

He shook his head. "No. Indeed, I find myself very pleased with the outcome. I can rest easy knowing that you are proficient in that area of flirting. Indeed, I am rather impressed with my teaching skills."

"Your teaching had nothing to do with my skills, my lord." Sarah huffed. "If not to apologize, why did you bring me here?" What else was there about the evening that he wished to speak to her about?

"It is about Lady Mary. She attended with Lord Ragsdale."

Sarah stared at him. What did Lady Mary have to do with anything? She was quite ignorant and seemed unaware of how others perceived her. But what did that have to do with Sarah? "What about Lady Mary?"

His mouth dropped open in protest. "Oh, come now. Do not tell me you did not pay her any mind. I saw you watching her with a look of pity on your face. The girl came across as quite brainless." He looked over at Sarah. "I know you witnessed what I did."

She nodded. "How could I miss it? She had nothing to say about everything."

His brow furrowed. "How does one say nothing to everything?"

Sarah dropped her head to the side. "I mean she said nothing of consequence. The conversations were not enhanced—indeed, in some cases, I believe she detracted from them—by anything she added. In essence, she said nothing about everything. I do not think it possible to keep her quiet."

His eyes lit and he raised his hands up in front of him as if he were about to reach out and cup her face. *Was* he about to hold her face? Now that she had thought it, she hoped he would. How would it feel?

He nodded. "Precisely. I knew you had noticed." He shook his head. "What you may not know is that Lady Mary, while not the cleverest of people, is not as brainless as she appeared last evening."

Sarah nodded, pushing her disappointment down. "You know Lady Mary, then?" She was still uncertain what Lady Mary had to do with her.

"I do not know her well, but I have seen her enough to know she is not the dimwit she appeared last evening."

"Then I am sorry for her," Sarah sighed and looked at her feet walking slowly down the pebbled path. "But I must confess, I still have no idea what Lady Mary has to do with me. Why was she so important that we needed to take a turn about the park to discuss her?"

Reginald looked over at her. "You do not understand? It is another element of flirting."

"Looking like a complete nodcock is considered flirting?" As soon as the words were out of her mouth, Sarah realized the truth of them. Indeed, she could hear in her head Mariah's voice telling her that to draw a man's favor, a woman must hide her intellect. *No man wishes for a bluestocking, Sarah.*

"Yes. It seems to be a widespread notion by women that a man only wants a dimwit." His brow creased and he looked ahead. "While I am certain this is true of some men—men like Muckrake would be threatened by a woman with wit. But then no woman with intelligence would ever seek after his affections." He stopped walking and turned, staring hard at her. "No man worthy of you would ever ask you to pretend to be less than you are."

Sarah was quiet for a moment, thinking through what Reginald had just said. While she did not take the opinion that a woman must be brainless, she also knew of men who would not appreciate a woman with greater intellect than their own. But if Reginald was correct, there were men who wished for a woman who could think. "Then this is your next lesson?"

"Yes," his brow furrowed but his lips turned up. "Although, I am not certain how to demonstrate it." He glanced at her from the corner of his eye. "At least not as proficiently as I did last evening's lesson."

"I have had enough of your demonstrations for now." Sarah fought the grin threatening to come. She did not wish for him to see that she had enjoyed last evening as much as she had. "Perhaps I am the one that must demonstrate this one."

Reginald nodded pensively. "Indeed, I find my interest piqued."

She grinned and tapped her finger to her chin. She dropped her gaze to him. "My lord, are you aware that a grouping of hippos is called a pod?"

His brow creased slightly and then his eyes widened. "But you called them a herd last evening." His mouth dropped open in feigned indignation. "You lied to me."

"It was not a lie. A herd is an acceptable name. But a pod is more accurate." She shrugged. "But it worked for my objective. And all is fair in love and flirting, my lord."

A soft smile turned his lips. "Were you flirting with me, Sarah?"

Her cheeks blazed. But the softness of his tone made her heart race. Did he want her to flirt with him? Her chest tightened and she licked her lips.

His gaze dropped to her mouth, and he stood staring at her for a moment.

She cleared her throat. "I was not flirting with you. I was practicing, my lord, as any good student would."

He pulled his gaze up to her face and sighed. "It seems you know all you need to about not being brainless, but there is another aspect that you should know about."

They started walking again and Sarah glanced over at him. "There is more? What else is there to know?"

"It is not just about what you know. But what you both know together."

What they both knew together? Sometimes it felt like Reginald spoke in a language Sarah did not understand. She understood the individual words on their own, but when he put them together, they sounded like complete gibberish.

"You can't be the only one who has knowledge to impart. At some point, you need to discover things that you have in common. Sharing those experiences is where the relationship grows into something more." He looked straight ahead.

Sarah frowned. "To discover such things will require extensive conversations. How is one to gain such information in the course of a set at a ball or with a table full of people at a card party?"

Reginald rolled his lips between his teeth. "That is where the other things I've taught you come into play. You must do things to convince the man that he wishes to spend more time with you. You will only learn what you have in common while on a turn about a park or garden or perhaps on a carriage ride."

Sarah nodded slowly. "Then I must become proficient in touching and whispering," her face heated at the way it sounded, "if I am to have the opportunity to come to know the gentleman more intimately?"

Reginald nodded. "Although, as you saw last night, the theater can prove to be an effective place for conversation also." He raised his brows. "Or in the case of Lady Mary, it may be the place that determines there will be no further acquaintance."

Sarah clasped her hands tightly in front of her, chewing on the side of her lip. She had not realized when she came to London what all it would entail. She had imagined they would be invited to many events. Perhaps not every night of the week, but more than they had to date. While she had not believed men would line up to make her acquaintance, she had hoped someone might show an interest in her. But it was all coming to naught.

If she could not find a match among the thousands of gentlemen in London, how was she to find one among only a few dozen gentlemen in Stoke-on-Trent? And how was she to find a match like what her parents had? That kind of luck seemed almost impossible—in London or outside of it.

She looked ahead. What could she have done differently in preparing for her Season? As much as Reginald touted his teachings, she knew even learning them before she came would not have changed how woefully unprepared she felt.

Chapter Seventeen

Reginald stepped into the entryway of Charles Bancroft's Berkeley Square townhome. Mariah was in front of him, already unbuttoning her pelisse and untying her bonnet.

He sucked in a deep breath. Tonight was to be a quieter night with just friends in attendance. Which was precisely what he needed after the crushes of the last few weeks. He was not only physically tired but mentally tired as well. The London Season was not for the faint of heart.

Apart from his time at his club and his lessons with Sarah, he had little to look forward to. At least until this invitation had arrived.

The butler led them down a well-lit corridor and into a cozy parlor. Reginald smiled and released a breath. All his friends stood in the room, talking and laughing. Several ladies stood with the group, but even then, there were little more than a dozen people in the room. A far cry from the hundreds that turned out for the various balls and parties he usually attended.

"Reg," Charlie called from the other side of the room.

"I'm glad you and Lady Mariah could attend tonight. With how late the invitations went out, I worried you may already have plans to attend another party."

Reginald strode over, taking the glass Charlie offered him, and grinned. "I felt not a moment's regret in declining the invitation from Lady Portsmouth. It has been barely a month since I've been in London, and I am already tired of society. It is all so taxing."

Several of the men raised their glasses to him, calling out words of agreement.

Mariah stayed close to his side. She likely did not know any of the ladies in attendance. And as they all looked to be several years her senior, he could understand her slight hesitation. While most would think his sister was rather high in the instep and overly confident, Reginald knew better. She tended to overcompensate for her insecurities by acting confident and at times rather arrogant.

Reginald motioned with his head to a girl standing next to the pianoforte. She kept to herself. He took a step closer to Mariah and lowered his voice. "Do you see the young lady standing by the pianoforte?"

Mariah nodded, her eyes drifting over to the girl.

"That is Charlie's sister, Madeleine. She has only just arrived from Cornwall. You and she are of similar ages. Perhaps you could go and speak to her. Make a new friend."

Mariah swallowed and pulled her bottom lip between her teeth. "Perhaps after dinner we may be introduced."

A rustling at the doorway drew Reginald's attention away from his sister. Sir Winston and Lady Brown, along with Sarah, stood in the doorway.

Reginald sucked in a deep breath. The evening kept getting better and better. Sarah looked lovely in a deep green gown. He could not help but notice her neck was completely exposed. Surely there was some sort of lesson he could impart to her while they were there together.

138

Charlie moved away from Reginald and made his way toward his new guests. "Sir Winston… Lady Brown. I am so glad you could join us this evening." He bowed deeply to Sarah. "And you too, Miss Brown."

Charlie returned to Reginald's side. "I hope you do not mind, Reg. But I thought perhaps your sister might be more at ease if her friend was invited."

Reginald shook his head, his grin growing. "Quite the opposite, Charlie. You figured it just right. I have no objections."

Charlie clapped Reginald on the shoulder. "It was not completely selfless. I admit to hoping they may take a liking to Madeleine. She is dreadfully shy and has had difficulty finding friends since arriving with her companion last week. It is one of the difficulties of her not being out yet. I had hoped to take her to a few smaller gatherings this Season so she might make some friends before her come out next Season."

"I'm certain they will be giggling together before the evening is over." Reginald grimaced.

Charlie chuckled. "I hope so. I find I am forced to remain at home more than I wish since their arrival. She does not wish to go anywhere. I'm beginning to wonder if my mother has had too much influence on her." He turned and waved to Ragsdale who was seated on the couch by the fire. "Rags is scowling more than usual tonight. Perhaps I should go discover what the matter is." He rolled his eyes before moving away.

Reginald wanted to go to Sarah, but it would not seem right, so he walked over to the couch where his sister sat quietly watching the other ladies speaking to each other.

He extended his hand to her. "Mariah, look who has just arrived."

She stood up and turned, just as Sarah approached.

Mariah sagged in relief. "Oh, it is as if my thoughts have

come true. I was just wishing you were here with me. I am no longer dreading the evening."

Sarah leaned forward and embraced his sister. "Mariah, I was hoping you would be here." She glanced around the room. "I do not believe I know a single lady beside you."

Mariah leaned in even closer to Sarah and whispered to her, but Reginald did not hear what she said. Sarah's eyes flicked to his and he wondered if they might be speaking of him. Most likely Mariah was complaining about something he had done of late.

Sir Winston and Lady Brown came and stood beside them. She clicked open her fan, waving it furiously in front of her chest. "I believe we have you to thank for this invitation, my lord." She smiled genuinely at Reginald. "Thank you."

Reginald shook his head. "Indeed, I had nothing to do with this. I only learned of your invitation when you walked through the door." His gaze traveled over to Sarah. "I believe it is your daughter you must thank. Mr. Bancroft's sister has arrived, and I believe Miss Brown made an impression on him. He wishes for the ladies to become better acquainted."

"I am certain you played a part, nonetheless." Lady Brown gushed.

Reginald shrugged off the praise and lifted his glass to his mouth.

The butler entered the room and announced dinner.

Charlie stepped forward and clapped his hands together. "As this is a group of friends, I am certain no one will object if we dispense with the formalities." He glanced over at Ragsdale and grinned. "Except for Rags. As most of us know, he disdains the idea."

Ragsdale smirked at Charlie. "I do not mind. As it means I will not have to sit next to you."

Reginald laughed. He knew it was likely Ragsdale would sit beside Charlie, even though precedent was not being observed. It would not be because he had to but because he wanted to.

Charlie led his sister over. He dipped his head to Mariah and Sarah. "Lady Mariah, Miss Brown. I wish to introduce you to my sister, Miss Madeleine Bancroft."

Both Mariah and Sarah curtsied, muttering at the same time, "Pleased to meet you."

Miss Bancroft smiled warmly. "I was very happy when my brother told me he was to invite the two of you. While I am not officially out—Charlie does not wish to present me in court until next Season—he thought it might be nice if I knew a few young ladies. He believes I stay indoors too much and hopes if I meet some people, they might entice me out of the house."

Mariah shrugged. "I believe you have the right of it. The weather is far too cold to do much outside."

Sarah smiled. "Come now, Mariah. Did we not enjoy ourselves at the museum? It was not so very cold."

"Yes, but we were indoors most of the time." Mariah shrugged. "I will wait to venture out of doors until Spring when walks and carriage rides about the parks will be much more enjoyable."

Charlie held his arms wide to his side as if he were a gamesman herding a bunch of cattle or deer. "Come along, we may carry on the conversation once we are seated. But you know Mrs. Mercy will ring a peal if we allow the soup to chill by dillydallying."

Miss Bancroft put her balled hands on her hips. "If you did not wish us to speak to each other now, why did you not wait to introduce us until after dinner?"

Mr. Bancroft cleared his throat and glanced at Reginald. "I certainly see the error of my ways." He shook his head. "Although, I'm pleased to see that you are getting on with each other."

They all moved toward the doorway and into the corridor. Mariah leaned in close to Sarah and whispered, although not as quietly as she likely thought. "Now is your chance. We must see that you are seated next to him at dinner."

Reginald fell back a step. Sit next to him at dinner? Was the gentleman Sarah hoped to flirt with there? He hurried to catch up, hoping Mariah might expound on who he was. It was obvious that it was one of Reginald's friends who had caught Sarah's attention. But which one? He stared at the back of each man walking in front of him. He hoped it was not Rags. As much as Reginald praised her intellect and qualities, Rags would never look twice at her. Montcort and Ponsonby might look twice, but they were even more intent to avoid marriage than Reginald was. And Berwick was not better. That left only Bancroft. Reginald shook his head. That was no good either. Bancroft did not desire a wife. None of his friends did. But how did she think to try and change their mind about such things?

He shook his head. It was no use trying to figure it out. He supposed he would just have to see which gentlemen she tried to sit next to at the table.

They entered the dining room, one that was more suited to the family rather than a large dinner party. While they did not sit in order of precedence, everyone tended to sit so that a gentleman sat on either side of a lady. Mariah chose the seat across the table from Sarah, while Miss Bancroft sat to her brother's right at the head of the table. Sir Winston and Lady Brown sat at the opposite end.

Reginald took the seat next to Mariah, and Lady Josephine sat on his other side. Sarah sat across from him with Berwick on one side and Ponsy on the other. Reginald looked between the two men. Which one had she wished to sit next to? Or had she not been able to secure a seat next to the man she wanted? Blast it. This had not answered any questions at all. Indeed, it had only raised new ones.

He sat back in his seat, feeling rather irritated by the whole thing. He glanced across the table at Sarah and a smile slowly started to form. Perhaps the evening was not completely objectionable. He was in a good position to watch and speak with her. Maybe he could see how she interacted with the men on either side of her and see if she paid them any special attention.

Ponsy leaned toward Sarah as the footman ladled soup into his bowl. Why had he leaned toward Sarah rather than Miss Duncan on his other side?

Sarah said something and they both smiled.

Was she flirting with him? She did not appear to touch him, and she was not whispering as much as she was just speaking in a lower tone to him. If she was flirting, it was not anything Reginald had taught her, but he supposed she might have gained some knowledge of her own.

He leaned to the side, paying no attention to the soup being ladled into his bowl. He watched them as he lifted the spoon to his lips.

Berwick reached for his fork at the same time Sarah reached for her spoon and their small fingers brushed each other.

Reginald narrowed his eyes. Had that been on purpose? It was precisely what he had taught her. He was not certain he liked his lessons being used on his best friend.

Sarah smiled at Berwick and apologized.

Berwick chuckled and returned her smile. "No harm done," he said. Harm? How could rubbing their fingers together cause harm? Or was it just a pretense to cover up what they were really doing?

Sarah's shoulders rose with a sigh, and she stared down at her plate. Was it Berwick? Was that the man Mariah had been teaching Sarah to flirt with? And in turn, Reginald had taught her how to flirt with him even better. He pressed his fingers to his chest, a pinch squeezing it tightly.

Lady Josephine spoke at his side, but he kept his answers short, afraid he might miss something going on across the table. It was not that he cared a wit that Sarah desired the affections of Berwick. He merely wished to see if what he had taught her worked. And he wanted to make sure that Berwick did not hurt her. That was the only reason he continued to watch. Although, he need not watch to know that things would not work out as Sarah and Mariah hoped. Berwick was not looking for a wife. None of his friends were. He thought they knew that.

When dessert was served, Reginald watched as Sarah leaned in close to Berwick and whispered something in his ear. Berwick grabbed a plate of tarts from the center of the table and waited while she took one.

He returned the plate and then turned to Miss Turner on his other side and said something to her. What was wrong with the man? Could he not see how hard Sarah was trying? Could he not see how intelligent and humorous she was? Did he not see she was perfectly lovely in every way? Why did he not pay her more mind?

It pained Reginald to see her looking down at her plate in resignation. And while he did not think Berwick was worthy of her, if he was the man she had chosen, Reginald would do what he could to help her. He kicked out his foot under the table, hoping to draw Berwick's attention away from Miss Turner.

Sarah let out a gasp and leaned forward with a pained look on her face.

Reginald's eyes widened. Lud, how had he managed to kick her?

She looked across the table and he dropped his gaze to his plate, his face surely showing his guilt.

He looked up under his lashes, afraid if she saw him full on, she would know of his crimes.

Sarah stared at him for a moment, before turning her attention back to her plate.

And she was not the only one looking. Ponsy had stopped his conversation with Lady Martha and stared at Reginald. As did Berwick. Even Mariah, who was usually completely oblivious to anything that did not involve her, was watching him.

Reginald grunted quietly. His plan had worked in a sense. He had distracted Berwick away from Miss Turner.

Ben watched Reginald for several heartbeats, then shifted his gaze to Sarah. But then he returned it to Reginald.

It seemed rather obvious what had happened and who had done it. Reginald did not know why he pretended nothing had happened. All it did was make him look more guilty. Why had he not made up an excuse? Leg spasms or some such nonsense? That would certainly have been better than what had transpired.

Lud, he was an idiot!

Reginald vowed to keep his feet to himself at dinner from now on. No matter what should happen across the table.

The women adjourned to the drawing room and all the men stayed behind for drinks.

"Reg, did you do something to Miss Brown?" Ponsy asked.

Reginald tried to look confused. He could not rightly admit to kicking her when he had acted as if nothing happened during dinner. "What would I have done to Miss Brown?"

Berwick came to stand next to Ponsy. "Yes, what happened to Miss Brown? She seemed rather distressed."

Ponsy raised a shoulder. "I don't know. Reg was glaring at me and then Miss Brown yelled. From the way she leaned over and rubbed her hand over her leg, I suspect she was *kicked*." He raised a brow.

Reginald chuckled awkwardly. "Why should I kick Miss Brown?"

"That is what I am wondering. I had thought the two of you were friends."

"We are friends." Reginald looked over Ponsy's shoulder. Where was Ragsdale when you needed him—someone to speak of things that no one else cared about? Ragsdale was a master of nonsense. And nonsense is just what Reginald needed.

"Then why did you kick her?" Ponsy eyed him.

Reginald opened his mouth to protest.

"Unless…" Ponsy did not continue the thought, but the look in his eyes said he knew the truth. He continued to watch Reginald with far too much interest.

Reginald had yet to have a drink of his port when Charlie suggested the men rejoin the ladies in the drawing room.

Finally. He let out a breath as he placed his glass on the sideboard. Surely there would be fewer questions once they rejoined the ladies.

He hung back, allowing the other men to lead the way into the drawing room.

When he stepped into the room, Reginald could not keep his eyes from seeking out Sarah. He wanted to ensure she was well. What if he had hurt her terribly? He had meant to hurt Berwick, so it followed that he had kicked Sarah rather forcefully.

She sat on the chair next to Mariah. Miss Bancroft sat on the couch on Sarah's other side. The three were chatting quite amiably. Charlie had been correct in his assumption that they would become fast friends.

Reginald moved over to stand behind Mariah's chair. "Good evening, ladies."

Miss Bancroft smiled up at him, but both Sarah and Mariah gave him less pleasant looks.

Thankfully, Charlie clapped his hands, and everyone turned to look at him. "I thought a friendly game of cards might be enjoyable."

146

"Friendly? Since when have you ever been friendly in cards?" Montcort shouted.

Charlie grinned. "That is only when I play with you. When ladies are present, I am always on my best behavior."

Everyone stood as servants stepped in and set about moving couches and setting up card tables.

Sarah leaned over to Reginald. "I have a problem," she whispered in his ear. His breath hitched. Lud, she was good at this. Perhaps he should not have been so thorough in his teaching.

"I did not bring any fish with me." Sarah looked at him with wide eyes. "And this time it was not even on purpose."

"I find it best if I always have at least a small set with me. Especially with small parties such as this. Cards are often the chosen activity following dinner."

Sarah nodded. "Yes, I had the same thought. But then my mother suggested I change my wrap, and I set my fish down to change. I forgot to grab them again on our way out."

"What are you two whispering about?" Miss Bancroft asked.

Sarah released a sigh. "I seem to have left my fish at home."

Miss Bancroft smiled. "Oh, there is no need for you to be upset. We have many sets. I am certain Charlie would not mind you borrowing some."

Miss Bancroft turned to leave, but Reginald reached out a hand to stop her. Hopefully, Sarah would not think he was flirting with Miss Bancroft. His eyes widened. Lud, hopefully, Miss Bancroft did not believe it either. "If you will tell me where they are, I will go fetch them. There is no need for you to miss any of the party. After all, you are the hostess."

Miss Bancroft nodded. "Thank you. That is very kind of you. They are in the top right cupboard closest to the fireplace, in the library."

Reginald nodded. "Yes. I know just the place."

He turned away, intent on fetching the fish. But Sarah reached out a hand and pulled him to a stop. His arm heated from the tips of his fingers to his shoulder. "You need not go get them. I can fetch them myself. It was my mistake."

He waved her words away. "But you do not know where the library is. It is no problem, Sarah. It is the least I can do."

Sarah shook her head. "You could just tell me how to get to the library."

Why was she being so stubborn? Reginald shook his head. "No. It will be much faster if I just go." He headed toward the door, but when he stepped out into the corridor, Sarah stepped out beside him.

"It is my fault I forgot them. At least let me come with you to fetch them."

He looked over her shoulder into the room of people. "I am sure you will be missed."

She glanced over her shoulder and shrugged. "You are mistaken. Only Mariah and Miss Bancroft know me. And they believe I am fetching some lemonade."

"What of your parents?"

She dropped a heavy sigh, her hands tightening at her sides. "Please? If we hurry, no one will be the wiser."

"Why…"

"I just need a moment away. A moment when I am not worried about every word I speak or every move I make."

"Why do you feel you need to worry about what you say or do? These people are friends."

"They are your friends, not mine. They are heirs to dukedoms and marquessates. I am just the daughter of a gentleman. What I say among them matters."

"You are welcome to take a moment out here in the corridor." He knew it sounded lame.

"Do you not wish me to come? Are you unhappy with me?" Worry replaced the exhaustion he had seen there only moments ago. "Is that why you kicked me under the table?"

Reginald's face burned. "That was an accident."

She smirked. "Then it was you?" He scowled at her. She had tricked him into confessing.

"Very well, Sarah. Follow me." He started down the corridor. Unless he wished to confess every wrong he'd ever done, it might just be best if he did not argue with her anymore.

Chapter Eighteen

They walked quickly down a brightly lit corridor, turning from it into a much darker one. "Are you certain you know where you are going?" Sarah whispered.

"Of course I know where I'm going," Reginald countered. "I've been coming to this house for nearly seven years. I believe I know where the library is."

"I did not mean anything by it. You simply seemed unsure."

Reginald stopped in front of the door and smirked down at her. "This is the library. I will now accept your apology for your lack of faith in me."

She sighed. "It was not that I lacked faith in you. Indeed, I have never had more faith in a gentleman other than my father."

His hand paused on the door handle, and he stared down at her in the dim lighting. Was she in earnest? Why did that notion make him feel as though he could slay a dragon? "Is that the truth?"

Sarah swallowed and looked at the floor "Indeed, you have never done anything to make me doubt you." She gave him a smirk very similar to the one he'd given her. "Except, for the night at the theater."

He shook his head. "Are you never going to forgive me for that?"

"Perhaps I would if you ever apologized. But as you have no regrets," she mimicked his words from their walk in the park, "I find that notion unlikely."

He took a step toward her, eliminating most of the space between them. "Then let me apologize now. While I do not regret what I did, I do regret that I made you feel ill at ease. That was not my intent." That was not entirely true. He had rather enjoyed her unease. Which, looking back on it now, had not been kind of him. Although he did not believe she disliked all of it.

Sarah shook her head. "I find that hard to believe, my lord."

Reginald grinned. "Then perhaps I need to apologize for that as well."

They stood staring at each other for several heartbeats. What would it be like to kiss her? He knew he could not do something so untoward, especially not in an open corridor, but he could not help but wonder. And not for the first time.

He shook off the thought and turned the handle, pushing open the door.

He stepped inside, a breeze of cool air meeting him. Reaching back, he grabbed Sarah's hand and pulled her in behind him.

But he didn't let go once she was inside. He enjoyed the feel of the warmth spreading through each of his fingers and up his arm far too much. And while he did not hold her hand tightly, he could feel a slight pulse. It thumped quickly in a similar rhythm to his own.

He pulled her toward the fireplace and regretfully dropped her hand so he could open the cupboard to the right.

Sarah pulled her hand in front of her, rubbing lightly at

her fingers. Was she cold? Should he retake her hand or perhaps even wrap his arms around her? He liked the thought of that.

She took a step to the side, and he pushed his thoughts away. If she wanted his warmth, would she not step closer?

He rummaged through the cupboard. What were all these things inside? How was he to find— "Ah ha, victory." He held up a box, a grin on his face.

Sarah returned his smile.

The moonlight filtered through the light sheers on the windows, casting a pale white light across her face. The thought of her brushing her fingers against Berwick's came unbidden to his mind. Berwick? What did she see in him?

Reginald clenched his jaw. What had he done? Why had he been such an accomplished instructor? If she did end up marrying Berwick, he had no one to blame but himself. He should have just allowed Mariah and her fans to continue Sarah's training.

He handed the box over and she grasped hold of it lightly.

Perhaps he needed to show her what real flirting was like —show her that Berwick was not the right man for her. He took a step closer to her and ran the back of his finger lightly across her jawbone.

"What are you doing?" She asked in a shaky voice.

"I'm giving you another lesson on flirting. Is that not what you asked for?"

Sarah swallowed and focused her gaze on his Adam's apple. "This feels like more than flirting, my lord."

"I assure you, Miss Brown. This is the best kind of flirting." He took a step closer and leaned in slightly. "And you seem to learn best when I demonstrate." His whispered voice tickled her neck sending a shiver through her body.

"Are you sure a demonstration is necessary?" She stood still as a statue, except for her eyelids, which fluttered wildly.

"Trust me. This is the best kind of demonstration."

The same intoxicating scent that had nearly undone him at the theater filled his nostrils and the desire to kiss her came again, but with far more intensity than in the corridor.

He pulled back from her slightly. What if she did not want it?

Her eyes were still closed but her head tilted to the side, leaving the slope of her neck fully exposed. That was an invitation, was it not? He leaned in and placed a feather-light kiss just below her earlobe.

Sarah shuddered and sighed.

Reginald grinned as he placed another kiss on her neck. But that wasn't enough. He wanted to feel her lips on his. He trailed a line of kisses up her neck and along her jaw until he came to the crease at the side of her mouth. For a moment, he considered stopping there. But what was the point? If he stopped now, he would forever wonder what her lips felt like… tasted like. It would eventually drive him to bedlam. Of that, he was quite certain.

The box of fish clattered to the floor.

Reginald moved his hands up her arms and placed them on either side of her face. He paused a moment longer, then leaned in and captured her lips with his. His mouth moved over hers, wanting to explore every crease and dimple.

He moved closer pressing his body against hers. She wrapped her arms around his neck, thrusting her hands into his hair. He let out a shiver and a soft moan.

She whimpered and pulled back. Her eyes were wide. Was it with confusion? Or perhaps embarrassment? No, he swallowed. It was shame. "This was a mistake," she whispered. Her words were like a splash of cold water on his face.

What had he done?

She dropped down and gathered the fish with trembling fingers.

"Sarah, I—" He dropped down with her.

She brushed the fish into the box and slammed it shut, shoving them into his hands. She stood, not giving him a second glance, and she fled from the room.

Reginald swore. Never had he behaved in such a despicable manner. And to Sarah. How could he have done such a thing to her? She was like a sister to him.

He shook his head. No, what he had experienced—the emotions and reactions that had just flooded his body—they were not the feelings one had for a sister.

No, he wanted Sarah in a way he had never wanted another person. He wanted all of her—mind, body, and soul. It felt selfish, but he could not help it. He wanted her for himself.

But she had left, and he felt as if she had taken a part of him with her. It was almost as if he lo… He shook his head. No. That was not possible. He was very happy with his life as a bachelor. He did not wish for a wife…did he?

But if he did not lo—he could not say that word—Sarah, then what he had just done made him no better than Muckrake. Bile rose in his throat. He collapsed into a nearby chair and dropped his head back, staring at the ceiling as thoughts flitted in and out of his mind. Could it be he was no different than that rake? His throat felt thick.

Or could it be he…loved…he tried the word out in his mind, testing it to feel its truth. He was surprised to discover that it did not feel as foreign as he had thought it would. Could he love her? His chest warmed. It was possible. But his discovery may have come too late. He could not say that she would ever speak to him again.

Would she still come to visit Mariah? A warmth of hope spread throughout his chest. If she came to visit Mariah, perhaps there was a chance he could explain to her—apologize to her for everything.

The door to the library swung quietly open. Reginald did not turn around. He hoped it was Sarah, but he knew deep down it wasn't. And whoever it was need not witness Reginald's disappointment.

"Reg?" Ponsy's deep voice sounded from behind.

"What?"

"You have been away from the party for some time. Are you well?" His voice was softer than normal.

"No, I am most unwell."

"What happened?" Ponsy settled into the chair next to him.

Reginald sighed. Heatherton was usually the man he confided in. They were closer friends than any of the others. Just as Montcort and Berwick and Ragsdale and Bancroft were.

Ponsonby was the lone man out. He did not have a single best friend but rather was a best friend to all of them. He was the fill-in when someone was missing. And while Reginald would have preferred Heath was there, he wasn't. He was somewhere on the continent with his mother. There was no way Reginald could speak of this with the others. No, Ponsy was the only one present that Reginald trusted not to make light of his situation.

"How is Miss Brown?" Reginald could not get her wide-eyed face out of his mind.

"She and her parents left early. Miss Brown claimed to have a headache."

"She left?" Reginald straightened in his chair, unable to help the pitiful tone of his voice.

"I think it best. She did not look well when she returned —" He trailed off.

Ponsonby was implying that he did not know where she had come from. Already there was speculation. That could not be advantageous.

"Lemonade. She told Mariah and Miss Bancroft she would fetch them lemonade." Reginald's voice was firm. He had hurt her enough. She need not suffer the censure of the *ton* also.

Ponsy nodded. "Her head must have ached enough that she forgot the lemonade."

"Must have." Reginald ran a hand over his face.

Ponsy sighed. "You wouldn't happen to know anything about her headache, would you?"

Reginald shrugged. What could he say? It was not just him in this story. If people outside this room learned what he had done... Suffice it to say, Sarah would have to return to Stoke.

"You may confide in me, Reg. Your story is safe."

"I know, Ponsy. It's just..."

"Miss Brown?"

Reginald nodded. "I'm a terrible person."

"I doubt that." A soft smile rested on Ponsy's lips. "You are one of the most honorable gentlemen I know. And I know a lot of gentlemen."

Reginald's head shook back and forth. "No, I'm not. You don't know what I've done."

"Why don't you tell me, and I'll be the judge."

Silence hung around them for several long moments. Finally, Reginald sighed. "It all started when I inadvertently heard Mariah telling Sarah—"

"Sarah?"

Reginald ran a hand through his hair. "Miss Brown."

Ponsy nodded and motioned for Reginald to continue.

"Mariah was instructing Sarah," there was no use in calling her Miss Brown as Ponsy knew he was way beyond that kind of propriety, "on the proper way to gain a gentleman's attention. The suggestions were ridiculous, Ponsy. Some included fans. I had no choice but to intervene. I had to volunteer to teach Sarah myself."

A hint of a smile flitted across Ponsonby's face and he

nodded. "You had no other choice." He said it matter-of-factly, but it felt as if he was teasing.

Reginald nearly stopped talking, but then Ponsonby's face became serious again. "Continue."

Reginald found himself telling his friend everything. The story poured out and before he knew it, he was telling Ponsonby about the kiss.

"That is when she fled from the room. But her face…" Reginald sighed, his head shaking and his shoulders stooping. "She looked…"

"Quite unwell. Yes. I saw her." Ponsonby nodded slowly.

"What am I to do?" Reginald's voice was quiet.

"That all depends."

Reginald looked up at him. "What do you mean? It depends on what?"

"If you do not care for the lady, then you do nothing. You carry on as if it never happened."

Reginald looked at his friend hardly believing the man could suggest something so cold and calculating. "Nothing?"

"However," his brows rose, "if it is as I suspect, and you do care for the lady, you must take a more careful approach."

Reginald studied Ponsonby. "What kind of careful approach?"

"Then you do care for her?" Ponsonby leaned forward, placing his elbows on his knees and his chin in his palms.

"Of course, I care for her. I have known her since she was born. How could I not care for her?"

Ponsonby raised a brow and stared. His quiet observation left Reginald feeling fidgety.

"That is it? You care for her simply as a neighbor?" Ponsonby pushed to his feet. "I don't have time for this, Reg. I'm returning to the drawing room."

"Wait." Reginald looked at his fingernails picking at a piece of skin at the side. What was he to say?

Ponsonby took a few steps and stopped. "Let me ask you this, Reg. Do you kiss all your neighbors?"

Reginald smirked. "Of course I do not kiss all my neighbors. What a ridiculous notion."

"Then why Miss Brown? What was it that made her special?"

Ponsonby's gaze held on Reginald. It was rather disconcerting how intense the man could stare. Indeed, Reginald's skin itched under the scrutiny. But perhaps Ponsonby's gaze had nothing to do with the state of Reginald's skin.

Why had he kissed Sarah? He crossed his knee over his leg, trying for a more comfortable position. But it did not seem to help, nor did it answer the question.

He felt things when she was near that he had never felt before. He woke up each morning anticipating her arrival and he thought about her when he fell asleep. He had spent more time in the past month coming up with things to teach her than he had spent looking at his ledgers. He had even tried his hand at creating a charade, just to see if she would enjoy it. He just… sighed. He just loved her. That was it.

He pulled in a long, slow breath. He could admit it to himself, but could he admit it to Ponsy? He didn't think he was ready for that yet.

"There is much to appreciate in Miss Brown. But she is not so very special." Hearing the words come out of his mouth pierced his soul. How could he say such a thing about her? How could he minimize her like that? At that very moment, he wondered how he was even breathing normally without her there. How could he say she was nothing special?

"If she is not special, *why did you kiss her*? You already said you are not in the habit of kissing your neighbors. And from what I've seen, you are not in the habit of kissing many ladies, either."

"Kissing ladies brings complications," Reginald quoted the motto of his friends—of their little league of bachelors. He leaned back in his chair and allowed his head to drop to the seatback, his hands interlaced around his neck.

"Indeed, it does. Which begs the question, why Miss Brown? Why did you kiss her even with the complications? Because I should think kissing her would bring even more complications than kissing any other lady of society." Ponsonby returned to his seat.

Reginald let out a long moan. "I know. It would have been much easier had I kissed the likes of Lady Clara."

Ponsonby sighed heavily, obviously frustrated by the conversation. "Then why did you do it? Why did you kiss her, Reg?" He nearly shouted.

"Because I love her." Reginald snapped out. "Because I cannot stop thinking about her. Because I never want her out of my sight. Because *it made me insane* thinking she might have set her sights on Ben."

"By Jove, it's about time you admitted it," Ponsonby reached over and patted Reginald on the shoulder. "Now, that wasn't so hard, was it? I've known it for quite some time. I am surprised it took you so long. But then you always were a bit slower than the rest of us." Ponsy threw his head back and laughed.

Reginald straightened in his seat. "That was one examination, and it was more than seven years ago. I am not slow."

Ponsy twisted his head to the side and smirked. "You are if you think she has set her eyes on Ben. I believe she was intent on Charlie, in the beginning."

"Charlie?" Reginald stared at his friend with a critical gaze, but then thought about everything he had said. "Wait. You knew how I felt about her? And what precisely led you to your conclusion? I have only tonight realized my feelings. How could you have known before I did?"

Ponsonby grinned widely. "After watching the two of you at the theater, it did not take much of an imagination to discover the truth."

The heat drained from Reginald's face. "You saw us at the theater?" He cleared his throat. To the average onlooker, it must have looked very intimate. Indeed, even with the ridiculousness of their whispered conversation, it had felt intimate. He swallowed hard. "But then I was simply teaching her."

Ponsonby laughed again. "You and she may be the only ones who believe that. You were flirting every bit as much as you were teaching."

Reginald allowed a smile to emerge. "I really was a very good teacher."

"Perhaps it was more that you had a willing student."

Reginald leaned forward all humor gone from his face. "Do you think so? Do you think she is amiable towards me… towards the idea of us?"

Ponsy put a finger to his lips, as if in thought. "I should say she was at the theater, but after tonight—" he shrugged.

Reginald sagged back into the chair. Running his hand through his hair. Gads, how could one man make such a mess of his life in such a short amount of time?

"Then I ask you again, Ponsy. What am I to do?"

Ponsy steepled his fingers. "Perhaps you need to stop being her teacher and try to be her suitor. Show her you are what she needs, not Charlie or Ben."

Stop being the teacher. The man had a point. The plan had all the perks of teaching with the added perk of winning the lady's hand. Perhaps Ponsonby was wiser than Reginald had given him credit.

Chapter Nineteen

Sarah stared out the window at the gray morning sky. She had yet to dress for the day or even to break her fast. Indeed, she should already be on her way to Mariah's for morning calls. But she couldn't do it today.

She dropped her head against the window and sighed. Unfortunately, going to Mariah's meant the risk of seeing Reginald. And after last evening's kiss—after last evening's life-altering kiss—Sarah did not know if she could ever look Reginald in the eye again.

The evening was both the best and worst of her entire life. She had always held a special place in her heart for Reginald. It was a hidden place. One she did not speak about, even to Mariah...especially to Mariah. She would not understand. And she would certainly not wish to share Reginald. As much as Mariah talked of them being like sisters, Sarah did not think Mariah wished them to be actual sisters. Especially if that meant Sarah would take a bit of Reginald's time from Mariah.

But never, in all her dreams, had she imagined what had happened last evening. She closed her eyes, feeling the warmth of his lips on hers. The tingling of her skin where he caressed her arms. It was more than a dream come true.

She brushed her fingertips across her lips. But had her dreams really come true? In her dreams, Reginald kissed her because he loved her. Because she meant something to him. Not because he was pushing to see how much he could fluster her under the guise of teaching her how to flirt. Indeed, she did not believe he could have meant anything by the kiss. It was just another joke to him.

And while she could not imagine the kiss meant anything to Reginald, it had meant everything to her. But what was she to do now? How was she to look at him, knowing that he had released something inside her that she did not know how to cage again? How was she to hide her desire for him so he was not aware of it? How was she to pretend it had never happened?

One thing was for certain. She no longer wished to flirt with Mr. Bancroft. Indeed, Sarah was resigned to the idea that she might never marry at all.

She put a hand to her temple as her head began to throb again. Perhaps it would be best if she returned to bed.

Sarah laid down, pulling the counterpane up to her chin, and stared up at the ceiling. Flashes of the evening jumped in and out of her thoughts. Reginald leaning in closer. Her leaning in to meet him. The soft brush of his lips. The pressure as he deepened it. The feel of his hair against her fingers. She moaned.

Saints above. She had kissed him as much as he had kissed her. And therein was the problem. She had behaved most improperly. And now he knew what kind of woman she was— wanton and undisciplined.

She rolled to her side and closed her eyes hoping to block the images, but it only made them more vivid against the darkness of her closed lids. How was she to get any sleep when all she could think of was that kiss? Of Reginald? Of what she had done?

She tightly pinched her eyes closed, forcing herself to think of anything but last evening. In her mind, she put every one of her bonnets to pieces, rebuilding them into a dozen different designs. The ruse worked until she pictured herself trying the new bonnets on. Every time she did Reginald appeared and kissed her soundly, then laughed at the hurt on her face.

Sarah shooed him away, but it did not keep the hollow feeling in her stomach at bay. Finally, she gave up on her bonnets and simply pinched her eyes shut and pushed every thought from her mind. Focusing only on the blank, black void behind her lids. When an image tried to creep in, she pushed it out. It was exhausting, but it was just what she needed to finally fall back to sleep.

Sarah and her parents stepped into the large saloon. Rows of chairs were set up facing a pianoforte and a harp at the front. Lord Ponsonby's home was quite stunning. While he might only be a baron, he was obviously a very wealthy one.

"Where shall we sit?" Her mother glanced around the room.

Sarah put a hand to her head. The thudding behind her eyes had not completely gone away, but she had not been able to deny her mother the chance of coming to the musicale. Hopefully the evening would be uneventful, and Sarah could relax to the music.

"It does not matter. We should sit in the middle of the row. As none of us will be performing, we need not worry about being on an end." Sarah enjoyed attending musicales, even if she never performed. Indeed, perhaps that was why she liked them. She never had to worry about a performance.

While she played the pianoforte, she did not play it with enough proficiency to justify performing publicly. And her singing voice... even her mother would not persuade her it was adequate. *God did not give all ladies the ability to sing.* And Sarah was at peace with that. It enabled her to attend musicales and enjoy what others had to share.

She motioned to a group of chairs in the middle of a row towards the back. While she led her mother to believe she was doing it for those who were to perform, that was not entirely true. Sarah knew Mariah was to perform, which meant she and Reginald would sit on the aisle. Sitting in the middle ensured Sarah would not have to worry about sitting too close to him.

She moved into the row and took her seat, glancing around and trying to push the guilt away. Not sitting close to Reginald also meant she would not be sitting close to Mariah. Could she still offer the support Mariah needed from the center of the row? While Mariah liked people to believe she was confident, Sarah knew that this type of display was intimidating to her when they were in the country. She could not imagine the nerves Mariah was feeling tonight.

But it was not as if Mariah was completely alone. She would have Reginald by her side. Which was something Sarah did *not* need.

"Miss Brown." Sarah heard her name called through the crowd. She looked around, trying to discern where it had come from. Her mother nudged her arm and dipped her head forward, motioning to Mariah who stood waving her arms several rows in front of them. "We have already saved you seats with us."

"Oh, look how kind." Mariah's father stood and helped her mother to her feet.

Sarah released a heavy breath. "But we are already settled here, Papa." She could hear the slight pout in her voice. Something she had obviously learned from Mariah.

Her mother looked down with a determined expression. "But it would be improper for us not to join them when they have singled us out. Lord Stoke and Lady Mariah hold a high place in society. We would do well to not offend them."

Sarah clenched her fists at her side. It seemed Mariah was not as skilled a teacher as her brother. Sarah had not learned to pout as well as her friend.

She closed her eyes and shook her head. "Very well." She pushed herself to her feet and trudged along behind her parents. Perhaps she could sit on the opposite side, making them a barrier between her and Reginald. That way there would be no chance that Reginald could lean over and flirt with her.

But it was for naught. Mariah patted the chair next to her. "I saved this seat especially for you."

"Do you not wish for Reginald to sit there? I can sit on the other side of my parents to give him room."

Mariah guffawed. "Regi may sit on your other side. I should far prefer to have you next to me."

Sarah's jaw clenched even as she smiled and settled in next to Mariah. Thankfully, Reginald was not within sight. Perhaps if Sarah were living a righteous life, he would not join them at all. Her mind flashed to the kiss, and she knew there was no chance of that.

"Sarah, I am so glad you are here. After you left last night, I feared you might not feel well enough to attend tonight." Mariah wrapped her hands around Sarah's arms and squeezed. "But I so wanted you to hear me perform."

There were times when Sarah tired of being Mariah's confidant and disciple. It was a taxing role to play. But then Sarah looked down the row at her mother and father and her unkind feelings subsided. Who else did Mariah have? While Reginald was a kind and attentive guardian, it was not the same as having a mother or a sister.

Sarah smiled, partially turning so she could embrace

Mariah lightly. "I was determined I would not miss your performance. I do so enjoy listening to you play the harp."

"As do I."

Sarah's heart jumped into her throat, and she found it difficult to swallow.

Reginald came to a stop just behind Mariah. He looked at Sarah, a soft smile barely turning the corners of his lips. Could he sense her feelings? Was he mocking her? She looked in his eyes and relaxed, seeing nothing mean-spirited. Indeed, she thought she saw concern but also perhaps joy. Was he happy to see her?

"Miss Brown, I hope you are feeling better. I was disheartened to learn of your early departure last evening."

Sarah smiled tentatively, watching him for any signs that he was toying with her. "I am feeling much better. Thank you, my lord."

Lady Ponsonby stood at the front of the room and clapped her hands. The room quieted and all eyes turned to her. "Everyone please find a seat."

Sarah took the opportunity to glance at Reginald from the corner of her eye. He did not look at Lady Ponsonby, as everyone else did, but rather stared at her with that same soft smile on his lips.

A flutter flared up in her stomach. Could it be last night had meant something to him also? Had she been wrong to think he kissed other ladies the way he kissed her? She looked down at her hands in her lap, scolding herself for latching on to even the smallest hint that he might care for her. It was a smile, that was all. And she would do well to remember it. Else, in the end, it would surely only cause her pain.

166

Chapter Twenty

"We would like to begin our evening's program shortly." Lady Ponsonby beamed out at the crowd. Her son, Lord Ponsonby, stood at her side, far less beaming. Indeed, he looked rather annoyed by the whole situation. "If everyone could please find a seat."

His mother turned to take her seat but elbowed him in the side before she left. A scowl replaced his annoyance as he followed behind her.

Reginald chuckled. "This evening is very near Purgatory for poor Ponsy."

Mr. Bancroft and his sister waved and hurried over to them. "Lady Mariah. Miss Brown. I am so glad to see you here." Miss Bancroft looked eagerly at them.

"You see, there are enough chairs for us to sit with them. You were worried about nothing." Mr. Bancroft rolled his eyes behind his sister's back.

Reginald grinned. "Sisters. I completely understand."

Sarah had not heard the words as much as read them on his lips.

Mariah and Miss Bancroft compared their musical numbers in low tones.

"Normally, Charlie would not allow me to attend this type of event until I am out, but as Lord Ponsonby is the host, he felt he could make an exception this one time." Miss Bancroft turned her eyes on Sarah. "Miss Brown, are you to perform?"

Both Reginald and Mr. Bancroft turned their attention to Sarah. It unnerved her to see all their eyes focused on her. She shook her head. "No. I am not musically inclined."

Mr. Bancroft put a hand on Sarah's arm and she noticed Reginald bristle. "Surely you are just being modest. I wish you would change your mind and perform."

Sarah shook her head, looking down at his hand. "Uh, no…" She stuttered.

He removed his hand from her arm and Sarah stared at the spot it had been. There was no heat or tingles dancing up her arm. While she did not seek his affections any longer, she was confused by the lack of reaction when he touched her. She had felt nothing when his hand had touched her arm, and yet, when Reginald did it, she could not think straight nor keep herself upright. What was she doing wrong that Reginald was not affected by her touch? She would have asked him about it if she was not so worried he would give her another demonstration. She didn't know if her vulnerable heart could take another lesson.

Sarah pulled her gaze away and looked at Reginald. Could it have anything to do with her feelings for him? That thought did nothing to lift her spirits. If she had to marry for convenience, was the Mr. Bancroft reaction what she had to look forward to? How would she stand it knowing what a man's touch could do to her, only to have it not?

"She is not being modest, I assure you. She really is rather dreadful." Mariah tilted her head to the side with a slow nod and a slight pout on her lips. "It would be embarrassing."

"Mariah," Reginald looked angrily at his sister. "How could you say such a thing about our friend?"

Mariah looked affronted. She turned and looked at Sarah.

"I was not being unkind, was I, Sarah? Did you not say the same thing?"

Sarah smiled. Although what Mariah said was true, hearing it spoken aloud in front of other people stung. But she was not about to admit as much to anyone standing there. "Indeed, you are not mistaken."

Reginald's head shook. "Regardless, Mar. You should not have spoken it aloud." He looked up at Sarah. "Please accept my apology on my sister's behalf."

Mariah let out a little huff. "You need not apologize for me, Regi. I am perfectly capable of doing it on my own."

"And yet, you have not." His face looked stern, not a look Sarah often saw on Reginald. He was one of the few people she knew whose face stayed in a perpetual grin. It was not of the large toothy variety, but it was a smile nonetheless, and it was one of the things she loved about him. She clenched a fist. She really must stop thinking of him like that.

"Sarah, I apologize if I was rude. That was not my intention. I simply knew you did not wish to perform and was trying to help them see why it was out of the question." She looked at Reginald and gave a quick smirk. "You, see? I am perfectly capable." Without giving him or Sarah another look, Mariah sat down in the chair on the aisle and looked toward the front.

Reginald looked to Mr. Bancroft and mouthed, *sisters*. His head shook and his eyes rolled theatrically.

Mr. Bancroft grinned.

"If you do not play, what do you do?" Miss Bancroft eyed Sarah critically.

"Madi!" Mr. Bancroft now looked at his sister with wide eyes. "Music is not the only pastime a lady may enjoy. I am certain Miss Brown has plenty of other interests." He smiled down at Sarah, "Please excuse my sister. It seems tonight is the night for sisters to speak without thinking through their words." He glared at Miss Bancroft. "Besides, she is still new to society and does not always know when she is being impertinent."

Miss Bancroft's brow furrowed, and her cheeks turned a rosy shade of pink. Her brother had embarrassed her by pointing out her folly.

Sarah shook her head. Reaching out, she placed a hand on the girl's arm. "It is no matter. I took no offense." She smiled when she felt Miss Bancroft relax. "You are not the first to ask the question."

Mr. Bancroft grinned sheepishly. "At the risk of sounding like my sister, what types of activities do interest you?" His tone held a note of curiosity, but she could detect no partiality. Perhaps friendship could develop between them, but she could no longer imagine more. She smiled up at him, hoping she did not look as if she were flirting.

Her gaze flitted over to Reginald. His lips no longer held the soft smile and his brow furrowed as he looked at his friend. Was he angry at Miss Bancroft and, by association, her brother? Or had something else raised his ire?

She cleared her throat. "I quite enjoy charades and puzzles."

"Puzzles?" Mr. Bancroft folded his arms across his chest, his gaze downturned. "You mean dissected maps to teach children geography?"

Sarah grinned. "It started with those. But I like all kinds of puzzles. Rebuses, charades, and riddles. They are all very enjoyable." She smiled. "When I was a little girl, my uncle made me a puzzle out of wooden blocks. The blocks had to be placed in a certain order for them to form a cube. It took me hours to figure it out. But once I started on it, I could not stop until it was complete."

Mr. Bancroft's brow still furled, but Reginald stared at her, the soft smile back in place. "She is really very good at them. Much better than I. She had to break the charade down into pieces and explain each part before I could see the answer."

He held her gaze the entire time he spoke. He seemed sincere, but was she simply seeing what she wished to see?

"Puzzles? Is that really a hobby?" Miss Bancroft flicked her gaze to her brother, her cheeks pinking once again. "I'm sorry, I did not intend to sound impertinent. I simply have not heard it referred to in such a manner."

"I should think any pursuit one finds enjoyable, would be considered a hobby." Reginald's gaze still did not leave Sarah's face.

"We will begin with our first performer." Lady Ponsonby directed a scowl at Reginald and Mr. Bancroft. "Our first number will be by Miss Winters on the pianoforte." Lady Ponsonby's voice carried over the low murmurs. She motioned to the piano as a young lady made her way up the aisle.

Miss Bancroft, Mr. Bancroft, and Reginald scooted into the row. Sarah sighed. Reginald was next to her parents and Mr. Bancroft and Miss Bancroft sat between her and Reginald. Perhaps she did not need to sit in the center of the row to be safe.

Miss Bancroft leaned forward and motioned to Sarah. "Would you mind terribly if I sat by Lady Mariah? I should hate to step on your foot when it is my turn to perform." She cast a worried look at her brother as if she were afraid she had said something wrong again.

Sarah caught sight of the empty chair on the other side of her father. "It is no problem. I was about to move and sit next to my parents." Sarah stood, but Reginald caught hold of her wrist. Tingles danced their way up her arm and into her chest and stomach. Even her knees seemed less steady. She thought perhaps her reaction to Mr. Bancroft's touch might be preferable.

"Why do you not sit here? I will not be performing and that will allow Bancroft to sit by his sister and offer encouragement. There is no reason for you to move farther in." He held her gaze. The piano gave its first strains, and Sarah slid into the seat between Mr. Bancroft and Reginald. He pulled his hand back, but the heat stayed for several minutes longer.

Sarah glanced down at her arm, pulling her lip between her teeth. There was no doubt. She much preferred Reginald's touch to Mr. Bancroft's.

She looked to the front, trying to focus on the performance, but she could not concentrate on the music. Every time Reginald shifted, she glanced at him from the corner of her eye. Why did her entire body react to Reginald's slightest touch? While she could not elicit even a single spark in him? Sarah shook her head in frustration.

Mariah and Miss Bancroft watched Miss Winters perform, every so often bending their heads together and speaking in whispered tones.

Reginald shifted in his seat, his leg and shoulder brushing against Sarah's. The whole side of her body shivered. She wanted to look over at him, but she did not dare. Was he giving her another lesson? Or was he practicing what he taught? She closed her eyes, trying to focus her mind on the performance. But still her lids cracked open at his every move.

She opened her eyes and looked straight ahead, afraid of what she would see if she looked at him. What if he smirked at her? What if this was just another lesson and he meant nothing by it?

Reginald shifted again, but this time he leaned in close, draping his arm over the back of her chair. "Why did you say you are not proficient on the pianoforte? I have heard you play, and I found the experience quite delightful." His breath warmed her ears and tickled her neck. It was the theater all over again. Except this time was so much more excruciating because she knew what those lips next to her ear were capable of doing to her.

She closed her eyes again. Never had she felt more vexed and excited at the same time. "You must be misremembering, my lord."

"I think you might be surprised just how much I remember about you, Sarah." He sat back in his chair, but he continued to look at her in a way that nearly undid her.

What did that mean? He may have been sitting upright, but his arm was still draped over the back of her chair. While his thumb did not perform its magic on her arm, it did periodically brush against her, making her flinch erratically.

Sarah released a stress-filled breath and her leg brushed against Reginald. More tingles traveled the length of her body. Why had Lady Ponsonby placed the chairs so close together? Sarah felt as though she was nearly sitting on Reginald's lap.

Her face heated as she thought on that for a moment. She brushed jerkily at her skirt and her reticule fell from her lap, landing on the floor with a soft thump.

She leaned over to pick it up, just as Reginald did. His hand rested on hers and he glanced over.

"What are you doing?" Sarah whispered.

He grinned. "Helping a lady in distress."

"I am not in distress. I simply dropped my reticule." She scowled at him, hoping he would release her hand.

"You *look* distressed."

"You are what is distressing me. Please release my hand. You are causing a disturbance." She hissed at him. She did not need to look to know that most of their row was leaning forward to look at them.

He grinned wider. "Very well." He sat up in his chair, folding his arms across his chest with a satisfied smile on his lips.

Sarah snatched her fan and handkerchief that had managed to work their way out of her ridicule and shoved them both back inside. She sat up just in time to hear the applause for Miss Winters.

Gracious, she had not heard a single note and it was all Reginald's fault. She clasped her hands tightly in her lap, her nerves nearly frayed to their breaking point.

A tall man made his way into the row in front of them, settling into the seat in front of her.

"Our next performer is Miss Lavendry." Lady Ponsonby announced.

Sarah watched the young lady make her way up to the front but was not able to see her face. She stood just in front of the piano, and just out of Sarah's view.

Another woman took her place at the instrument and played the first chord.

Miss Lavendry began to sing, and Sarah strained to see her. It was no use. The man in front of her was too tall for her to see anything. She tilted toward Mr. Bancroft but could gain no better view.

Glancing out of the side of her eye at Reginald she wondered if she dared lean toward him? He had a rather devilish look in his eye that she did not quite trust. Must she see the performer to enjoy the performance?

Sarah frowned. She at least wished to put a name to the face. Slowly she leaned over but moved back when the distance between them closed faster than it should have.

She released a frustrated grunt. Putting the strings of her reticule around her wrist, she placed her hands on either side of the chair and lifted herself up slightly so she might see above the gentleman's head in front of her.

But that was no better of an idea. She had barely caught sight of the performer when warmth enveloped her hand. She sat down hard, jerking her head around to stare at Reginald. He looked straight ahead, but his hand completely covered hers. Sarah tried to move her hand, but his fingers intertwined with hers forcing her to keep her hand where it was.

Gah! He was a sneaky one. There was little she could do without making a scene.

Her arm felt hot. Not like she was engulfed in flames, more like she was just sitting so close to the fire that it warmed her all the way through to her bones.

The flutter in her stomach was like nothing she had ever experienced. She could not decide if she was on the verge of expelling her dinner or grabbing his face in her hands and kissing him again. Neither was an acceptable option. Her brain screamed that this should not be happening, but her heart would shush her brain and happily thump along.

With both reluctance and joy the number ended and the applause sounded. Now he would release her hand. While she wanted it to go on all night, she knew it couldn't, so she would have to make sure that her hand remained out of his reach.

Only he didn't let go. He slapped his free hand on his leg keeping his hand firmly over hers. Sarah swallowed. Would not Mr. Bancroft notice? What of her father? She was certain people would notice their intertwined fingers. He was bound to either ruin her or force himself into unwanted matrimony.

Sarah shifted and Reginald loosened his hold. Grudgingly seeing this as her chance, Sarah pulled her hand free clasping it tightly in her lap.

She dared not look at Reginald for fear he would see her true desires in her eyes. Although, would that be so bad? He did not seem to be laughing. Could it be he was using his flirting methods on her? Could he mean it? But as soon as the thought came, she pushed it away.

Reginald had vowed he would not marry. At least not in the foreseeable future. Which meant only one thing...he was simply playing with her.

Chapter Twenty-One

The applause subsided and Sarah shot out of her seat, more than ready for the intermission Lady Ponsonby had requested.

Sarah needed to speak to Reginald. She could spend the rest of her life questioning his motives, but she would never truly know what his intentions were unless she spoke to him. And while that made her knees shake, she knew she did not have a choice.

Reginald stood up beside her. He clasped his hands behind his back, which was a relief. At this point, she could not predict what he might do with them.

He moved his neck from side to side. "Lud, it's stifling in here." He grinned down at her. "I am going to get a breath of air. Would you care to join me, Miss Brown?"

The way he said her name nearly made Sarah shiver from head to toe. She had heard him say her name many times, but this was the first time his tone of voice matched the mischievous look in his eyes.

Sarah shrugged. "Perhaps in a moment. I told my parents I would fetch them some refreshments." She had not, but he need not know it was a lie. Now that the time was there, she felt uncertain about their discussion. She pulled her bottom lip between her teeth before letting it slide back out.

Reginald watched her, his lips moving slowly but no sound came out.

Gracious. She just needed to stiffen her back and speak to him. "There is something I wish to discuss with you, my lord. Perhaps after I am done with my mother, we might have a word?"

"I am looking forward to it." Reginald waggled his brows at her. "You know where to find me."

Sarah placed a hand on her nervous stomach as she moved to the far side of the room, picking up three glasses of lemonade and one plate. She placed several pieces of cake on the plate and turned to take them to her parents. Her hands shook and the glasses clattered together.

She did not *want* to speak to Reginald. Nothing good could come from it. But it had to be done. She had to put a stop to his demonstrations before they both found themselves in an unhappy situation—either her ruination or him unhappily married. And while she wanted nothing more than to be married to Reginald, she knew she could never be happy in marriage knowing he was not.

She delivered the refreshments to her parents and made her way slowly through the crowd of people to the terrace doors.

Deep male voices could be heard drifting through the door, but she could not hear what was being said.

Sarah took two steps outside and paused when she heard her name. A large topiary stood on either side of the doorway keeping her hidden. But it also hid those who were speaking.

"I wonder at your intentions with Miss Brown." The man's voice sounded familiar, but Sarah could not place from where.

"I do not see as it is any of your business, but as I suspect it will be public knowledge soon enough. I do not mind confiding in you that I am planning to ask for her hand."

Sarah's heart jumped into her throat. She recognized the second voice. Indeed, that voice had kept her up several nights that very week.

It was Reginald and he had just said he planned to ask her to marry him.

Sarah grinned so widely her cheeks hurt. Perhaps she would not need to speak with him after all. Perhaps it was him that would do the talking. She took a step forward but pulled back when the second man's voice sounded again.

"Are you daft, man?" The man gave a sort of chuckle. "You cannot marry the chit."

"And why not, pray tell?" While Sarah could not see it, she could picture Reginald folding his arms across his chest in defiance. It brought a smile to her face.

"Because she will not suit. Surely you see that? You are an earl. There are certain expectations of you, and she does not fit them."

Sarah swallowed, wanting to leave so she need not hear anymore. But her feet would not take her backwards.

"I do not see why she will not suit, Rags. She is a gentleman's daughter. Her father is a knight."

Sarah's chest tightened at the defiant tone of Reginald's voice.

"A gentleman's daughter? Hardly." Lord Ragsdale exhaled a deep breath. Sarah should have known it was him from the words he spoke. "Yes, technically she is a gentleman's daughter. But it is not the same as someone like Miss Bancroft. She has been trained from her youth on the protocols of society."

From behind the tree Sarah could hear Reginald's grunted breaths. "As has Sarah."

Lord Ragsdale sighed loudly. "But does she know precedence? Your wife will need to know such things. You will be expected to host parties and balls and other social events. Are you telling me Miss Brown knows whether to seat me or Montcort first?"

Reginald cleared his throat. "I am certain she realizes that Montcort is a viscount, and you are a marquess. The rest she will figure out. Besides, I can teach her. She is very intelligent, and she will learn."

Sarah slowly moved forward, peeking around the topiary. Just as she had imagined, Reginald stood stiff backed with his arms crossed.

Lord Ragsdale had a smug look. It was the same look she always saw on his face.

"It will be too much," Lord Ragsdale shook his head. "I know you think you love her, Reg, but you will grow to resent her if you marry her." Lord Ragsdale chuckled. "Although, she would make a fine mistress..."

Sarah twisted the strings on her reticule, willing the lemonade in her roiling stomach to stay down. The strings cut into her skin and disrupted the circulation to her hand. She could not hear anymore. Quietly, she backed away until she was in the saloon. Then she turned and hurried away as quickly as she could from the terrace doors.

She hurried to the opposite side of the room. Stepping out into the corridor, she looked both directions before hurrying down the longest, darkest one. When she was sure no one was around, she ducked into a doorway and pressed herself against the wall.

Her chest and throat ached, begging for her emotions to be released.

Reginald had said he loved her. How many times had she dreamed that would happen?

She shook her head, her brows creasing. No, that wasn't true. Reginald had never said he loved her. Lord Ragsdale had stated it. While Reginald had not disputed the accusation, neither had he voiced any agreement.

The pain in her throat climbed and intensified with each

breath...each swallow. While the words Lord Ragsdale had said hurt, what hurt most was that he was right.

In Stoke-on-Trent, the difference in their stations was not so noticeable. But since arriving in London, she had noticed how great their differences were. She'd felt out of place but had been willing to overlook it for the chance to be with Reginald.

Hearing Lord Ragsdale say it out loud, however, made it real. It didn't matter how much she loved Reginald. Or even if he loved her in return. She could never make him a proper wife.

Chapter Twenty-Two

"A mistress? How can you even make a joke about such a thing?" Reginald turned his back on Ragsdale, his jaw set firmly. "I don't care what you say. I will marry her if that is what I wish to do."

Ragsdale released a heavy sigh. "If you really love her, Reg, you can't do that to her. You will make a mockery of her. She is ill-prepared and will make a fool of herself and you."

Reginald closed his eyes. He wanted to believe Rags was only saying these things so that Reginald would not marry, and their little band of bachelors would not change. But deep down, he knew that Ragsdale was correct. At least partially.

He waved a dismissive hand at his friend and stepped inside the saloon. Where was Sarah? Had she fetched her parents' refreshments yet?

His mind churned. While Sarah was the daughter of a gentleman, she had not been trained to be the wife of an earl. Her upbringing had been sheltered. Her family did not associate with those of the nobility. Their dinner guests were more often successful shopkeepers and the local clergy than members of the aristocracy. Indeed, Reginald was likely the only member of the peerage Sarah had ever met before coming to London. He could not recall her ever even meeting his friends when they came to visit.

She had been trained to be the wife of a gentleman, although not one of very high standing. She knew how to behave in higher society, but Rags was right that she would not know who to seat where at any formal event.

He closed his eyes against the cold wind blowing in off the garden. But would it be as bad as Rags suggested? Would she really be ridiculed? Society could be harsh, he knew that. But would they ostracize her? Could he knowingly make her the joke of the Season?

A dull ache pounded just behind his right eye. What was he to do? Last evening, he had kissed her quite thoroughly. And then to make matters worse, he had flirted unrepentantly with her the entire first half of the musicale. He had not been discreet in the least, because he had not thought he needed to be. He had not cared who saw what he did. Their engagement was likely only days away. Or that is what he had thought.

Gads, he really was just like Muckrake! Although in his defense, he had flirted with her after deciding he wished to marry her. Muckrake could have no such intentions each time he ruined a lady.

Ruined a lady. Lud, was it that bad?

Reginald shook his head. He was not like Muckrake because, unlike Muckrake, Reginald intended to complete what he had started with Sarah. Indeed, the thought of dismissing her, as Ragsdale suggested, left him feeling empty and cold.

Perhaps he could move on and marry someone else if he did not love Sarah. But the more he thought about it, the more he knew he did love her. And knowing that, he could not go back to the way things were, nor could he move forward without her.

But what about Sarah? What were her feelings for him? When he kissed her, she seemed not only to want it but to enjoy it. She might have simply been caught up in the moment. Indeed, she had not said much before she fled from him.

His brow creased. Perhaps that was his answer. If she felt the same for him as he did for her, would she not have stayed? Would she have felt shame for what they did?

Reginald felt no shame. Although, his guilt was growing by the second.

He released a heavy sigh. He would not know unless he asked her.

What he did know was that he loved her, and his life was the better for it. The thought of spending hours upon hours at his club did not hold the same appeal as it once had. In truth, nothing held the same appeal if Sarah was not there to share it with him.

To the devil with it!

He would marry her if she would have him, and he did not care what Ragsdale thought. Ponsonby had not found the notion so reprehensible. Although, he was only a baron. He did not have the same expectations as some of the rest of them did.

His eyes scanned over the crowd. His lips turned upward as his gaze stopped on her. She was speaking with her parents, taking small sips from the drink in her hand.

He shook his head. How had he ignored her for so long? How had he not seen what was right in front of him his whole life?

Whatever the reason, he did not intend for it to continue any longer.

He approached the row where Sarah and her parents sat conversing and stood looking down at them, a smile on his face. "Are you enjoying the musicale, Sir Winston, Lady Brown?"

Lady Brown nodded her head enthusiastically. "I have never seen so many talented people in one room." She glanced over at Sarah. "Perhaps you should try again at the pianoforte. With more practice, you might be able to perform as well as some of these young ladies." Even Reginald could hear the doubt in Lady Brown's voice.

Sarah's whole being drooped. What had happened to her? While her mother's comment was not the most encouraging, she had not said anything so very lowering. Nothing that should cause the downcast look on Sarah's face. But regardless of the reason, seeing Sarah's distress caused an ache in Reginald's chest that he could not rub away.

"I see no need for it," Reginald defended. "Sarah need not try and be like the other ladies. She has her own strengths and talents that make her just as desirable."

Lady Brown's brows rose slowly to her hairline. She looked from Reginald to Sarah.

Sarah's brow creased as she looked up at Reginald, her expression not one of appreciation. Indeed, if anything, she looked even more disheartened than before.

She stood up abruptly, her head shaking. "My lord, might I have a word with you in private?"

Reginald grinned at the slight fire he saw in her eyes. She was not altogether happy with what he had said. Perhaps he had been impertinent and stated his opinion too openly, but he could not regret it.

Although, her knit brows may have more to do with who was listening than what he had said. After all, who could be angry at him for saying such kind things? Especially if he meant them.

He dipped his head and motioned toward the aisle. "Of course, Miss Brown."

They stepped into the corridor "Perhaps we could find a quiet room where we may speak in private."

She glanced over at him her eyes narrowed. "I have seen what happens with you in quiet rooms," she hissed.

Reginald grinned. Happy that the memory was still as

fresh for her as it was for him. But it fell away when he noticed her trembling fingers. "What if I were to promise not to kiss you until we have both had our say."

Her eyes widened and her cheeks turned a shade of puce. She turned and walked down another corridor.

"Where are we going?" He pulled her to a stop.

Sarah shook her head. "I have no idea. I just wish to put some distance between us and the saloon. It would not do to have someone come out and see us alone."

Reginald grinned. "No, you are right. It is far better if someone catches us in a darkened corridor." He winked at her.

She stopped walking and hit him on the arm with her fan. "What is that all about? I need no more of your lessons on flirting. You have done a very thorough job."

"What if I am no longer instructing you?" He took a few steps closer to her.

She took the same steps back, pasting herself against the wall. "No. Please don't say it."

Reginald shrugged. "Do not say that I am flirting with you? Could you not see that for yourself?" He tilted his head, giving her a side look. "You just told me you needed no more lessons."

Sarah closed her eyes. "I know you have been flirting with me. But you need to stop."

"No, I need you," Reginald ran both his hands lightly down her arms.

Her whole body shivered under his touch. "No, you don't." Her voice came out as a whisper.

Reginald put his finger on her lips to stop her from interrupting him until he had said what he needed to say. His stomach gave an excited flip. It felt as if his whole life was teetering on this one conversation. "I know you wished to speak to me, but there is something I wish to tell you also. And I think it best if I go first."

She looked down at the floor.

"For years you have been our neighbor. I thought I knew you...or at least what I needed to know about you. But since coming to London, I have realized I didn't really know you at all."

Her brow creased. She opened her mouth, but then closed it when he raised his finger. Instead, she bit her bottom lip.

Lud, if she kept doing that, he would not be responsible for what happened next. His pulse hammered rapidly in his neck, filling his ears with the muffled sound of waves.

When he did not speak, she took the opportunity. "There is little to know." Her gaze dropped to his neck. She seemed rather fascinated with the knot on his cravat. "I am the daughter of an insignificant knight. There is nothing exceptional about me."

"You and I seem to have very differing opinions on that matter." He took one of her hands in his, intertwining their fingers. "I think you are exceptional, and I wish to show you just how exceptional you truly are."

She shook her head. "You are imagining too much. No one of your acquaintance will see what you think you see."

Reginald opened his mouth, "But—"

She placed her finger over his lips. "Please, do not say any more, my lord. It will be best for both of us if you do not continue."

It felt as though she had plunged a dagger into his heart when she called him "my lord." She used his title as a defense, telling him she did not wish for the intimacies he desired.

He squeezed her hand. "Answer me one question and I will do what you wish, whatever that is."

She leaned back, standing flush against the wall as if trying to put more distance between them. But he held fast to her hand. "Very well, what is your question?"

"Do you love me?" He stared intently at her, hoping he

186

would know the truth even if her words said the opposite of what he wanted.

Her brow knitted and her bottom lip pulled between her teeth. She stared at him for a long while and he could see the indecision in her gaze. Why would she not tell him? Perhaps he had misjudged, and she felt nothing for him. Was she worried she would hurt him? Or was she worried he would damage her reputation when she spoke the truth?

He released her hand and leaned back on his heels, waiting for her answer, but bracing himself also.

She closed her eyes and nodded. "Yes, I do, even though I know it was silly and dim of me to have allowed it."

Reginald's breath pushed from his lungs, and he grinned wider than he believed possible. She loved him! This was the best news he'd ever heard. He leaned forward, placing his hands on both sides of her face and lowering his lips to hers.

She put her hands on his chest and he paused as the warmth radiated though his body. He brushed his lips against hers.

But it was a very short-lived kiss. She pushed him away from her, shaking her head. "No. You can't do this. You said if I answered your question, you would do as I wished."

He leaned forward and dropped his head, resting his forehead against hers. "I thought I was doing what you wished." He brushed his thumb against her jawline.

She pushed him away again. "No. I answered your question. Now you must leave me alone. I stand by what I said before. Nothing good can come of this."

Reginald stepped back, crossing his arms over his chest. "What do you mean? You said you love me. How can you turn me away when you know I feel the same?"

"Don't you see? It will never work. *We* will never work. I was never trained to be the wife of an earl. I do not even know what I do not know. How could I be Mistress of Oakdale when I do not even know how to host a dinner party?"

Reginald guffawed. "Your mother taught you how to properly host a dinner party."

"Perhaps for the curate and the constable. I might even be able to manage to seat the Squire correctly. But I have no notion how to seat all of your friends. And I would imagine, while in London, even more aristocracy would be invited than just your friends." She closed her eyes and dropped her head back against the wall. "I would appear the fool for my attempt, and you would look the fool for choosing me."

Reginald frowned. That was almost exactly what Ragsdale had said. Recognition dawned. Sarah had heard his conversation on the terrace.

He stared at her, ready to refute her. But when she met his gaze, he saw the look of determination and resolution in her eyes. She would not be moved. At least not yet.

Reginald sighed. "I cannot convince you otherwise?"

Sarah lowered her gaze, looking at her clasped hands. "No. You cannot."

"Very well." His words may have said he would do as she wished, but he had no intention of giving up. He would not stand by and watch her marry another. Not when he knew they loved each other. She may not realize how rare their feelings for each other were, but he did. And he could be just as stubborn as Miss Sarah Brown. "I will do as you wish. But may we at least remain friends?"

Sarah eyed him warily. "Friends?"

"Friends," Reginald nodded.

"I suppose," she said although, she didn't look convinced.

Had they not been friends at the theater? And in the parlor? A grin slid across his face. Perhaps Sarah needed to see what a good friend Reginald could be.

Chapter Twenty-Three

Sarah held the invitation in her hand. She looked down at it again, wondering how they had come across it.

"Miss Brown, Lady Mariah is here to see you. I have put her in the blue parlor."

Sarah smiled at Chadwick. "Thank you, Chadwick. I will be along shortly."

"Very good, miss." The butler turned and disappeared into the corridor.

Sarah looked down at the invitation one more time. How had they received an invitation to Lord Carrington's dinner party? She had never met the man, and she could not imagine her parents had either. Unless they had met him on one of their park walks, Sarah did not see how they could have come across him. She had been to many more social events than her parents since coming to London.

Perhaps Reginald or Mariah had something to do with it. Sarah sighed. While she appreciated their help, she was tired of feeling like she was an act of charity for them. Indeed, if Reginald would be in attendance, perhaps it would be better if Sarah declined the invitation and stayed at home.

It had been four days since Reginald had told her he loved

her. Four days since she had told him she loved him in return. And, if anything, the pain had only grown. As much as she told herself it could not happen, her heart did not seem to understand or accept the decision.

With a sigh, she pushed herself off the couch. If she did not go to Mariah soon, her friend would surely come in search of her.

The blue parlor was only a few doors down the corridor. Sarah stood outside watching Mariah from behind. Her friend sat on the couch, looking around the room.

Sarah could not help thinking that Mariah must see everything lacking in the room.

While the house itself was above a store, Sarah had been relatively surprised at its pleasing decor. There was nothing shabby about the wallpaper or paint, and most of the mill-work was of fine craftsmanship. But still, it was nothing to Reginald's townhouse in Berkeley Square.

She released a breath, more loudly than she had anticipated, and Mariah turned around.

A large smile turned Mariah's lips. She stood and walked around the couch, meeting Sarah halfway. "This room is so lovely. I should think I would spend all my time in it if I lived here."

Sarah's nerves settled slightly. "Good morning, Mariah. I am surprised to see you."

Mariah frowned. "Did you not receive my note?"

Sarah shook her head, but then looked down at her hands. A card she had not yet opened lay beneath the invitation from Lord Carrington. She pulled it out and held it up. "Is this it?"

Mariah's shoulders slumped and she looked at Sarah with a bland expression. "Yes. Why have you not looked at it yet?"

Sarah held up the invitation. "I'm sorry, but I opened this invitation first and it had me so befuddled, I forgot there was another."

Mariah pushed her lips out slightly. "And just whose invitation was so captivating it made you forget to even look at mine?"

Sarah handed it over.

Mariah looked down at it. "Oh, Lord Carrington. We received an invitation to this party last week." She frowned. "I wonder why yours only came today. The party is not more than four days away."

Sarah nodded. "And how did he come across our names?" She tilted her head to the side. "Did either you or Lord Stoke happen to make mention of us?"

Mariah's brow creased and her head shook. "No. I have not seen Lord Carrington since he visited Oakdale shortly after my parent's death." She shrugged. "He came to pay his respects, but that was the last time I saw him."

"What about your brother? Do you think he asked that a special invitation be extended to us?"

Mariah eyed her suspiciously. "Why should he do that? I cannot imagine Regi cares one way or another if you are present."

Sarah's smile dropped away, and she looked at her hands. If only Mariah knew how her words could cut, perhaps she would not say such a thing.

Mariah clapped her hands together. "I knew it. You have discarded Mr. Bancroft in favor of Regi, have you not?" Mariah collapsed onto the sofa with a dreamy sigh. "I have seen the way he looks at you. Oh, Sarah. Just imagine. If you should marry him, we would be sisters! Not just dear friends as we are now but actual sisters! It is the best news!"

There was so much enthusiasm, Sarah almost did not put a stop to it. But she knew she must. Mariah needed to know that nothing would come of the harmless—she winced at the word—flirting they had done.

She tilted her head to the side. "Mariah, you must see it could never be."

"I most certainly do not." Mariah sat up stiffly on the

couch, staring at Sarah in unbelief. "Why could it never be?"

Sarah sighed. She had gone over it so many times in her head, she was tired of even thinking about it. Why was it that only Lord Ragsdale could see the problems when everyone else around her felt the problem could be overcome? "Mariah, society would never accept me as your brother's wife."

"Why not? You are the daughter of a gentleman. It is not as if your father is in trade or something so scandalous as that."

Sarah shook her head and closed her eyes. Both Reginald and Mariah made it sound so simple. But it was far from simple. "Mariah, surely you see that our upbringings were very different. You were taught things I never even imagined."

Mariah's brow crinkled. "I cannot believe I learned so much more than you. You had good tutors."

"But tutors did not teach me precedence or the way of the nobility. I would be a mockery among the *ton*. And, in turn, make a mockery out of Reginald. It would only take a single dinner party for them to realize just how much I was lacking."

Mariah batted Sarah's words away. "All you need to do is learn a few names and dates. You have always been very good with numbers. I do not see it should be any trouble at all for you to learn such things."

"That will not matter Mariah. I was born into a different social sphere than you. It is not proper for me to believe I can change that simply because I have fallen in love with a peer. Society will not understand or accept that."

"But you are in love." Mariah lifted her chin. "You care too much about propriety and society."

"And you often care too little. It is easy for you to say it is not important. You are the daughter of an earl. You are already a part of that society. Besides, I hardly think you are the one to give me advice when you rarely behave properly." As soon as the words escaped her lips, Sarah wished them back.

And when she saw Mariah's eyes widen and her mouth open slightly, Sarah knew she had spoken out of turn.

"What do you mean I rarely behave properly?" There was irritation mixed with hurt in Mariah's voice.

Sarah clasped her hands tightly in her lap. What was she to say? It was true, Mariah ofttimes showed little care for propriety. But was it really Sarah's place to correct her? "I meant nothing by it. I misspoke."

Mariah's head shook slowly. Gracious, were those tears in her eyes?

Sarah dipped her head, scrubbing her fingers over her brow. Why had she not thought before she spoke? The outburst was simply another example of how unfit she was to marry someone of Reginald's status.

"You did not misspeak. And you did mean something by it, else you would not have said it." Mariah chewed at the side of her cheek. "And just what did I do that you found so improper?"

Sarah sucked in a slow deep breath. Perhaps it would be best if she just said it. It was not a lie if it happened, but did that mean it would hurt less? As one who had been on the receiving end of Mariah's sometimes less-than-thoughtful help, Sarah knew that the truth was sometimes painful. "You speak to your brother and call him by his nickname, even when others who do not know him or are not so closely tied to him are present."

"That is it? The name by which I call my brother has deemed me improper in your eyes?"

Sarah looked at her hands, unable to look Mariah in the eye. "It is not only that. You completely disregard proper introductions. I am certain your mother taught you how it was to be done, but you do not abide by it. You speak of things publicly that should be spoken only in private. And you oft neglect to send your regrets to invitations you receive." Sarah bit her lip. She need not mention any of the other examples.

Mariah wiped a quick hand across her eyes and lifted her chin. "This has been quite an enlightening discussion. I had no idea you found me so lacking."

She pushed herself to her feet, clutching at her reticule so tightly she left wrinkles in the fabric. "I shall be on my way. I apparently have many things I need to study up on if I am to attend Lord Carrington's dinner party on Friday."

Sarah stood and reached out a hand but pulled it back when Mariah shrugged away. "Mariah, please. I did not mean to hurt you."

Mariah gave her a mocking smile. "Did you not? For some reason, I feel as though your set down has been coming for quite some time." She turned on her heel and headed for the door, stopping just before the corridor. She turned back and stared at Sarah. "In light of my new desire to behave properly, I should prefer if you call me Lady Mariah from now on."

Sarah's mouth dropped open. Never, in all her life, had she referred to her friend in such proper terms in private. Although, from the look on Mariah's face, Sarah was not certain she could use the term "friend" anymore.

"Please don't go... Lady Mariah." Sarah knew she was begging, but she did not care. If it took begging to get Mariah to accept her apology, she would do it. Mariah was her best friend. Her only friend in London. And while there were times when Mariah was not as kind as perhaps she should be, she never meant it to be hurtful.

Mariah either did not hear or more likely ignored Sarah's plea. She rounded the door frame into the corridor without so much as a look back.

Sarah sank onto the couch and dropped her head into her hands. What had she done? And how did she move forward? It seemed in the course of a few short days, she had succeeded in losing her best friend and the man she loved. Why, in the name of all that was holy, did anyone wish to come to London?

Chapter Twenty-Four

Reginald set his pen to the side and sat back in his chair, rubbing at his eyes. The ledgers were balanced for the month and all the expenses had been paid. Perhaps he would go to the club and see who was about.

He grunted. And sat back in his seat. The thought held little appeal.

A knock sounded at his door but before he could answer, it swung open and Mariah stormed in. The look on her face made his stomach sink. This was not to be a friendly sort of conversation, if her scowl was any indication.

She put her hands on her hips and stared at him. "Did you make Miss Brown an offer of marriage?"

Miss Brown? Since when did Mariah refer to Sarah as Miss Brown? Mariah and Sarah had used Christian names for as long as they could speak. His stomach sank a little more. What had happened?

"A good afternoon to you as well, Mariah." Perhaps avoiding the question for a moment would help her to calm down before she received the answer that she likely did not want.

"You did not answer my question, Regi. Did you make an offer of marriage to Miss Brown?" Her shoulders rose and fell with deep angry huffs.

Reginald shook his head, feeling as though he had entered a story at the midpoint, rather than from the beginning. He had no context or point of reference in which to know how to answer the question. "And why do you wish to know?"

"I am your sister. I believe I am entitled to know if you have asked Miss Brown to marry you. If you have, it will affect me as much as it does you."

Reginald shook his head. "I quite doubt that." He squinted, trying to discern where this conversation would end. "No. I did not ask her to marry me."

Her shoulders relaxed and she released a deep breath. "I am glad to hear it. If you have not made it official, then you need not proceed with it." She turned on her heel as if the conversation was over.

Reginald shot out of his seat and leaned over his desk. "Wait a moment, Mariah. We are not done here."

"But we are." She tossed over her shoulder.

"Mariah Eloise Margaret Thornbeck, turn around and come back in this room immediately." Reginald did not often pull out his father voice, but Mariah left him little choice. Did she think she could march into his study, demand answers of him, and then leave without so much as an explanation? She was much mistaken if that was her belief.

Mariah stopped at the doorway, and her shoulders slouched. She turned slowly and made her way back to him. "Mama and Papa were the only ones to ever use my full name." She scowled up at him. "And you are neither Mama nor Papa."

"And I have never pretended to be. If you had responded when I first asked you to stay, I should not have had to use that tone."

Mariah slid into the chair in front of his desk, putting her elbow on the arm and dropping her chin into her hand. "What else did you wish to discuss, Regi?"

Reginald sat back in his seat, but leaned forward on his desk, his fingers intertwined. "I wish to know what is going on. You march into my study and ask if I have asked Sarah to marry me?" He held up a finger. "Excuse me, you asked me if I have asked Miss Brown to marry me. When did you start referring to Sarah as Miss Brown?"

"When Miss Brown decided to give me a lecture on all my improprieties. If she sees me so improper, I do not intend to continue to be so improper as to use our Christian names."

Reginald shook his head, her explanation not making complete sense. "When did Sarah give you a lecture on propriety?"

Mariah bit down on the side of her cheek. "I just came from her house, in *Cheapside*. While I was there, she informed me of the many times she has witnessed me behaving improperly."

Reginald frowned. "You were simply visiting, and she began to criticize you for your past improprieties?" That did not sound like something Sarah would do. Indeed, she held her tongue with Mariah far more often than he did.

Mariah looked down at her hands. "In a sense."

Reginald leaned back in his chair and folded his arms across his chest. "Perhaps it would be best if you started at the beginning so I might get an idea of what this *sense* really was."

Mariah told Reginald about her trip to see Sarah. She told her about the invitation to Lord Carrington's party and Sarah's question as to whether Reginald had used his influence to secure the invitation. And then she recalled her excitement over learning that Sarah was in love with Reginald.

Reginald unfolded his arms and placed his elbows on the arms of the chair, his fingers clasped together and his index fingers steepled in front of his lips. Sarah had admitted to Mariah that she loved him? That was something, was it not? It was more than he expected from her, considering their last conversation.

"She told you she loves me?"

Mariah scowled at him. "That is all the questions you have?"

He slowly shook his head. He had many questions. Indeed, more seemed to spring into his mind before any previous questions had even been answered.

"Well, did she actually tell you she loves me?"

Mariah rolled her eyes. "I don't recall if she actually said the words, but she did not dispute it."

Reginald frowned. Had she not said it because she did not wish Mariah to know? Or had she changed her mind since the night of the musicale? He raised a brow at his sister and motioned her to continue. "How did this turn into a lecture?"

Mariah huffed and looked back at her fingers. "I told her I was excited for you to marry her because when you married, we would become sisters. But then she told me it would never work. That you could never be married. And, therefore, we would never be sisters." Mariah looked utterly annoyed by the conversation.

Reginald swallowed hard. She had not changed her stance on that then. That was rather disappointing.

"She told me it would not be proper. And when I told her she need not worry about that, she told me she would not take advice from someone who regularly acted in an improper manner." Mariah's voice hitched up an octave, as she did a poor imitation of Sarah.

"And that is why you asked if I had asked her to marry me?"

Mariah nodded. "I am relieved to know you have not actually asked her."

"That is not to say I have given up hope of marrying her. Indeed, I can think of myself married to none other."

Mariah's eyes widened, and her lips flattened into a thin

white line. "I will not give you my blessing. I do not care if you love her or if she loves you, I do not wish for her to be my sister."

Reginald closed his eyes, rubbing his fingers at the wrinkle between them. Why could all the ladies in his life never be of one accord? Although, it seemed right now none of the ladies were even in negotiations with him. "While that is regretful, Mariah, it will not change my mind. I do love her, and I believe once you choose to overlook her words, you will see it is good for all of us."

"And why should I overlook her unkind words?"

"Because she overlooks all of yours. You have spoken far more unkind words to her than she has ever spoken to you." He ran a hand through his hair. "Indeed, Mariah, if Sarah stopped speaking to you after every unkind thing you said to her, I daresay you wouldn't have made it past a week of friendship."

Mariah's mouth dropped open and tears pooled in the bottom of her eyes. Lud, he had not meant to make her cry. But regardless she needed to hear the truth. Especially if he hoped to ever marry Sarah. It would not do for his wife and his sister to be at odds.

REGINALD CHECKED himself in the mirror one last time, pulling down on his pale green waistcoat. Thanks to Mariah and her explanation the other day, Reginald knew almost for certain that Sarah would attend Lord Carrington's dinner party.

While he had not asked for Sarah to be invited, he was certainly glad the invitation had been extended. It had been days since he had seen her, as she and Mariah had not yet made amends. Her absence had been felt keenly, both by

Reginald and by Mariah. Although Mariah was not likely to admit it.

Reginald ran a hand through his hair, just as Jones stepped out of the dressing room. He let out a sigh. "My lord, I just finished with your hair. If you do not stop running your fingers through it, it shall never lay flat."

Reginald scrunched up his nose. "My apologies, Jones. I did not mean it. I am simply distracted."

His valet raised an eyebrow but then quickly schooled his features. "You are distracted? I have never seen you fidget so."

"I have never been so uncertain about meeting a lady at a ball." He ran another hand through his hair, and Jones released another sigh. Reginald dropped his hand to his side, shaking out his fingers to keep them from his hair. "I am concerned she will not be as eager to see me as I am to see her."

Jones shook his head. "I cannot imagine any woman would not be eager to be with you, my lord."

Reginald raised an eyebrow at his reflection in the mirror. He knew it was what Jones must say to him, but still, the words were surprisingly calming.

"Do you wish for me to attempt your hair again, my lord?"

Reginald shook his head. "Perhaps if I did not run my hand through my hair again, it would be advisable. But as I cannot imagine I will not, I do not see the point."

Jones's lips quivered slightly. "Very good, sir. Have a pleasant evening." He gathered the last few things off the bed and moved into the dressing room, closing the door behind him.

Reginald sucked in a deep breath. He felt as though this was either the beginning or the end of the rest of his life. If things did not change with Sarah tonight, it certainly did not mean the end, did it?

He gave his hands one last shake, then turned and headed toward the door.

Mariah was already standing in the entryway, her wrap draped over her shoulders and arms. She had a lovely string of pearls braided into her hair. "You look very handsome tonight, Mariah."

She dipped into a curtsy. "Thank you, my lord."

Reginald raised a brow. "My lord? Is that not going a bit far, Mariah?"

She smirked. "I am simply practicing proper behavior."

Reginald simply nodded. Ah, she was not yet over her disagreement with Sarah. He only hoped it did not affect their evening. He had plans for the evening and he could not be managing their disagreement at the same time. He led her out the door and handed her up into the carriage. As he sat on the bench, he could not help but lament the fact that they were not to pick up Sarah on the way.

He sighed. But at least she would be meeting them there. Or he hoped she was. After her disagreement with Mariah, he worried she had decided to forgo the party. And having not seen her for nearly a week had just about undone him.

Mariah kept to herself on the ride to Lord Carrington's. Reginald would have enjoyed the peace, but Mariah's loud sighs radiated irritation and unhappiness.

When they finally arrived at Lord Carrington's Mayfair townhouse, Reginald handed Mariah out and escorted her into the entryway.

"It is a lovely home, is it not, my lord?" Mariah smirked at Reginald.

"Yes, Mariah. It is very fashionable."

A footman led them to a large drawing room, where people talked and laughed as they waited for dinner to be announced.

Reginald craned his neck looking about the room for Sarah.

"Would you stop being so obvious that you are looking for her?" Mariah growled next to him.

He smiled over at her. "Only if you will stop looking as though you will bite anyone who approaches you." He shook his head. "How do you expect any gentlemen to approach if you look as though you might injure them should they try to speak with you?"

Mariah shrugged. "I am not interested in any gentleman here. Therefore, I do not care what they should think about me."

Reginald's brow creased. How did she know she was not interested in anyone in attendance? Did she have a specific person she was referring to? It is not as if she had a guest list. Reginald ran a hand across the back of his neck. Had she formed a tendré for someone and he had not noticed? Had he not been paying her proper attention?

Sarah and her parents entered the room and Reginald's mind went blank. It felt as if he were finally drinking a cup of water after thirsting for many days.

He could worry about Mariah later. Especially knowing she was not interested in any gentleman here. It made Reginald's job much easier and meant he could spend his time watching Sarah.

Mariah stepped away from him, mumbling something that he did not pay heed to. He moved toward Sarah and her parents at the far side of the room.

"Sir Winston, Lady Brown, I am so pleased to see you here tonight." He dipped his head but kept his eyes trained on Sarah. "Miss Brown, you look exceptionally lovely this evening."

Sarah's cheeks pinked, but she avoided looking directly into his eyes. Was she angry with him or was this simply her way of dealing with their current situation?

"Good evening to you, my lord." Sir Winston patted Reginald on the arm in a friendly way. The man grinned, as was his normal look.

Lady Brown fluttered her fan in front of her and smiled. "We are all glad to see you here this evening, my lord. Aside from Lord Carrington, who only Sir Winston is acquainted with, I'm afraid we are acquainted with very few people here."

Then Lord Carrington had invited the Browns of his own accord. For a moment, Reginald wondered how Sir Winston knew the Viscount. But then he glanced back at Sarah and forgot about it. It did not really matter as long as she was there.

Lord Daley walked past their group, and Reginald leaned down toward Sarah. "That is Lord Daley, he is a baron, so he will be seated before Lord Giles but after Lord Markham." He looked around the room to see who else was in attendance. "That man in the yellow waistcoat is Lord Thurgood. He is a marquess. And aside from Lord Berwick, he seems to be the highest-ranking title here this evening."

"Is not Lord Ragsdale attending?" Sarah pulled her bottom lip between her teeth and her brow creased.

"No. Lord Carrington and Ragsdale's father had a falling out several years ago. The duke has forbidden Ragsdale from even speaking to Lord Carrington or anyone in his family."

Sarah nodded as if that made sense, which it didn't. The whole feud was rather silly and had gone on for far too long.

"Is Lord Berwick here?" Sarah glanced around the room. But why was she asking about Berwick?

Reginald nodded and dipped his head to his left. "He is there, speaking with Lord Montcort."

"If Berwick and Thurgood are both marquesses, which one will go first?"

"Berwick. His title is at least a hundred years older than Thurgood's."

Sarah dropped her head, shaking it back-and-forth and

rubbing her fingers between her brows. "It is no use. I shall never understand or remember any of this."

Reginald put his hand on the small of her back, biting back a sigh as heat raged up his arm. "You will. It will simply take some time."

"Time is what I will not have. Once our engagement was made public, everyone would expect it immediately." She shook her head.

Reginald tapped down any hope bubbling inside at her mention of an engagement. They were not engaged. And her comments made him believe it was not likely to happen. At least not anytime soon.

Anytime soon.

He rubbed his thumb back and forth along the small of her back. She gave a barely perceptible shiver, and he grinned. "Then I shall simply wait."

She looked up at him. "I beg your pardon?"

"You said it will take time. That is something I have plenty of. As I did not intend to marry for quite some time anyway, I am in no hurry to do it now. If you need time, I shall give it to you." He met her gaze. "You are worth the wait, Sarah."

Her mouth opened as if she meant to reply, but no words came out.

The butler stepped into the room and announced dinner.

Reginald removed his hand but winked as he took a step away to collect Mariah before they moved into the dining room.

Chapter Twenty-Five

Sarah lay in her bed staring at the ceiling. She had been staring for what seemed like an hour, yet nothing had changed. The plaster design had not changed. Her feelings had not changed. Her situation had not changed. And from what Reginald had said last evening, his feelings had not changed either. Which left her in the same situation as yesterday morning and the morning before that. Indeed, nothing had changed since the day Reginald had told her he loved her.

She dropped her hands heavily onto the bed and heaved out a groan.

Her brow furrowed. Perhaps *something* had changed. Reginald had said he would wait for her. He had said she was worth the wait.

Her chest tightened.

That was new.

He seemed to think it was only a matter of her training that prohibited her from accepting his offer that he had not, in actuality, made.

But there was more to it than that, was there not? It was not simply a matter of knowing some names and the dates they were created. She was not of the same social standing as Reginald. And nothing would change that.

Yet, she could not seem to stop herself from holding on tightly to the idea of time. They simply needed more of it. Perhaps given enough time, something would happen to make the match acceptable.

A soft knock sounded on her door and her mother poked her head in. "Dearest? Are you well?" Her mother opened the door wider and stepped inside, coming to the bed and putting a hand to Sarah's face. "You do not feel feverish. Is something else the matter? It is not like you to stay in bed this late."

Sarah shook her head. "No, Mama. I am well."

Her mother narrowed her eyes at her. "Then why are you still in bed? And why do you sound as though you have lost a cherished toy?"

Sarah looked back up at the ceiling, slightly annoyed that it looked the same as it always did. "I was simply thinking."

Her mother looked up and frowned. "What you are you looking at? I do not see anything interesting enough to hold one's attention."

"I am not looking at anything in particular, just the ceiling."

Her mother rounded the bed and carefully positioned herself on the mattress next to Sarah. She folded her arms crossed her middle and stared up at the ceiling. "What is it you are thinking about? It must be something very heavy indeed."

Sarah closed her eyes, taking in a long deep breath. "I was simply thinking about my education."

Her mother glanced over at her. "What about your education? Do you not feel we provided you with the best we could?"

Sarah offered her mother a small smile and squeezed her hand. "I know you did, Mama. It is just that I am not certain I learned what I need to know to fulfill the dreams I have."

"What dreams? What are you lacking?"

Sarah sighed. What was she thinking? Now she was only making her mother feel as though she had not provided her with an adequate education. Which was not true. It would have been very out of place for a tutor to teach Sarah something that was deemed out of her reach. "Nothing, Mama. I received a very good education, and I am happy for it."

Her mother turned to the side, studying Sarah. "Dearest, what do you wish you would've learned that you did not."

"I am simply being silly. You need not worry about it a moment longer." She closed her eyes. Why had she even mentioned it? And why could she not put the whole thing out of her mind and move on?

She had realized Mr. Bancroft—while he was a very affable gentleman—simply was not suitable for her. The expectations of a marriage with him were not so very different from Reginald. The only real difference between the two, besides Reginald's title, was that Sarah did not love Mr. Bancroft and he did not love her.

But certainly there was someone else suitable for her to marry—perhaps a vicar or a country gentleman of slightly lesser status who would never have the opportunity of entertaining the likes of an earl or a marquess.

Her mother stayed where she was. "You used to tell me what was on your mind, dearest. When did that change?"

Sarah sighed. There had been a time when she told her mother everything. But this felt like something her mother would never understand. She would only see Reginald as an eligible bachelor in want of a wife. But with Mariah angry with her, who else did Sarah have to talk to? Except for perhaps Mills. But Sarah could not see herself confiding in the woman.

She pulled her lip between her teeth. "I believe Lord Stoke loves me and wishes to marry me." She hurried through the words, hoping they would not sound as ridiculous as they felt when she said them.

Her mother let out the tiniest squeal of delight. "I had my suspicions." She took Sarah's hand in hers, squeezing it lightly. "Why do you seem so disheartened by it? I should think you would be overjoyed."

Sarah continued to stare at the ceiling, her head moving side to side. "Why does no one but Lord Ragsdale and me see the problems with it?"

"Lord Ragsdale? What has he to do with this?"

Sarah did not know if she could bear to hear another person tell her she was being silly or that society's expectations did not matter. They all saw daily proof it was not true. And simply because she and Reginald wished to do contrary to what society deemed acceptable did not mean it would not have consequences. "Lord Ragsdale told Lord Stoke that if he went ahead and married me, society would make a mockery of me and Lord Stoke would grow to resent me because I could do nothing but bring him down in society."

Her mother bit at her lower lip and Sarah smiled at the inherited trait. "He is not completely wrong."

Sarah released a heavy breath. She had not expected her mother to understand and found she was disappointed not to hear that everything would work out in the end. Over the years, Sarah had come to rely on her mother's optimism, even if she rarely believed it.

"However," her mother tapped at her lip with her finger, "I believe Lord Stoke is not ignorant of society's expectations. If he believes he can overcome them, I do not see why you should not trust him. He is not without influence."

There was the optimism Sarah had expected. "Mama, do you not see? He is allowing love to overpower his good judgment. But in time, perhaps his love will dim, and then what will happen? Who will he blame when he has lost his status?"

Her mother laughed. "Oh dearest, you think too highly of yourself. If you think you can bring an earl to his knees, you are far overestimating your importance."

Sarah did not know whether to be relieved or offended by her mother's words.

"What I am trying to say is there have been others before him who have married far beneath them, and I dare say they survived to tell the tale."

Sarah sat up leaning back on her elbows. "What do you mean?"

"Lord Stoke would not be the first to marry outside the peerage. Indeed, you are not so very far below him. Your father is a gentleman, one who has been knighted even. You will not be disdained by all who see you. There will be some who will not give you the respect you deserve —perhaps those who wish to be in your situation but have failed—but I daresay the average nobleman, if you treat them with the respect they deserve, will not dismiss you out of turn." Her mother rolled off the bed in a rather unladylike fashion. She stood and ran her hands down the front of her skirt, smoothing out any wrinkles. "But it does provide some enlightenment for me. I assume you wish you had learned more about precedence and other information you might need when interacting with nobility."

Sarah nodded.

Her mother shrugged. "I should think you would be able to learn that information easily enough. But it may take some time. I suppose the question is whether Lord Stoke has the patience to wait for you." Her mother leaned over the bed and placed a kiss on Sarah's brow. "I'll leave you alone now, dearest. You have much to think about."

Her mother was correct. She did have much to think about. She threw back the covers, suddenly needing to do something—anything. Lying around in bed all day was doing nothing to help her situation. Indeed, it only seemed to make her feel worse.

Mills came from the dressing room, almost as if she had

been listening at the door and waiting to hear the rustle of sheets. "Are you ready to dress for the day, miss?"

Sarah nodded. She was not certain exactly what she was going to do, but she needed to find a teacher—who was not Reginald, her heart could not take that kind of teaching—to teach her what she was lacking. Perhaps if she had a knowledge of precedence to her credit, her other deficiencies would not be as noticeable.

But who could she ask? Mariah seemed the obvious choice, but she also was the last person Sarah believed would help her. While she did not believe their rift would last forever, she knew Mariah was not yet ready to forgive her.

Sarah sat at her dressing table as her maid unbraided her hair. She drummed her fingers on the tabletop, trying to think of someone who might help her. In truth, the only people with the kind of knowledge she needed were Mariah and Reginald's friends. But she had already overheard Lord Ragsdale's opinion. He seemed unlikely to help her. Surely the others felt the same.

She shook her head. Besides, it would not be proper for her to seek them out and ask them for such a personal favor. But if not them, who?

A slow smile slid across her face. Of course. Why had she not thought of her before?

Sarah stepped out of the carriage, running a hand down the front of her skirt and pelisse. She looked up at the front of the Berkeley Square townhouse, noting it looked much brighter in the daylight.

She ran a tongue across her lips, clutching her reticule tighter in her fist. She had sent a card to Miss Bancroft, asking if she might visit this afternoon, but she had not stated the reason. Miss Bancroft had replied promptly that she would adore seeing Sarah again.

But now the time had come, and Sarah hesitated, uncertain if she could ask Miss Bancroft for the favor.

She looked up at the facade and sighed.

Reginald was willing to wait for her. Could she not at least muster the courage to seek Miss Bancroft's assistance, for Reginald? Did she not love him enough to do that much?

She gave a sharp nod and moved to the door. Lifting the knocker, she dropped it several times. She took a step back and looked up and down the street, hoping she did not appear overly eager.

The street was not as busy as she had assumed it would be. Was it always this quiet, or was everyone out visiting Hyde Park or one of the other attractions? Perhaps it was simply Cheapside that was constantly filled with carriages.

The door swung open, and a footman looked at her expectantly. Sarah pulled a card from her reticule and handed it over. The footman opened the door wider and motioned her inside. "Miss Brown, Miss Bancroft is expecting you. If you will follow me."

He moved to a corridor off to the left side of the entryway. They passed several doors before he stopped, motioning Sarah into one on the right. They stepped just inside the door and the footman bowed. "Miss Bancroft, Miss Brown is here to see you."

Miss Bancroft sat on a couch near the window, a book held up in front of her face. At the sound of the footman's voice, she lowered the book and turned, looking over her shoulder.

Any misgivings Sarah had felt about interrupting the girl fled when she saw the smile covering the young lady's face. She jumped to her feet and met Sarah halfway, giving her a small embrace. "Oh, Miss Brown, you do not know how excited I was to receive your note. I have been wishing to see you again."

If she wished to see Sarah so badly, why had she not sent a card herself?

Sarah pushed the question away, knowing it did not really matter. She was not here on a social call, per se. While it may seem like one to Miss Bancroft, Sarah looked at it as more of a business dealing.

Miss Bancroft motioned to the couch. "Please, do sit down." She looked back over her shoulder at the footman. "Robert, we will have tea now."

The footman dipped his head. "Right away, miss."

Once they were both seated, Miss Bancroft leaned forward, putting her hands on Sarah's. "Your note did not indicate a reason for your visit." Her nose scrunched up. "And while I wanted to believe you simply wish to see me, I have a feeling there is more to it than that."

Sarah's brow creased and guilt burrowed a hole in her stomach. Had she been so obvious? Perhaps she should not ask for the favor right at the beginning. Perhaps it would be best if she chatted with Miss Bancroft for a few moments. Surely there would be something said that would lead her to the true reason for her visit.

She smiled. "I had hoped I would hear from you sooner, but when I did not, I decided I must make the effort myself to come and see you."

Miss Bancroft's shoulders relaxed. "Oh, I am so pleased to hear it. I was certain I had offended you. Every time we see each other, I seem to say the exact wrong thing."

Sarah's heart melted a bit. She knew exactly how Miss Bancroft felt, especially when she was in the company of those she felt were above her. She pulled one hand out from under Miss Bancroft's and placed it on top, offering the girl's hand a little squeeze. "I can assure you, Miss Bancroft, nothing you've said has offended me. Especially not enough to keep me from forming a friendship with you."

Sarah pulled her lip between her teeth, feeling rather

disingenuous. She had not come to foster a new friendship. She had come for a specific purpose—a specific favor. Perhaps it would be best if she just asked for it, and then they could relax and enjoy a pleasant visit afterward.

Sarah took in a deep breath and plunged ahead. "However, you were right. There was a reason for my note to you."

Miss Bancroft's smile faltered.

"Not that I did not wish to visit with you, but I had also hoped you might be able to help me with something. You are one of the few people I know who might be in a position to do so."

As she had hoped, the smile returned to Miss Bancroft's face. "I do not believe I have ever been singled out to do a favor for someone. Or at least I have never been only one of a few who might accomplish it."

"Before you become too overcome, I must warn you it is not anything that is immensely exciting. I worry I have now set your expectations too high." She should just ask what she came to ask, but for some reason, she could not seem to blurt out the question.

Miss Bancroft stared, smiling, her head nodding slightly as she seemed to anticipate Sarah's words.

Sarah looked at the ceiling for a moment, gathering her courage. "I wish to learn the rules of precedence. It is not something I was taught in my education, but it is something I feel I should know."

Miss Bancroft smiled even larger, almost bouncing on the couch. She leaned forward offering a knowing look. "It is because of Lord Stoke, is it not?"

Sarah's smile dropped—as did her confidence—and heat filled her cheeks. What did Miss Bancroft know of Reginald? "Whatever could you mean?"

Miss Bancroft patted her hand. "Come now, Miss Brown. One must only see the two of you together to know of your partiality for one another. You are a bit more guarded, but I suspect the affection is not only on Lord Stoke's part."

Sarah, while she did not wish for Mr. Bancroft to hear this conversation, did miss his stern reprimands at his sister's often inappropriate words. In many ways, Miss Bancroft reminded Sarah of Mariah.

"Yes, well, it is not strictly for Lord Stoke. I do spend a great deal of time with Lady Mariah. And as she has asked me to accompany her to several dinner parties, I thought it only proper for me to understand precedence." The excuse sounded lame even to her ears, but she was not certain Miss Bancroft was the cleverest of girls.

Miss Bancroft pulled her hands free from the pile on Sarah's lap and stood up. She moved to a table at the far side of the room and pulled open a drawer, pushing things to the side. Finally, she straightened with a book in her hand. Slowly and with a slightly raised brow, as if trying to add a theatrical flair, Miss Bancroft returned to the couch and set the book on the cushion between them.

Sarah looked down at the worn leather cover. There was no inscription on the front or the spine.

Miss Bancroft put her finger on top of the book and pushed it slowly towards Sarah. "I am not certain this was the proper way to teach me, but Charlie did it anyway." She shrugged. "Mother objected at first, but she finally gave up and allowed me to use this. It was hard for me to remember all the names. But perhaps it will help you with what you need."

Sarah reached over and picked up the book, flipping it open to see many blank pages. It was a journal of sorts. She opened the book to the front cover, carefully turning the first few pages. Long rows of names and titles with dates beside them covered page after page.

She looked up at Miss Bancroft. "Is this everyone in the peerage?"

Miss Bancroft scooted closer to her, pointing at a set of names. "This is the name of the titleholder," her finger moved to the other side of the page. "And this is the date of creation. They are all listed in order. You need only memorize this, and you should have no problem knowing who belongs where at a dinner table. In time you will put faces with the names and that is all you need to know."

Miss Bancroft made it sound far easier than it likely was, but for the first time in more than a week, Sarah had hope. She held the book to her chest, hardly believing she had it in her hands. Could this be the answer to her troubles? Could this really be all she needed for her dreams to become reality?

She leaned over and pulled Miss Bancroft into a hug. Sarah owed this young lady much for her help. She grinned. And there had been absolutely no demonstrations involved—although if she was being honest, she had missed Reginald's demonstrations a great deal.

She sucked in a breath. While she did not have an easy time memorizing information, it also was not impossible for her. If she disciplined herself, she might be able to memorize it within a week or two. But even if it took longer, Reginald had promised he would wait. Hope bubbled up in her chest.

But would it be enough? Would learning every name and date inside the book enable her to be with Reginald? She released a breath. If it only gave her a small chance of being with him, it would be worth it. He was worth it.

Chapter Twenty-Six

It had been nearly a fortnight since Reginald had last seen Sarah.

She had been conspicuously missing from all the parties he had attended, and it had been the longest, most vexing two weeks of his entire life.

He shoved his hand through his hair, questioning for the hundredth time why he had not realized he loved Sarah until she was in an argument with Mariah. While knowing she was set against them being together would have been hard to think about every time he saw her at his home, it could not have been worse than simply not seeing her at all. Why had he not taken advantage of her presence for all those weeks when he had the chance?

He entered Lord Derby's house and searched the faces of people milling about the entryway. But it was all for naught as he did not see her about.

Mariah let out a huff next to him. It was rather a common noise from her of late. "Why must you be so obvious?"

Reginald ignored her. It was the same question she asked as they arrived at every party. "I should not have to be obvious if you would simply apologize and allow her to come with us," he said absently.

A dinner party hosted by Lord Derby was not a place he would normally expect to see Sarah. And as Mariah still refused to speak to her, Reginald had gone to great pains to ensure Sarah and her parents received an invitation.

It had not been an easy task. Lord Derby had not been inclined to extend an invitation to a little-known gentleman from Stoke—even if he had been recently knighted. But Reginald had not hesitated to use his father's name and the friendship the two men had shared in order to secure the invitation for the Browns.

He knew it was rather beneath him to resort to such means, but if it meant Sarah was in attendance, he could have no regrets.

But where were they? Reginald only knew that the invitation had been extended—he had told Lord Derby to send the invitation to him, so as not to disclose her Cheapside address —but he had no notion if it had been accepted. Were they not coming? Or were they simply already in the drawing room?

Reginald had been grateful Derby was hosting a dinner party because it seemed unlikely the earl would have agreed to invite the Browns to a ball.

He frowned. Such thoughts led him to wonder if Sarah and Ragsdale might have the right of it. But dwelling on that made him far too depressed, so he did not allow himself to think about it for long.

A footman led the group down a corridor and Reginald followed behind until they stepped into a long drawing room. Couches and chairs sat in clusters throughout, most of them already occupied by people. More people stood in groups along the perimeter.

"Reginald, do you mind if I go speak with Miss Waters? She will be seated rather far away from me at dinner, so I will not be able to speak with her then." Mariah touched his arm, drawing his attention to her for a moment.

He waved her away. "Yes, yes. Go ahead. I will see you when dinner is called." Another huff sounded before Mariah moved off toward a cluster of ladies.

Reginald looked at everyone, trying to find Sarah in the sea of people. He growled low in his throat when he did not see her. What if she did not come?

Montcort lifted a hand and waved Reginald over to their group standing at the far end of the room.

Grudgingly, Reginald moved over toward his friends. If he could not be with Sarah, they would be a desirable second option.

He reached the others and smiled half-heartedly. "Good evening, gents. How are you all?"

"Better than you, from the look on your face." Berwick raised a brow. "What has you in such a state?"

"I am not in a state," Reginald grumbled.

"I would beg to differ. And where have you been? You have been rather scarce these last few weeks." Bancroft asked before finishing the rest of his drink.

"I am guessing it has to do with a certain lady?" Berwick waggled his brows.

"This is neither the time nor the place to discuss such things, Ben," Reginald growled and looked over his shoulder.

Berwick nodded toward the terrace doors. "Then why do we not excuse ourselves? We should have some privacy outside. And as you have been avoiding the club, this seems our only chance to talk. The ladies will find it far too chilly out, and the gentleman will surely stay where the ladies are."

Reginald shrugged. Indeed, he was interested in speaking with his friends about his situation with Sarah. He knew Ragsdale's opinion but what of the others? Did he dare ask them their opinion?

"Where is Rags?" Reginald glanced over his shoulder, looking for their missing friend.

Charlie flicked his brows up. "The duke ordered him to Kent to check in with their steward there."

Reginald grinned for the first time that evening. "I'm certain Rags was thrilled."

"His usual scowl was downright menacing. I should worry about any highwayman that decides to make Rags his prey." Berwick chuckled.

Reginald nodded toward the doors. "If we need not wait for him, why do we not move our conversation out of doors?"

They moved as a group, walking to the farthest point of the terrace—away from the doors and prying ears.

Berwick crossed his arms and leaned his hip against the weighty stone baluster. "Now, I am certain most of us know the reason you are out of sorts, but why do you not tell us exactly what it is about Miss Brown that has you so vexed? Is it just your behavior at the theater or is there more to it?"

Reginald ran a hand through his hair, silently apologizing to Jones. Just how much did Berwick know about the theater?

He glanced at Ponsonby who raised a shoulder and shook his head, indicating he had not mentioned anything to the others. What did it matter? Once Reginald finished speaking with them, they would all know the essence of it—except perhaps the kiss. He did not feel the need to share those details. "I wish to marry her."

At his words, the other men grimaced, but he guessed it was for the notion of marriage and had nothing to do with Sarah particularly. "The trouble is she overheard something Rags said to me, and now she is convinced that a match between us is impossible because we come from different social spheres."

Ponsonby twitched his lips to the side. "She overheard Rags? That could not have ended well."

Montcort settled against the hand railing. "We all know he

219

is rather high in the instep, but that does not mean he is right. What is important is what you believe, Reg. Do you believe marrying her would be a mismatch?"

Reginald shook his head. "Her most ardent argument is that she does not know precedence. But I know she is intelligent. She could learn such things quickly. Once that is in hand, I see no reason why she should not be accepted. But she disagrees. She fears our marriage would only lower me in the sight of other peers and, in time, I would grow to resent her for it."

Bancroft shifted and all eyes turned to him.

"You have something to say, Charlie?" Reginald asked warily.

Bancroft shrugged. "As the only one of us who does not hold a title, I can understand her concern, to a certain degree."

Montcort snorted. "How is that, Charlie? You have more per year than Ponsonby, and when you host a party, you invite as many peers as the rest of us do."

Ponsonby frowned. "Thank you for the reminder, Cort."

Bancroft nodded, but it was reserved. "Yes, yes, I know. But it does not mean that I see myself as an equal to those that I invite. There are times, even with you gents, that I feel my inferiority. I understand there is a distinction between us. And I can imagine Miss Brown feels it far more keenly than even I do."

"Then you believe that she will be looked on with disdain by those of society?" The tightness that had gripped Reginald's chest for weeks increased.

Bancroft shrugged. "I believe she will have her critics. Not everyone will be watching to see if she fails. But there will be those that do."

"Take heart, Reg," Berwick lifted his chin. "We will simply have to ensure she does not fail. Once others see us embrace her, they will follow suit. Especially if Rags does."

"But will he? He has already told me I should turn my attention elsewhere."

Bancroft shook his head. "If you decide in favor of Miss Brown, Rags will come around. He may speak of superiority, but you know he is loyal above all else."

The tightness eased slightly. "You do not see it as a problem not to be overcome, then?" Reginald looked at all his friends, trying to discover if they were hiding their true feelings.

Berwick frowned. "Reg, if you love her, I cannot advise you to turn your back on that. Love is a rarity, especially in our world. I believe all our parents married for convenience or for political reasons." They all nodded. "When one finds that person who makes them whole, they should move toward it, not away. From what I have seen, Miss Brown makes you whole."

Reginald swallowed hard at the sincerity he saw on Berwick's face. He turned his gaze on the rest of them. "What about the rest of you?"

Ponsonby grinned. "You already know my opinion."

Charlie nodded.

"I am in agreement with Ben." Montcort added.

Reginald clapped Ben on the shoulder. "Thank you. I am grateful to have your support." He looked at all of them. "All of you."

Berwick smirked. "If you had not been staying away from the club of late, you may have discovered our support weeks ago."

Reginald ducked his head sheepishly. "I should have known you would not think as Rags. But I did not know how I should manage if you did."

Ponsonby motioned toward the door. "Dinner cannot be far off. We had best move inside, lest we miss the meal altogether."

Reginald followed his friends inside, feeling lighter than he had in weeks. If he could convince his friends that Sarah was right for him, perhaps he might be able to convince her of it also.

He stepped into the drawing room and his eyes immediately met Sarah's gaze from across the room.

A slight smile appeared on her lips, and it gave him hope that perhaps all was not lost. How could she deny him when they both felt such joy at simply seeing one another?

He moved in her direction, but just before he reached her, Mariah intercepted him. "Reginald, there is a gentleman I wish you to introduce me to."

"In a moment, Mariah."

She stepped in front of him, blocking his way to Sarah. "I cannot imagine mother and father would approve of you placing Miss Brown's needs ahead of mine." She crossed her arms over her chest and jutted out her hip.

"Mother and father would be pleased that I am making an effort to ensure an heir." Even as he said it, he was not completely certain it was the truth. Would his parents think him neglectful? Or would they approve of him doing what he could to secure a match? Even if it was with Sarah? He was certain his parents had never envisioned him marrying their neighbor. They were more like-minded with Rags. But they were not here. And he could not let their *past* desires for him dictate his *future* happiness. "Mariah, step aside. You are causing a scene."

"I am not the one causing a scene, Reginald." She hissed through her teeth. "It is you and your tendré for Miss Brown that is causing a scene."

He stopped and looked down at his sister. "If you wish me to act as your guardian, then I shall. And as your guardian I must ask why you have not yet apologized to Miss Brown? I know for certain that she has apologized to you, numerous times. And yet, you have not accepted it. Why is that? It is not proper to withhold your acceptance."

Mariah's face pinked. "Do not speak to me of propriety. You know as well as I that now is not the time for that discussion." She scowled up at him.

"Indeed, it is not." Reginald looked hard at her. "But you will apologize, Mariah. I will make certain of it." He turned away from her. "Now, if you will excuse me."

"But what about introducing me to Mr. Cleverly?"

Reginald shook his hand. "His is not an acquaintance I wish for you to make. Now step aside. I wish to speak to Miss Brown. I have not seen her in weeks, and I wish to make Sarah and her parents feel as comfortable as possible in this crush."

"Lady Mariah," Ponsonby lifted his arm for Mariah to take and gave Reginald a knowing smile. "I hoped you might come and help settle a dispute between Lord Berwick and me."

Mariah glanced over her shoulder and scowled as Ponsonby led her away.

Reginald smiled. He did not think anyone in all of England had better friends than he.

He turned back, catching Sarah watching him. A swarm —would Miss Brown know the correct word—of butterflies erupted inside of him.

He continued his way over to her and her parents. "Good day, Sir Winston and Lady Brown." He bowed to them, but his eyes stayed on Sarah. "Miss Brown, I am very pleased to see you here this evening."

She looked down at the floor, but he did not miss her grin.

His heartbeat picked up speed and he allowed hope to warm his belly.

He straightened and looked down at her, hoping she could see how happy he was to see her. "Miss Brown, I wondered if you might know what a swarm of butterflies is called?"

She grinned up at him. "Indeed, my lord. They are called a swarm."

"Ah, it was just as I thought." He could not seem to pull his gaze away from her. The sight of her had been withheld from him for so long, he did not know if he could allow her out of his view again.

"Lord Stoke," an older man approached Reginald, and he grudgingly turned toward the voice. "I have wanted to speak with you, but I was unable to find you after Lords."

"Lord Haverly," Reginald glanced over at Sarah and her parents. "I do not believe you have met Sir Winston and his wife, Lady Brown."

Lord Haverly nodded to them. "It is a pleasure to meet you." He glanced back at Reginald. "I should like to meet with you privately."

Reginald nodded. "And have you met their daughter, Miss Sarah Brown?"

Lord Haverly let out an exasperated sigh. "I have not had the pleasure." He dipped his head quickly. "Miss Brown."

He glanced back at Reginald.

"It is a pleasure to meet you, my lord. I hope your daughters, Lady Brunswick and Lady Isabel are in good health." Sarah inclined her head, the perfect example of propriety.

Lord Haverly turned his gaze from Reginald and focused on Sarah. "Indeed, they are both in excellent health. I thank you." His lips turned up in the barest hint of a smile—something that did not happen often—and he slowly pulled his gaze back to Reginald. "As I was saying, I wish to meet with you privately to discuss several matters which have come up in Lords over the last fortnight."

Reginald nodded, unable to hold the smile from his face. "Yes. If you will contact my secretary, I am certain we will find an amiable time for both of us to meet."

The earl nodded firmly, flicking a glance back to Sarah. "I shall look forward to our discussion."

"As will I," Reginald lied. He never looked forward to anything regarding Lord Haverly.

The old earl turned and disappeared into the crowd.

Reginald turned and leaned in toward Sarah. "That was very well done, Sarah. Tell me, how did you know about his daughters?"

"The same way I know about Lord Kendal and Lord Brinton." Sarah bit her lip, obviously trying to hide her pleased smile. "I learned about them in one of my lessons."

He raised a brow. "You've been receiving lessons from someone else? I thought we established that I am the best teacher."

Sarah blushed to the tips of her ears. "I could not afford the distraction of your instruction, my lord."

He frowned, hoping it looked more feigned than it really was. "I hope your lessons are not as demonstrative as our lessons were."

A quiet laugh escaped Sarah's lips and she placed a hand to her mouth. "No, indeed, my lord. If you must know, I am instructing myself this time."

He raised both his brows at her. "Are you, now? And where did you procure your study materials?"

"A friend was kind enough to lend them to me." Sarah glanced up at him.

The warmth in his belly radiated outward to his chest and his arms.

"And has your study proven effective? Has it opened your mind to other possibilities?" Sarah had been stubborn in her position on their relationship, so he mentally prepared himself for the answer he did not wish to hear.

She nodded slowly. "I must admit, it has allowed me to hope for things I previously believed impossible."

Reginald released a stuttering breath. Could it be she had changed her mind? If he asked for her hand, would she now accept him?

But after she had put forth such great effort for him, a simple *"will you marry me"* did not seem sufficient. An idea began to form in his mind. The least he could do was ask her to marry him in a way that was meant just for her.

The butler entered the room and announced dinner was ready.

Sarah looked around the room. "Is Lord Keatings in attendance?"

Reginald shrugged. "I have not seen him, but I do not know for certain. Why?"

She raised her chin and stared him in the eye. "I asked because his is the only earldom older than yours. I simply wondered where you might be sitting this evening."

While he had never considered the order of precedence a very romantic topic, he realized he might just have to reconsider the notion. Listening to Sarah speak of titles and creation dates made his breath a bit shallow. He had the overwhelming desire you wrap her up in his arms and kiss her quite thoroughly.

Lud, was it possible to love her even more now than he had ten minutes ago?

Chapter Twenty-Seven

Sarah looked in the mirror as Mills pinned up her hair. After last night's dinner at Lord Derby's, Sarah had awakened with a newfound confidence, and she liked the way it looked on her. She also liked the way Reginald had looked at her. He was proud of her. She knew that without a doubt. And while he had not asked for her hand last evening, she did think it might be coming soon.

And after last evening's success, she had almost convinced herself to accept. While her new knowledge did not change the station to which she was born, it did disguise it slightly. Lord Haverly had not seemed to care that she was only the daughter of a knight. He had looked at her respectfully once he learned she knew about his importance and that of his daughters.

And while their engagement would be announced in the papers and the banns would be read in Stoke, Sarah thought it possible she could quietly become accustomed to being Reginald's wife and a countess before the most critical of society could expose her. Hopefully, by then, she would have established herself enough that both she and Reginald could weather whatever storm might come their way. Truthfully, she knew she could weather any storm if Reginald was at her side. She just hoped he felt the same.

She stood up and ran her hands down her gown. "Thank you, Mills."

"You're welcome, miss." The maid gathered the night clothes from the end of the bed and moved toward the dressing room.

Sarah set out in search of her mother. She descended the staircase and happened upon a footman on the first-floor landing. "James, have you seen my mother?"

He nodded. "She went out, Miss."

"Did she say when she would return?"

"She said not to expect her back before teatime, Miss."

Sarah released a sigh. "Thank you, James."

"There is a missive for you on the tray in the parlor. It arrived a few moments ago."

Was it a letter from Reginald? Did he want to see her today? Perhaps he would call on her for tea or they would go for a drive in Hyde Park.

By the time she reached the parlor, her hands were shaking, and her heart was racing.

She gathered up the folded note off the tray and read the front.

Her name was written in a wide, flowing hand. But the handwriting was not Reginald's as she had expected. Instead, it was Mariah's handwriting that looked up at Sarah.

She cracked open the seal and unfolded the paper, reading the words before she had completely unfolded it.

She looked down at the paper and read it for a third time.

Mariah had finally accepted her apology, although the writing felt stilted and rather cold. Had Mariah truly forgiven her, or had Reginald forced her to apologize?

Sarah shrugged. Perhaps it did not matter. If her apology had been accepted, then perhaps even if it was not completely sincere, they could at least start to mend their friendship.

Sarah took out a paper from the writing desk and sharpened her quill. She would see how forgiven she was by inviting Mariah over for tea. If the invitation was accepted, Sarah would know there was room to mend the friendship. If it was declined, then the answer would be clear. And while Sarah was not ready to forsake the friendship for good, she would not force herself or her friendship on Mariah.

She scrawled out an invitation for Mariah to join her for tea the following day, before folding it up and sealing it with wax.

Now, she would just need to wait for Mariah's response.

Was it too much to hope that Mariah not only accepted the invitation but that she also brought Reginald?

Sarah nodded. Indeed, that seemed like far too much to hope for. She needed to be patient. Once she and Mariah were back on friendly terms, it seemed likely Sarah would again spend most of her days at Mariah's townhouse. And that meant she would see Reginald far more often. She gave a little shiver at the thought.

When she had told Reginald that they could never be together, she had not anticipated how difficult it would be not to see him. Her fight with Mariah could not have come at a worse time. The weeks without seeing him had been far more difficult than her memorization of the peerage.

The door opened behind her, and Sarah looked over her shoulder. Chadwick stood just inside the door. "Miss Brown, Lady Mariah is here to see you. She presented me with her card and asked if you might spare her a moment or two of your time."

Sarah's brow creased and she looked down at the note she had written, the wax had not even completely cooled yet. How had Mariah known Sarah was going to invite her over?

"Please show her in, Chadwick."

Perhaps their relationship would not take weeks or months to heal.

A few moments later, Mariah breezed into the room behind Chadwick. "Thank you, Chadwick," Mariah called over her shoulder. She grinned at Sarah. "Good morning, Sarah. I hope you slept well."

Sarah nodded, uncertain what to make of it all. Mariah acted as if nothing had happened between them. As if she had not ignored Sarah's letters of apology and had not scowled at her at every meeting, as sparce as they had been, for the last fortnight.

"I did sleep well, Lady Mariah. I hope you did as well."

Mariah waved Sarah's words away. "Oh, Sarah. You are a goose. You know I did not really mean for you to call me Lady Mariah." She giggled behind her gloved hand. "Especially not when we are at home."

She floated over and sat on the settee. Looking down at her hand for a moment, she sucked in a deep breath. "Regi says that I need to accept your apology and that I must offer one in return." She paused, but her gaze remained down. "While I disagreed with him initially, I have thought about it these past few days and I realized he was correct."

Mariah looked up as Sarah slipped down onto the settee next to her.

Sarah shook her head. "No, Mariah. You need not apologize."

Mariah's brow creased. "I do. Reginald pointed out to me that I do not always speak kindly to you. And while I have never intended to hurt you, he feels—as do I—that you deserve an apology."

Sarah put her hand atop Mariah's and smiled. "Let us forget all about it and start anew, shall we?"

Mariah smiled, and for the first time in weeks, it reached her eyes. "I believe that is the best idea I have heard in a fortnight, at least." She leaned over and embraced Sarah tightly. "I do hate it when we fight, Sarah."

"As do I, Mariah. Let's agree not to do it again."

Mariah nodded firmly. "Oh, yes. I completely agree." She sighed. "I have missed you these past weeks, but I believe Regi has missed you even more."

Sarah's cheeks felt hot, and she dropped her face into her hands to help hide the blush. "I am certain he has been able to entertain himself."

Mariah shook her head. "No. Indeed, he has hardly even been to his club."

That hardly seemed truthful. The club was where Reginald and his friends met to talk. Why would he have stayed away from them? Unless he knew they would not approve of his feelings for her either.

That thought brought a sinking feeling to her stomach.

Mariah smiled at her. "But I think that is all about to end. Have you read the post this morning?" Mariah pulled out the poorly folded newspaper and handed it over to her. "There is a paid advertisement on the front page that I believe will interest you."

Sarah looked at her friend with a creased brow. Why would she think an advertisement should interest Sarah? She had read the post several times since they arrived in London and had found very little to interest her. She opened the paper and carefully spread it out on the low table in front of her. Skimming over the page, she saw nothing so extraordinary as to catch her eye.

She glanced up at Mariah. "I do not see anything interesting here."

Mariah smiled knowingly. "It is in the second column, the fifth from the top and it begins, '*For SB from RT.*'" Mariah paused as Sarah skimmed down the page.

Sarah nodded and pointed to the advertisement. "Oh, yes. Here it is." She smiled. "It is a charade." She glanced up at Mariah. "You are right. I do find this intriguing. Do you wish to solve it with me?"

Mariah shook her head. "I have already seen it. But you should surely try to solve it."

Mariah read aloud.

> *"My first is a word that comes with glee,*
> *My second each day in the mirror I see,*
> *My whole with the parson we soon will be."*

SHE LOOKED UP EXCITEDLY at Mariah. "Did you already figure it out?"

Mariah nodded. "Indeed, I believe most of London has."

Sarah chuckled. "It is not a very difficult charade. 'My first is a word that comes with glee'? That is obviously *'merry.'* And, 'My second each day in the mirror I see'? That would be 'me.' My whole with the parson we soon will be." Sarah clapped her hands. "It is a marriage proposal, Mariah. Is that not romantic? I wonder who it is for?"

Mariah's face fell. "Did you not read the first part?"

Sarah frowned. "I thought I did." She turned back to the paper. "Yes, I did. It says for SB from RT. Who do you think they are?"

Mariah threw her hands up in the air. "You can decipher charades, but you cannot figure out initials? SB...Sarah Brown?"

Sarah's smile fell away and she looked back at the paper. Her hands shook as she lifted it off the table. To SB from RT...Reginald Thornbeck. Gracious! He had asked for her hand in the newspaper? What had he hoped to gain by doing it so publicly? Any hope Sarah had of quietly assuming the role of countess and Reginald's wife had now slipped through her fingers.

"Why would he do this? Especially when he knew I was so uncertain?"

Mariah shrugged her shoulders. "I would have thought you would be happy. You will be married before the Season is done." Mariah frowned.

"Mariah, what is wrong? Have you changed your mind about wishing for us to be sisters?" Sarah swallowed at the thought of her next words. "If you do not want me to marry him, I will not. I do not wish for another rift in our friendship."

Mariah laughed, but it was strained. "No, I am very happy you are to marry Regi. I only thought that I—" She shook her head. "Do not fret over me. I am very happy for you."

Sarah looked at her for a moment and then nodded slowly. Mariah had thought she would marry before Sarah. It seemed a logical assumption. Mariah had a larger dowry and a better bloodline. And she was quite five times prettier than Sarah.

While the thought did not bolster Sarah's confidence, she was pleased to know that Mariah had shown some restraint and thought about her words before she uttered them. Perhaps Mariah was learning and growing, just as Sarah had this Season.

She placed a hand on Mariah's arm. "I am certain if Lord Heatherton had been here this Season, that you would also be married before the Season was over. I hope you do not see it as a competition, for there is no one else in London I think worthy of you."

Mariah swiped a hand across her face. "Thank you, Sarah. I truly have missed you these last few weeks."

Sarah wiped quickly at her eyes too. "And I, you."

Mariah patted her hand. "Do you not think you should go in search of my brother? I should think he is rather anxious to receive your answer."

Sarah nodded. "We should go to him immediately." She moved toward the door, but Mariah sat still on the settee. "Mariah, are you not to come with me?"

Mariah shook her head. "I believe you need to do this on

your own. I will be here when you return, and you may tell me all of the particulars."

Sarah put a hand to her heart. Was she really going to accept him? Just learning some names and dates did not really change that much, did it? She closed her eyes and took in a calming breath.

"I know you are questioning this, Sarah, but you must stop. Regi loves you and you love him. Nothing, not even propriety, should keep you apart. Now go find him and accept his offer!" Mariah waved her hand toward the door, shooing Sarah out.

Sarah nodded and raced from the room. Mariah was right. She had successfully mounted the biggest hurdle. The rest she could handle—they could handle—together.

Chapter Twenty-Eight

Sarah stood at the door of Reginald's townhouse, her hand raised and ready to lift the knocker. But she paused. What was she to say? What if Mariah had it wrong and those were not either hers or Reginald's initials? What if Roger Thompson had bought the ad for Suzanne Buckley? How was Mariah so certain the proposal was for Sarah?

Even as Sarah thought it, she knew the chances of it being for someone else were not likely. Reginald had created that charade just for her because he knew how much she enjoyed them.

Her chest swelled at the thought that he knew her so well.

No, the notion that it was not meant for her was not what was troubling her. It was that he had placed the charade on the front page in the morning paper of one of the most-read newspapers in London. That idea alone made her question if he knew her at all. He could easily have given her the charade in the privacy of his home or on a carriage ride. The sentiment would have been the same—better, even, because it would have been intimate and romantic.

So why then had he done it in such an open and public

way? It was as if his intimate, romantic gesture had been completely undone by his outlandish delivery method.

She placed her hand flat against the door and sucked in a slow, calming breath. There had to be a reason he had done what he did. Reginald, for all his attempts to appear unaffected and carefree, never did anything without a reason.

But what that reason could be, she had no idea. And she would never know until she knocked on the door and spoke to him.

With a new resolve, Sarah lifted the knocker and dropped it several times.

Taking a step back, she clasped her hands in front of her and glanced discreetly down the street. How many people had deciphered the charade already today? What did they think of her? Of Reginald? Had Lord Ragsdale seen it? Was he even now inside lecturing Reginald on his folly?

The door swung wide, and the butler nodded to her. "Miss Brown. Lord Stoke has been expecting you. Please come this way."

Sarah tried to swallow past the knot forming in her throat. What was she going to say to him? They had spoken only once in the last fortnight, and even then it had only been for a moment. How did one start such a conversation? Did she simply ask why he had placed it in the paper right from the beginning or was it better to ease into the conversation first?

The butler stepped into the library, a room Sarah knew well, and cleared his throat. "My lord, Miss Brown is here to see you."

Reginald looked up from the book he was reading, and his face smoothed into a soft smile. Lawkes, how she loved that smile. "Thank you, Maxwell."

The butler bowed and turned back into the corridor.

Sarah stayed rooted in place just inside the doorway. What was the proper thing to do in this situation? Did she wait for him to come to her? Or maybe it would be better if she walked casually over to him. What she wished to do was run toward him and throw her arms around him, never to let him go.

And while that was a rather welcome idea, it was not the proper thing to do. And she was nothing if not proper. Except it seemed where Reginald was concerned. She bit the side of her cheek.

As if making the decision for her, Reginald set his book on the side table and stood up, walking slowly toward her with his hands clasped behind his back. Did he mean to drive her mad with his tortoise-like pace or was he simply giving her time to flee? If he thought she wished to flee, he did not know her in the least.

His eyes danced with merriment, but she also saw an intense longing. Had the last fortnight been as hard on him as it had been on her? "Miss Brown, I was hoping I would see you today."

Sarah licked her lips but quickly stopped when Reginald's gaze traced the path of her tongue. Her knees went a little weak and she shook herself mentally. She had to control herself or she would launch herself into his arms and never know the answer to the question she had come to discover.

She released a breath. "How could I not come after reading the morning paper?"

Reginald's grin increased and Sarah dropped her head to the side. How had she stayed away from him for so long? It had been torture, but she had not realized just how torturous until he smiled at her with *that* smile. She felt as if she had not seen it in years. Was the answer to her question so very important? At that moment, feeling his lips against hers seemed of far more import than the particulars of a silly ad.

"I admit I was a little concerned you might not read the paper today." He came to stop just in front of her. He was close enough to touch her, but not close enough to kiss her—a rather unpleasant discovery. "And then where would I be?"

"I thought the great teacher had an answer to everything." Sarah pulled her lip in and shrugged. "Mariah made certain I saw it."

His brows rose. "Mariah? I had thought she was still angry with you."

"She sent a note this morning accepting my previous apologies."

Reginald chuckled. "*She* accepted *your* apologies? But she offered none of her own?" He shook his head. "How was I so negligent in her upbringing?"

Sarah reached out a hand and placed it on his arm. They both fell silent as Sarah basked in the warmth flowing up her arm and filling her body. "You need not worry. She apologized when she came to visit shortly after the letter arrived. That is when she showed me the paper."

He relaxed. "She visited you in Cheapside?"

Sarah nodded. "Indeed, she is still there now."

"And she apologized?"

Sarah nodded but frowned. How had this conversation become about Mariah? "Yes. We are friends once again."

Reginald took a step closer. Still not close enough to kiss her, but the warmth radiating from him told her it would not take much to close the distance. "I am glad to hear it. It will make things easier for us, that is for certain." He lifted his hands to her arms and gripped her lightly, his thumbs doing their delightfully evil dance along the front of her arms. "I hoped you would come today and tell me the answer to the charade I composed for you. I hope it was not too difficult."

"I managed it well enough, my lord."

He shook his head. "Come now, Sarah. After what we've done at the theater and in Bancroft's library? I believe Christian names are in order." He winked at her.

Her face heated as the memories flitting through her mind, and she almost wished they could go back to the days when they spoke only about Mariah or the weather. But then she saw the inviting look in Reginald's eyes, and she wanted to be nowhere else but there. "I figured out your charade rather quickly, Reginald."

"And what did you think?" He waggled his brows at her. "I knew it would not take you long. You are far too intelligent. Besides, I did not wish to wait any longer than was necessary for you to discover what I wanted to ask you."

"Before I give you my answer, I have a question." Sarah looked down at her hands. "Why did you place the charade in the newspaper, Reginald? You created it just for me and then presented it in a way that was decidedly *not* me. Everyone will know of your proposal to me by this evening. Everyone will be speaking of it. Why, when you know I have been so tentative about it, did you make it such a spectacle?" She played with the tips of her gloves.

He placed his finger beneath her chin and gently lifted her face up until their gazes locked. "That is precisely why I did it, Sarah. You seem to think that we need to quietly slip off to the ceremony so society will not know what has happened. But I don't want that. I love you and I want all of London—all of England—to know it. Lud, Sarah, I would stand on the roof and shout it for all to hear if I could."

Sarah blushed, but she was nearly undone by the grandness of it. "But it is all rather embarrassing."

Reginald shook his head. "Not from where I'm standing. I will never be embarrassed to have you on my arm or to introduce you as my wife. And I could see no better way of convincing you of that than by proposing to you in the morning paper."

"But what if it only causes—"

Reginald placed his hands on each side of her face and lowered his lips down to hers. He kissed her slowly and tenderly, pulling back for only a moment. "I don't care what Rags or anyone else thinks of us, Sarah. I only care about you and what you think," he whispered. He dropped his forehead to hers, running his thumb gently across her lower lip. "Do you think you can marry me and be my wife?"

Sarah kissed his thumb as it brushed against her lip. She looked up into his eyes and nodded. "It's all I've ever wanted. I accept your offer, if you will have me."

Reginald dropped a firm kiss on her lips, and she wrapped her arms around his neck, tangling her fingers into his hair and leaning into him. She did not feel the frantic need to discover everything about his lips as she had when they had kissed in the library. She had a lifetime to learn all there was to know about him.

He sighed and pushed her gently away, but not *too* far away. "I must make an appointment—for today, if possible—with the Archbishop so I might have you as my own posthaste."

Epilogue

Sarah sat in the supper box and looked out toward the Orchestra. When she and Mariah had planned their adventures in London, they had never made plans to attend Vauxhall. Looking around her now, she could see the error in their plans.

Reginald slipped into the seat beside her and placed a light kiss on her temple. "How are you enjoying the evening, my dear?"

Sarah smiled up at him. "I could be just as happy in our parlor, reading a book. As long as you are with me, I care not where we dine."

He took her hand in his, intertwining their fingers. His thumb slowly brushed up and down the side of her finger.

She looked over at him and smiled. "My lord, are you flirting with me?" She whispered.

"The two of you are rather nauseating." Lord Ragsdale plucked a roll off the platter and stuffed a piece into his mouth.

"Indeed," Montcliff nodded. "It is bad enough that you have abandoned us in favor of matrimony, but must you display it so brazenly?"

Sarah's face warmed and she knew she was blushing.

"There will come a day, gents—you mark my words—when you will find a lady that you will not find so nauseating. And then I shall have the last laugh."

"What are you laughing about, now?" Everyone turned toward the new voice.

Reginald leapt from his chair and clapped the man on the back. "Colin! When did you return from the continent?"

Sarah stood, as the other men called out greetings and made their way around the table toward the newcomer.

The man whom Sarah could only assume was Lord Heatherton, grinned broadly at Reginald. "I arrived in London only this morning. It has taken me some time to track you gents down." He cast a glance at all of them, but then turned his gaze on Reginald. "What is this I hear about you marrying?"

Sarah took a step back. Reginald had never seemed embarrassed by her around his other friends. He had said he never would be embarrassed by her. That was, after all, the reason he had put her charade in the paper.

But she knew that he was closer friends with Lord Heatherton than any of the other men. Perhaps he would realize his mistake now that his friend was back in town.

Reginald turned toward her, his smile bigger than before and his gaze full of love and appreciation. "Indeed, I have. There is only one woman in all of England capable of enticing me out of bachelorhood." He moved the few steps over and rested his hand on Sarah's lower back. "Lord Heatherton, I would like to introduce you to my wife, Lady Stoke."

Sarah curtsied and smiled up at Lord Heatherton. "I am pleased to meet you, my lord. My husband speaks very fondly of you."

Lord Heatherton laughed. "Hopefully he has not told you

all of my secrets." He raised a brow. "Although, if he has, I am certain there are a few about him I could share with you."

Reginald dropped his head to the side. "Come, now. There is nothing you could tell her that she does not already know. We have no secrets, do we, my love."

"Gah," a piece of roll flew and hit Reginald in the chest. "Must you continue with the '*my love*' blather?" Lord Ragsdale grunted from the far end of the table.

Lord Ponsonby smirked. "You must excuse Rags. His father has cut back his living until he is engaged and he has had rather too much Arrack."

He sputtered. "Heatherton, you should be grateful you no longer have to deal with your father." Lord Ragsdale scowled at the piece of mutton on his plate. "They are nothing but tyrants."

Sarah did not know Lord Heatherton other than what she had heard from Reginald, but even she could see the hurt in his eyes. His relationship with his father must have been very different than that of Lord Ragsdale.

Lord Berwick must have sensed the tension. He clapped Lord Heatherton on the arm and smiled at him. "We are glad you are returned, Colin. Sit and have something to eat. There is plenty to be had."

Lord Heatherton flicked one last glance at Ragsdale, then pulled out a chair and sat on Reginald's other side.

"How is your mother doing, my lord?" Sarah asked, hoping to steer the conversation onto friendlier grounds.

"She is very well. I believe the tour was just what she need-ed." Lord Heatherton smiled at Sarah.

He seemed a nice enough man. And if he was Reginald's dearest friend, Sarah was certain he must be one of the finest men around.

"She enjoyed it so much she has let a house in France and plans to stay there."

Sarah blinked several times. "She is in France? When does she plan to return?"

Lord Heatherton shrugged. "I have no idea. I do not believe she does either. But there are no memories of my father in France. So perhaps she will stay for several years, or perhaps forever."

Sarah frowned. She had not meant for the conversation to come back around to his father.

Lord Heatherton looked around the tables. "Reg, where is Lady Mariah? I thought for certain she would be here with you this evening."

Sarah grinned. Mariah would be delighted to hear that Lord Heatherton asked after her.

Reginald nodded. "She is. She is listening to the orchestra with Miss Bancroft." He looked in that direction and frowned. Scooting back his chair, he stood, as if to find a better view. He placed his hand on Sarah's shoulders. "Charlie, do you see your sister?"

Mr. Bancroft turned and looked. "Yes, Madi is just over there." He squinted. "But I do not see Lady Mariah with her. Perhaps someone is just blocking her from view."

Reginald released a breath. "Yes, that is probably why I can't see her." His grip tightened.

Sarah scooted out of her seat. "I am certain she simply moved to the other side of the Orchestra. Why do I not go find her? Stay here and talk with your friends. I will go find her and bring her back to the box."

"Will you bring my sister along also?" Mr. Bancroft asked.

Sarah smiled and nodded. "Of course. I will be back shortly." Sarah dipped a curtsy to all the men and walked as quickly as was proper from the box. She moved toward the Orchestra, her gaze scanning the area for Mariah. She was wearing a deep blue gown, which should make her easier to see, should it not? But she could not see her anywhere.

Sarah moved up beside Miss Bancroft. "Are you enjoying the music, Miss Bancroft?"

She turned and looked over at Sarah in surprise. "Ah, Lady Stoke. You startled me." She grinned. "Indeed, I am. I should love to come here every night if I could."

Sarah looked toward the musicians. "It is good that your brother holds a season ticket then, is it not?"

Miss Bancroft nodded. "Still, I do not believe he will indulge me as often as I wish."

"He seems intent on making you happy. I am certain it would not take much for you to convince him." She looked around her, still trying to find Mariah. "Miss Bancroft, I have come to fetch you and," she leaned forward to peer around a large man. "Lady Mariah. Do you know where she is?"

Miss Bancroft bit down on her lip. "She was supposed to be back by now."

Sarah's brows rose. "Be back? Where has she gone?"

"She went for a turn on the Grand Walk." Miss Bancroft looked at the ground. "But she was only to be gone a moment."

"Alone? Did she go alone?" Sarah did not know if she hoped she was alone or not. Neither situation was desirable or proper in the least."

Miss Bancroft tipped her head to the side, but her gaze remained on the ground. "No, she did not go alone."

Sarah was about at her end. "What is the gentleman's name? How long have they been gone?" Sarah's heart raced as she thought about all that could be happening. Even now Sarah could be too late.

She took in a deep breath as she waited for Miss Bancroft to answer the questions. Perhaps it was not as bad as Sarah thought. Perhaps they were simply watching the orchestra from the other side and had lost track of the time.

"I had never met the gentleman before, but Lady Mariah

had." Miss Bancroft bit her lip again. "I believe she called him Lord Muckrake."

The air whooshed from Sarah's lungs. No. Not Lord Muckrake. How could Mariah do something so bacon-brained? "Which direction did they go?"

Miss Bancroft pointed toward the Grand Walk. "They went that direction."

Sarah put a hand to her head. She did not know Vauxhall well, but she was certain if Mariah and Lord Muckrake walked far enough on the Grand Walk, they would end up at the Dark Walk. And that was the last place Mariah should be, especially with the likes of Lord Muckrake.

"Thank you, Miss Bancroft. I will go in search of her. If you wait here, I will fetch you once I have found Mariah."

Miss Bancroft took several steps toward Sarah. "May I come with you?"

Sarah paused. This situation could be very bad, or it could be completely innocent—although with Lord Muckrake, inno-cent seemed hard to believe. If Sarah found Mariah in a compromising situation, it would be better that no one else was present. But then again, perhaps this would teach Miss Bancroft something that could prove very useful to her when she came out next Season. Besides, she should not leave the girl alone either.

Sarah grabbed her by the hand and pulled her toward the Grand Walk. "Come, we must hurry."

They walked quickly, dipping their heads and smiling at those they passed. The Grand Walk was full of people. Not so crowded that they could not move freely, but crowded enough that Sarah had to focus on watching for the dark blue gown. They passed the Center Cross Walk, and still, there was no glimpse of Mariah.

Sarah balled her hands at her side. What could Mariah have been thinking? She knew Reginald's opinion of Lord Muckrake. She had heard the accusations of the man. How could she go on a walk with him without the protection of a chaperone knowing what she did?

As they neared the Dark Walk, Sarah's eyes widened. There was Mariah and Lord Muckrake. They stood still, apparently intent in conversation.

Lord Muckrake motioned to the entrance to the Dark Walk, but Mariah shook her head. Lord Muckrake tipped his head to the side, but Sarah could not detect what he was saying. Mariah's brow furrowed, and her head slowly shook.

Lord Muckrake, took hold of her hand, pulling her toward the Dark Walk.

Sarah picked up her skirts, practically running toward Mariah. "Lady Mariah, there you are. I have been looking everywhere for you." She called out once they were close enough to not draw undue attention to themselves and still alert Lord Muckrake to their presence.

Mariah jerked around, her eyes wide.

Lord Muckrake dropped Mariah's hand and folded his arms across his chest.

Sarah smiled as she came to a stop in front of them. Miss Bancroft stopped also, breathing heavily.

"I am glad we found you. I am certain Lord Stoke is near bedlam with worry over us." She gave Mariah a knowing smile. "Come. Supper will be cold if we do not hurry."

Mariah looked at Lord Muckrake over her shoulder. "Thank you for the turn, my lord."

They walked in silence for many yards. Sarah's hands still hung fisted at her sides. What would have happened if they had not happened upon Mariah when they did? Mariah's carelessness had very nearly cost her reputation—if it had not already. Who knew what kind of fardiddles Lord Muckrake would spread about what had happened while he was alone with Mariah?

"Sarah, wait." Mariah pulled Sarah to a stop.

Sarah clasped her hands in front of her and stared at her best friend and now sister.

"Thank you for coming to find me." Mariah's voice was contrite.

Sarah simply continued to stare at her, her own anger building with every blink.

Mariah scowled. "Are you not to say anything?"

"*Say anything*? What would you have me say, Mariah?"

Mariah looked at the ground. "I do not know. But I can see it on your face that you wish to say something."

"You do not want to hear what I have to say."

Mariah jerked up her head. "And why is that?"

Sarah blinked, her jaw working as she held back. Finally, it was too much. "What were you thinking? How could you be so stupid and improper? Do you realize what could have happened? What almost happened if we had not come along when we did?" She hissed, trying not to attract attention.

Mariah flinched.

Sarah turned, resuming her walk up the Grand walk. The supper boxes were just ahead, and she could not be there soon enough.

A hand snaked around her arm and pulled her to a stop. Mariah stared, glaring at her. "Who are you to lecture me on propriety? Did you and Reginald not slip out into the corridor alone at Lord Ponsonby's musicale? You like to think yourself so proper, but we both know that even you are not proper all the time."

Sarah lifted her chin.

Mariah had a point.

Sarah looked back on her behavior, first in the library at Mr. Bancroft's card party—which Mariah did not seem to know about—and then at Lord Ponsonby's and knew she and Reginald had acted very improperly. But it was done, and there was nothing Sarah could do about it.

"Yes, I did. And I regret that decision. But it is not the

same. Reginald was planning to propose to me in that corridor. Besides, Reginald did not have the same reputation as Lord Muckrake." She sighed. "Come now, Mariah. You know what he is and still you willing went, unchaperoned, for a walk with him?"

Mariah folded her arms across her chest. "It was a walk, that was all. Nothing untoward happened. My reputation is still intact."

"Is it? You do not believe Lord Muckrake will not make up lies just to see you ruined? He despises Reginald. What better way to destroy him than by destroying your reputation after Reginald went to great pains to protect you."

Worry flashed through Mariah's eyes. "Even if he does, no one will believe it."

Sarah's shoulders drooped and all the anger washed away. "I hope, for your sake, that you are correct. But I have a hard time believing nothing will come of this." She turned, leaving Mariah standing with Miss Bancroft near the Octagon Rooms. They could find their way back to the supper box. Sarah was done for the evening.

As she neared the box, Reginald separated himself from the other men and came out to meet her on the grass. He slipped his arm around her and pressed a kiss into her hair. "Where have you been? I expected you back some time ago."

"It took me longer than I anticipated to find Mariah."

"To find Mariah?" Reginald sighed and looked back over his shoulder. "Where was she?"

Sarah shook her head. "Perhaps that is a discussion you should have with Mariah. She does not wish to listen to anything I have to say."

Reginald cursed under his breath. "Shall I take a turn with her, then?"

Sarah shrugged. "If you wish, but I believe I will return home. I feel a rather dreadful headache coming on."

Reginald looked over his shoulder one last time. "Perhaps

my talk with Mariah can wait. Why do I not see you home? Perhaps I can read you some charades before we retire to bed."

Sarah grinned. "You know I adore it when you read me charades."

"Just when I read you charades?"

Sarah lifted a hand to his cheek. "I adore you always. As you know."

He dropped his head to hers, running his hands down her arms. "And I adore you. I do not think I can ever thank Mariah enough."

"Thank Mariah?" Sarah leaned back to look at him. "For what, pray tell?" She was not in the mood to give Mariah much praise.

"If she had never tried to teach you to flirt, I might never have realized how deeply in love I am with you."

Sarah relaxed into his arms. "Yes, I suppose we shall always be in her debt."

"But we may thank her later." He dropped another kiss on her temple. "For now, let's get you home, my love."

Author's Notes

Thank you for reading Engaging the Earl. I hope it was an enjoyable experience.

In most of my books I try to keep very much to the customs and expectations of the time. However, in this book, there are several times when the rules may have been stretch slightly for the sake of the story. There are times when the characters may not have acted in character with the time. In most cases I tried to make my character aware of their improprieties, but there are a few times when I know they stepped over the Regency line, and I did it purposefully. I wanted this story to be fun and a bit more carefree, and not adhering to the proprieties of society helped that to happen. I hope you were able to overlook those instances and enjoy the story for what it was trying to convey...fun.

Special thanks to Sharon Lathan for the Regency Charades and their answers. Much like Reginald, most of them far too advanced for my way of thinking.

I hope that you will follow all of the League of Eligible Bachelors.

About the Author

Mindy loves all things history and love, which makes writing romance right up her alley. Since she was a little girl playing in her closet "elevator," she has always had stories running through her mind. But it wasn't until she was well into adulthood that she realized she could write those stories down.

Now they occupy her dreams and most every quiet moment she has.

Her kids are used to being called names they have never heard and they now use words like vexed and chagrined.

When she isn't living in her alternate realities, she is married to her real-life Mr. Darcy and trying to raise five proper boys. They live happily in the beautiful mountains of Utah.

You can connect with her on her website mindyburbidgestrunk.com.

Also by
Mindy Burbidge Strunk

The Mysteries of Hawthorn Hall

The Treasure of Owl's Roast Abbey

Want more? Sign up for Mindy's newsletter here to receive updates, deals, and new releases.

Made in the USA
Las Vegas, NV
19 February 2023

67768729R00152